DOUBLE DEALING IN DUBUQUE

FRANK DODGE MYSTERY #2

DEAN KLINKENBERG

Travel Passages

For Lucille.

CONTENTS

Chapter 1

Julien Hall, the main exhibit area of the Dubuque Convention Center, was packed with booths of boutique ice cream vendors, cupcake bakers, chocolatiers, craft beer brewers, vintage cheese makers, artisanal picklers, and small-batch whiskey distillers. Dubuque, the Iowa city that had begun as a crude mining camp in the early nineteenth century, was hosting the annual meeting of the hip Midwest Alliance of Craft Food Producers, an organization of chefs and restaurateurs and the small farmers who supply them.

I was happy to be there, and I was pretty sure Brian Jefferson was, too, fresh off a post-divorce vacation in Honolulu, where he'd bought the dreadful yellow and blue Hawaiian shirt he had on. Ruby Beck seemed a little confused by it all, like she'd never seen anything quite like it in her eighty-five years of small-town life. Maybe she just wasn't sure where to start.

I was supposed to be writing a story for New York–based *Wandering Gourmet* about the explosion of boutique food producers in Middle America. Middle America, where—in the mind of my editor—cultural trends arrive via Pony Express. But, hey, it's my home, where I keep my stuff—parachute pants, pet rock, and all.

Folks on the coasts might be excited today about food prepared with fresh, local ingredients, but here in Flyover Land we've had that all along. We just called it gardening. When my parents planted tomatoes, squash, beans, rosemary, thyme, and basil, they were boutique food producers; they just didn't know it. When Mom threw together a summer salad with greens, cucumbers, and cherry tomatoes from the backyard and served it with the trout that Dad had caught in a nearby stream, we didn't know we were at the forefront of a food revolution. We were just doing what we were raised to do, what our parents did and their parents had done.

What's different now, I guess, is that a lot of people stopped planting gardens, and fewer of us cook for ourselves, especially in our cities. At some point, though, we got tired of eating heavily salted Salisbury steak TV dinners and mashed potatoes reconstituted from sawdust. Some of us did, anyway. A few restaurants noticed that their customers were getting tired of eating the same burgers and steaks that every other restaurant served. A few chefs got creative—they probably had gardens when they were kids—and started serving dishes with fresh ingredients, sometimes buying from local farmers because they had the freshest produce. This was generally well received, so more restaurants started doing the same thing.

As big corporations took control of what we ate, many people—a minority, but still a lot—got sick of the way food and culture had become mass-produced and dumbed down. These folks transformed eating fresh, seasonal foods into a political movement, into a cause they could rally around, to separate themselves from a mass culture they didn't approve of. Soon freshness was no longer good enough; food had to be organically grown, an approach to farming that may have started with good intentions but quickly evolved into a marketing trick to get us to pay more for something we were already buying.

But it didn't stop there. Eating food from local producers became an end unto itself. The True Believers who embraced this philosophy, *locavores*, developed a compulsion to buy all their food from a producer who lived close enough to visit and get back home before finishing a half-caf, almond milk latte. In the same family tree of dietary zealots, there were people who would buy only food that was certified "cruelty-free." Cruelty-free. For me to eat, to live, something has to die, whether it's a pig or an asparagus plant. That fact is fundamentally cruel and doesn't change just because you gave it a name before you killed it.

So sure, I'm skeptical about many of today's food trends, but I can keep an open mind—open enough, anyway. I accepted the assignment to write about the boutique food movement in Middle America because I needed the cash, but I knew what they expected me to write. I was supposed to flatter the sensibilities of my New York–based editor and other coastal trendsetters with a piece about how folks in the cultural backwaters have adopted another one of their trends, all while shielding them from the truth that it's really the coastal elites who've been influenced by us. That's how we roll in the Midwest. When folks on the coasts adopt things that we've been doing all along, we're content to let them think they invented it. It's important to them to feel that way, and we're sensitive to other people's feelings.

Besides, how hard could it be to write? There was going to be some good food to sample at this conference, and I like to eat. And with a three-grand payday as my reward for writing the article, I'd be able to get back on my feet after a dry spell and the shit that went down in the Quad Cities. First, though, I had to peek in on the press conference. Few things are as much fun as kicking off a weekend by listening to politicians and marketing professionals rattle off focus-group tested talking points.

"You two go ahead and have fun," I told Jefferson and Ruby. "I'll catch up. Gotta do a little work."

I straightened up my fedora, then walked down a hallway until I found the press room, a space that looked like a drab high school classroom except that the desks had been replaced with metal folding chairs. I took a seat near the back and looked around. On one wall was a large black and white aerial photograph of Dubuque, with the Mississippi River cutting through the top right portion of the picture. On the opposite wall were signs and posters showing off the city's prominent businesses of the past and present: Cooper Wagon Works, John Deere, the Dubuque Packing Company, and the Dubuque Boat and Boiler Works. A podium was set up in the middle of a makeshift stage at the front of the room, with four metal folding chairs on either side of it. The lower part of the podium was decorated with a portrait of the city's namesake: Julien Dubuque. That portrait and the actual man symbolized much of what I felt about Dubuque.

Julien Dubuque had been born in Quebec around 1762. He traveled to the western frontier with his brother to get a foothold in the Indian trade. In 1788 he negotiated an exclusive deal with the Meskwaki Indians and their leader, Aquoqua, to mine lead from their lands; then he registered his claim with the European authority who claimed dominion over the territory west of the Mississippi, the Spanish governor of Louisiana. No one really knows exactly who Julien Dubuque was, though, or what kind of life he led. He didn't leave much of a paper trail.

He was probably married, but then again, maybe he wasn't. Even though he lived on the frontier, he was more of a middle-class gentleman than the backwoods roughneck or moral reprobate that later generations would make him out to be. While he must have made a good living from those mines, he kept his wealth carefully hidden. The only image of him, the portrait on the podium in front of me, was painted a hundred years after he died by the artist Charles Trudell. The man in the portrait, not surprisingly, looks an awful lot like Trudell.

Dubuque the man is a mystery, shrouded in myth and perhaps ultimately unknowable, which makes him a lot like Dubuque the city. I had been here a dozen or more times before this conference, chatted with people in dive bars and at champagne brunches. After all that time, all that effort, I didn't feel any closer to understanding the city than before my first visit. I didn't expect this time to be any different.

Inside the press room, the politicians and organizers were reading statements and congratulating one another. "We're excited to show off to the rest of the world the amazing people and creative food of our region," beamed Mike Andelfinger, the mayor of Dubuque. He was barely taller than the podium, dressed in a perfectly tailored suit, with gold cuff links flashing at the end of his shirtsleeves. I couldn't tell what distracted me more: his round cheeks and unnaturally youthful appearance or the long bangs he kept flipping back to cover a growing bald spot.

"These small producers, many of them dedicated families, reflect the values of our community: hard work, respect for the environment, and a commitment to giving back." He probably said something about God and the flag, too, but I tuned out the rest of his speech to look over the list of vendors. I already knew about Cathedral Ice Cream. I hoped to talk with Stella Mueller, the owner, after the press conference.

Dubuque's mayor stepped aside so Melissa Potts, the mayor of neighboring Galena, Illinois, could speak. As she stepped to the podium and around Mayor Andelfinger—he looked reluctant to give up the spotlight—she removed her glasses and let them dangle on a cord around her neck. She towered above the podium—and Andelfinger—and was dressed more casually than the Dubuque mayor, in black jeans and a tan blouse with the word "Galena" embroidered over her left breast. "We're proud to be a part of this event. Galena has a long history of incubating and supporting small businesses, unlike some communities who only recently discovered their virtues," she said, casting a subtle sideways glance at Andelfinger. "Our historic downtown is lined with small, locally owned businesses of the type we're celebrating here this weekend. Galena wouldn't be Galena were it not for them." I was tempted to ask the mayors whether they had their own gardens and, if so, whether they considered themselves boutique food producers, too.

The mayors' speeches were followed by more cheerleading from the head of the local chamber of commerce and some board members from the Midwest Alliance of Craft Food Producers, each person exceeding the previous speaker's insipidness. "Local food is the key to our future." "Where did your food come from today? Did you ask?" "Pat a small farmer on the back." "A local chicken is a happy chicken." I finally decided that I'd heard enough and was in need of some first-hand experience. I wasn't alone. Several reporters closed their notebooks and left before the last speaker was finished, probably to look for a happy chicken to choke.

I found the main exhibit hall and drifted around looking for Jefferson and Ruby, stopping to read a few brochures and to smile politely at the vendors while trying to appear aloof. The hall was blanketed with a dull fluorescent light that sank into the terrazzo floor. Aisles of vendors lined the hall, showing off their goods at booths separated by ten-foot-tall pole-and-drape walls. The scents of all of those edible wonders rose from each vendor's booth and mixed together into an all-you-can-eat buffet for the nose. I was trying to hold off on eating anything until I found Jefferson and Ruby, but the grumbling from my stomach was making restraint increasingly unlikely.

I walked on, trying to find Cathedral Ice Cream but with little luck. The booths didn't seem to be arranged in any particular order. I'd pass a bison farmer who was sitting next to a baker who was across the aisle from a coffee roaster, but there were several other livestock farmers, bakers, and coffee roasters in the hall. Maybe they were organized by the number of miles you had to travel from Dubuque to get to them.

I finally caught up to Jefferson and Ruby near a poultry farmer's booth and resisted the urge to ask how many of her chickens were self-actualized and self-basting. "Let's eat," I said. We walked a few feet down from the clucking hens and stepped up to a table where we sampled jerky from a guy who raised bison about thirty miles away, in Grant County, Wisconsin. He had several flavors of jerky laid out on the sheets of white paper that served as a table cover, each with a handwritten sign in front of it to let you know what he had to offer. There's a lot of bad jerky out there, especially at convenience stores. Too often it tastes like heavily salted leather. I stash those pieces away for later, in case I need help removing a loose tooth. This jerky was different, though. My first bite was chewy, a highly concentrated burst of essence of beef. I worked it over slowly, letting the flavors linger on my tongue. I tried the regular jerky; Jefferson raved about the Cajun-spiced version, while Ruby loved the teriyaki flavor. I bought a packet of each before we moved on to the next table.

I needed something to drink, so we found a woman who made root beer in her garage. Must have been one hell of a garage, given the number of six-packs and kegs that surrounded her tables. She poured samples into small paper cups from a steel tap she had set up just behind a table. It was a good choice. Her root beer wasn't highly carbonated and hardly sweet at all, a little silky with a hint of maple and just enough sassafras flavor so you knew it was there but not enough to make you think you'd just sunk your teeth into a compost pile. I bought a six-pack.

Next it was time to get serious: chocolate, at a place called Post-Modern Chocolates. When we first walked up, the young man at the booth seemed distracted; I had to clear my throat a couple of times to get him to turn away from the woman he was talking to. He gave us each a piece to sample. I slipped a truffle onto my tongue and let it rest there to melt: dark chocolate with a hint of espresso. Jefferson got a salted caramel truffle, his eyes opening wide as the flavors dissolved on his tongue. Ruby watched our reactions and smiled, then placed a dark chocolate caramel square topped with candied bacon in her mouth, chewed slowly, and said "Oh, my." Her eyes closed as she caressed the melting chocolate with her tongue, her knees nearly buckling. "I've never had anything like that!" she said. I blushed and suggested we move on, though we each bought a box of truffles first.

Just across the way I spotted an ice cream vendor, which seemed like a logical next course. As I turned toward that booth—Cathedral Ice Cream, I noticed—I heard a woman from there scream, "Take that!" and I felt a cold, slimy mass hit me in the cheek, slide down my neck, and land on my shirt. Rocky road, I thought.

"That look suits you well." I heard someone nearby say.

I recognized the voice right away. When I turned to my right, I saw Helen Kraft standing a few feet away from me. Damn! I should have known that she'd be here, too. I hadn't talked to her since she'd stolen my ecotourism story.

Chapter 2

Helen Kraft and I had been rivals for a while, not as long as hawks and mice but with a similar dynamic, except that I always ended up as the prey. She'd been a professional writer longer than I—been one most of her adult life, in fact. She seemed to know everyone in the profession, editors especially. They appreciated her engaging writing style—I called it banal—and the fact that she delivered on deadline. That might have explained why, even as more and more freelance writers struggled to get paid, she'd just bought a vacation home in Sedona. That and the fact that she stole content from other writers, like me.

I'd met her a couple of years before while sitting at the counter in a small café in Kellogg, Minnesota. She came in and sat next to me, fumbling a digital camera that she had just bought. I was researching my first travel guide. She was working on an article about pies of the Midwest—which sounded like a great idea for a calendar, I thought— but she had to shoot her own pictures and was having a hard time figuring out what all the buttons were for. I showed her how to get started with the camera and helped her take a shot of a slice of butterscotch walnut.

She offered to thank me by critiquing an article I was working on, with tips about what magazines to query and how to structure the pitch. She was sweet, like the sour cream raisin pie I was snacking on—or so I thought. I later sent her a piece I had drafted on the growing popularity of smoked carp, which included recommendations for three places that had the best, most consistent product. She responded with a couple of minor grammatical edits and suggested I look for a local or regional newspaper to publish it, that it wouldn't have a national audience. I thanked her and sent a couple of queries to newspapers and magazines in the Twin Cities but with no luck. About three months after Helen and I met, I got a quick e-mail from her, giving me a heads up that the next issue of *Budget Travel* would include a short article about smoked carp, crediting her as the author. Her e-mail ended with "SORRY!" and a note saying that she would explain later.

I was pissed, but by the time I saw her again several months later, I had moved on, even though she never bothered then to explain what happened. We met yet again at a wine tasting at the St. Paul Hotel. She had just gotten off the *Queen of the Mississippi*; she was researching an article on Mississippi River cruises. When she saw me talking to the host at the bar, she came over and quickly apologized. She explained that she had pitched the idea on my behalf, but the editor insisted that he wanted to work with a writer he knew, so he hired her. She wanted to involve me, she said, but she got an assignment to go to Botswana for four weeks, so she had to write it quickly. She promised to make it up to me.

After a couple glasses of wine—which, to her credit, she paid for—I believed her. Then again maybe it was just the wine that eroded my caution. I mentioned something about a couple of new eco-resorts on the Mississippi that I had just toured; then we went our separate ways. I wrote a story about those eco-resorts but had as much luck finding a home for it as I had for the piece on smoked carp. Some six months after I saw Helen in St. Paul, I picked up a copy of *Midwest Living* and saw one of those eco-resorts featured in a full-color spread. The article was written by Helen, of course. We crossed paths a couple of times after that article was published, but we didn't say a word to each other.

When I told Jefferson about her, he had no sympathy for me. He figured I was just jealous. It was just friendly competition, he said, which I should get used to or else quit whining and go back to being a therapist. Sure, I was jealous. I had a couple of good ideas that someone else took credit for. That might seem like friendly competition to some people, but to me it was downright theft.

"Isn't this conference wonderful?" Helen asked now, not looking at me for a response. "I think it's terrific how all these small businesses are thriving. It's truly a miracle!"

To Helen, everything was a fucking miracle. The way birds fly in a V-formation was a miracle. The way her long gray hair parted ever so slightly to the right—a miracle. Ice cream—a miracle. At least we agreed on that last one.

"So what brings you here, Helen? Trolling for content to steal?"

Jefferson handed me a couple of paper towels and shot me a look. I wiped off the ice cream, watching as Helen made no attempt to hide the smirk on her face.

"I just adore your sense of humor, Frank. It's so... unfiltered." She gave her hair a quick flip with her hand as she spoke the last word. "I bet you're upset about the *Midwest Living* photo spread, aren't you?"

"Why shouldn't I be?"

"Oh, poor, poor Frank! Perhaps you're a little too sensitive to be in this business. If I 'stole' anything from you, it was a vague idea about some interesting places to stay that you mentioned. You didn't have a finished piece that I copied. I just took an idea and fashioned it into a finished piece. A piece I knew would be of interest to a specific magazine. Had *you* pitched the same idea to *Midwest Living* before *I* did, it might have been your name on that byline instead of mine."

"I did more than just name a couple of eco-resorts. I told you the details of why they were special. Details that you included in your spread."

"Frank, those are details I would have found out very easily on my own. You didn't offer any unique insights that no one else could possibly have made. You just observed a couple of features that anyone with a little bit of travel experience would have noticed.

"But enough about that," she said and then paused. She turned to me and forced a smile. "I came here to relax and enjoy a mini-vacation. To taste some delicious food and be pampered. Not to lecture you on how to make a living as a travel writer." She followed that disclaimer with that damn hair flip.

"I found a lovely room in Galena at the Dent Bed and Breakfast," she continued, perking up. "The owners, Brett and Bart, have such refined tastes! They decorate with antiques, which even someone with simpler tastes, like you, could appreciate." She looked around the conference hall, then back at me. "For breakfast this morning they served ricotta-stuffed waffles with a lemon-raspberry compote and locally sourced pork sausage. Delightful!" She paused again. "How about you? Where are you staying?"

OK, so maybe Helen didn't technically steal content, but it sure felt like it. She'd stolen my idea, one that was more than just a casual thought. I'd talked about the angle, why those places had unusual appeal. She hadn't got it published because she'd developed the idea into a better pitch. Her piece was just as dull as everything else she wrote. She got it in *Midwest Living* because she had a long-standing relationship with the editor and I didn't.

"I felt like treating myself, too, Helen," I said, finally responding to her question after a token swipe at the ice cream stain on my shirt. "I got a room in the country, at a place called the Clear Lake Inn. It's also tastefully decorated. You'd approve."

The Clear Lake Inn was a budget motel, the cheapest I could find in the area, just fifty bucks a night, or a fifth of what I would guess Helen was spending. Like her, I got what I paid for. My room was scented with a spritz of stale cigarette smoke and illuminated by a single bulb hanging from an authentic Mid-Century Modern cord. Pieces of silver coating had flecked off the poorly executed Art Deco–inspired bathroom mirror. I washed my face three times before I figured out that the spots of dirt I thought were on my face were just small holes in the surface of the mirror. The pillows had as much substance as Helen's most recent travel piece ("Seven Spas for Seven Girlfriends").

Instead of being pampered by attentive hosts like Brett and Bart, I barely escaped public humiliation. When I'd taken a shower that morning, the steam from the hot water set off the smoke alarm. I ran out of the bathroom to make sure I wasn't about to burn to death, forgetting that I had opened the window and curtains to air out the room. That was no problem, though. The hookers who worked the room next to mine didn't seem fazed by the sight of a naked man jumping up and down on a bed while waving a magazine over the smoke alarm on the ceiling.

"Yes, quite the splurge!" I said, summing up my review of the Clear Lake Inn for Helen, flipping my own bangs back with a flick of my wrist.

"It must be delightful if you're staying there." She paused and zeroed in on me with those hawk-like eyes. "So what brings you here, Frank? Looking for the newest dive bar where you can hang out with the college kids and drink all night?" I guess she'd heard about the trouble I'd had in the Quad Cities.

"And here I thought you didn't have a sense of humor," I said, turning my attention back to the ice cream stain on my shirt. "I already know which bars

I'll be going to here. I've been here many times and got out on my own to explore. I don't need to steal that content—sorry: ideas, not content—from someone else. No, I'm interested in the food, too. I have an assignment for *Wandering Gourmet.* I'm writing a feature for them."

"Isn't that lovely, Frank! A miracle, even. Congratulations. So, you will finally get a chance to write for a *national* magazine. I'm sure you'll have no trouble producing an informative piece on deadline."

By my reckoning, I did have plenty of time. I didn't have to send them a draft until Tuesday, and all I had to do was eat and talk to people for the research. Piece of cake.

Ruby handed me a wet paper towel, which I used to dilute the chocolate on my shirt.

"I'm so sorry!" A woman wrapped in a blue-and-white-striped apron stepped between me and Helen, carrying a wet towel in one hand and an ice cream scoop in the other. "Let me help clean that off you." I had already taken care of the big bits, the marshmallows and walnuts. Rocky road with walnuts instead of almonds. Nice.

"I can't believe I did that," the woman continued, dabbing furiously. If she hadn't wasted so much time screaming at someone in the chocolate booth before coming to help me, maybe the stain on my shirt would have been a lot less visible by then. "I wasn't aiming at you," she said. "I really wasn't. It was meant for her," she snarled, pointing to the chocolate stand across the aisle, where we had just been.

Before my assailant could finish wiping the last of the ice cream residue off me, another woman came walking over. She was tall and thin, wearing both a black apron with gold strings and a grim expression, younger than the woman with the ice cream scoop. It was the same woman who'd been distracting the guy we'd gotten truffle samples from. "Nice aim, Stella," she said and crossed her arms. "At least your ice cream is finally a hit."

Stella raised the scoop and looked like she was trying to decide which of a range of disfiguring acts she wanted to commit on this woman, who took a step back. But Stella caught herself and lowered her arm.

"From what I could tell, the ice cream is delicious," I said to Stella. "I'm Frank Dodge, by the way. I think I'm supposed to interview you today."

Stella introduced herself with "Oh, shit!"

"Don't worry about it, Stella. If your ice cream is half as good on a cone as it is dripping down my face, I won't have anything but good to write."

Stella and I made plans to meet the next morning for breakfast at Brenda's Butter Cup. Helen flitted away in search of new marvelous experiences.

Jefferson, Ruby, and I decided it was time to move away from the conflict zone to check out the other vendors. "I don't know how you do it, Frank," Jefferson observed as we walked, "but you sure are good at landing in the middle of a shitstorm." He laughed and turned to me, catching a glimpse of Ruby in the process. Looking embarrassed, he said, "Sorry, Ruby. I need to watch my language."

"Oh, don't worry about me, Brian. I've heard a lot of shit in my eighty-five years."

I hated to end the day on a sour note, so we sampled a few more little bits of food that people had poured their heart and soul into—most of them, anyway. I was pretty sure the small-batch jelly bean manufacturer hadn't put a lot of thought or work into those tasteless blobs of snot.

"How was that press conference you went to?" Jefferson asked.

"About as useful as a cup of decaf."

"Who was there?" Ruby asked.

"The organizers of the conference, leaders of the Midwest Alliance of Food Whatever, plus the mayors of Dubuque and Galena."

"I can see how that might not be interesting," she said. "Did you know that Dubuque's mayor—what's his name?... something with finger in it..."

"Andelfinger," I said.

"Yes, that's right," she agreed. "Did you know he's running for Congress? I hear he's the favorite, but he has to beat the head of a local union. I forget her name, too, but she's the first woman to be elected president of the UAW in Dubuque. I think she's going to give him a good run."

"With a name like Handandfinger, he's going to have a hard time winning, I bet!" Jefferson said.

"Andelfinger," I corrected while looking around the hall.

"Whoever wins the primary, they'll have a tough fight in November," Ruby said. "We swing back and forth between electing Democrats and Republicans in this district. I guess we keep changing our minds about what we want."

"Enough about politics. What do you want to do now?" I asked Jefferson and Ruby.

"It's been so much fun this afternoon, Frank," Ruby said. "I haven't had a day out like this in a while. We have a nice little bakery in Friesburg, as you know, but nothing that comes close to the food these people create." She paused and looked at the booths around us, then rested a hand on the back of a chair. "It sure is tiring, though, eating all day. Before we go out this evening, I could use some rest."

"That sounds like a great idea to me, too," I said. We decided to head back to our respective rooms and meet at six thirty in the lobby of the Ice Harbor Inn, where Jefferson and Ruby were staying.

"How do we get out of this place?" Ruby asked. We were somewhere in the middle of the hall, from what I could tell, although the temporary walls between the vendor displays were tall enough to block our view of the layout.

"It was in that direction, I think," Jefferson said, pointing over the root beer table. Then his mood turned somber, and he scanned the hall. "But we should probably get out of here now. There's smoke rising between us and the exit."

Chapter 3

Smoke quickly began to fill the main exhibit hall, a black smoke thick with the smell of burning rubber and caramelized sugar. We thought we knew the way out, but in just a couple of minutes the smoke obscured the view ahead, and we had to stop to get our bearings. Crowds of people moved around us, casually at first, people looking inconvenienced if not a little annoyed. As the smoke billowed up and spread throughout the hall, though, bodies moved faster and less rhythmically, picking up speed as they broke up into smaller groups, abandoning the larger groups as they scrambled for an exit. They didn't necessarily fare any better on their own, though. I was pretty sure the same person bumped into me three times while we stood still looking around.

I felt as confused as most people looked. At first, I thought the small fire was almost funny, but when my throat began to burn from inhaling the smoke, I felt a more urgent need to get out of the hall. I looked at Jefferson and could see he was growing more and more concerned, too.

"Why hasn't the sprinkler system kicked on and sprayed us yet?" he asked. "We need to get out now. These folks are just a couple of minutes away from rioting."

He grabbed Ruby and started pushing his way through the crowd. I followed right behind them, trying to spot the closest exit while feeling bewildered by the panic and chaos that was growing around us. I heard a few screams and saw people cut a direct path to an exit door by pushing over vendor tables and knocking down the temporary walls between them.

A few people grabbed items from the abandoned tables. One guy slid two boxes of chocolates into his backpack. A woman ran her arm across a table, scooping little cubes of cheese into her purse. Bottles of wine disappeared into the complimentary shopping bags. As the smoke got thicker, some people gave up all pretense of hiding their booty. Several men ran around with six-packs of beer tucked under their arms. A young woman stuffed pints of ice cream into her pockets; I was pretty sure that wasn't going to turn out well.

We managed to get to the end of an aisle, where Jefferson took a hard right and led us to a group of exit doors. There was already a crowd around the doors when we got to them. More people piled in behind us, but nobody was moving forward. The din from the increasingly panicked crowd made it impossible to hear what anyone was saying, but I could see a couple of guys pushing hard on doors that were still closed.

Jefferson coughed a couple of times, then turned to me and told me to grab Ruby's hand. "Don't let go," he yelled. He forced his way through the crowd toward the closest pair of exit doors, lowered his shoulder, and rammed his body into a door, but he just bounced off it, falling back and nearly losing his balance. He righted himself and leaned into the door, putting his full weight into it, again with no luck. Fighting back through the crowd, he found us and pointed to his right. "Those doors won't open. Let's keep moving. There must be other ways to get out of this place."

"Let's move, then," Ruby said. "I'll keep up." She pulled a corner of her blouse up and around to cover her mouth and nose.

We couldn't see but three or four feet in front of us, so we followed the wall, passing another set of doors surrounded by another crowd of people who weren't going anywhere. "The doors won't open!" someone screamed. Another yelled "We're trapped in here!"

My throat was feeling scratchy, and my eyes were watering. I saw some people on the floor, but I couldn't tell if they had passed out or just slipped. I reached down to one, poking him to get his attention; I grabbed an arm and tugged lightly, but he didn't respond. I had to keep moving or else I'd lose Ruby and Jefferson, so I let go and pushed ahead. I tried to look back at him a minute or two later, but I couldn't see anything through the smoke.

With the smoke filling up more of the room and my eyes on fire, I was having a hard time seeing much of anything. People all around us were coughing, and I was about ready to tell Jefferson and Ruby to hit the deck, that we needed to crawl our way out before we suffocated. Then the sprinklers finally kicked on and sprayed cold water all over the exhibit hall, and all over us. It felt great.

The smoke thinned out enough so that we could see a set of three double doors, open, just ahead of us. We raced to them and got out of that damn exhibit hall. We didn't stop until we got through the outside doors. Then we stood on the sidewalk and caught our breath in the fresh outside air as people around us coughed and stumbled, looking for someplace to sit.

"What the fuck was that?" Jefferson asked.

"Honestly, what the hell just happened?" asked Ruby.

CHAPTER 4

The three of us—Jefferson, Ruby, and I—were lucky. We looked and smelled like we had just been tossed around in a barbecue pit, but other than irritated eyes and throats, we were fine. We sat down on the curb in the shade, just beyond where the emergency medical teams were working on people who weren't as lucky as we were.

"Look at all the people who are hurt," Ruby said after wiping her eyes. "How did this happen?"

"We didn't have much time to react after we saw the smoke," Jefferson said. He spat onto the street. "It spread so fast, it didn't hit me right away that we needed to rush out." He looked back at the building and slowly shook his head. "I don't understand why those side doors didn't open. That's what they're there for—emergency exits. Someone fucked up big time there."

The fire had torched whatever good intentions Jefferson had about watching his language around Ruby.

Someone handed us towels, and we gladly wiped the water and smoke off our faces and hands.

"I don't mean to sound unsympathetic," Ruby said, "but do you suppose we can leave now? I'd just like to go back to my room and rest for a while."

"Sure," I said. Ruby had looked tired before the fire broke out, so I imagined she was downright exhausted now. "Do you want a quick look-over from one of the med techs?"

"Oh, no. I don't want to be a bother. I'm fine, just tired." Ruby hated being a bother about anything; it was in her DNA. She didn't appear harmed, though, at least not outwardly, so I didn't feel the need to contradict her.

We made plans to meet up in the evening for dinner, and Jefferson took Ruby back to the Ice Harbor Inn.

I got word that Mayor Andelfinger was assembling a quick press conference at City Hall. I walked the three blocks down there to check it out, but either word had yet to get around or no one was bothered much by the fire. I was one of only five people in the press room who wasn't a city official. Helen was one of those five; I spotted her sitting in the front row. I sat down in the back just as the mayor began to express shock, outrage, indignation, sadness, and resolve, all in about two minutes and one long sentence. Mayor Potts, who hadn't yet made her way back to Galena, sat silently in a folding chair at stage right, looking down. Her face was ashen, her mouth and eyes frozen in disbelief. She didn't address the reporters. I'm not sure she even heard Mayor Andelfinger's comments.

The police chief itemized the damage, at least what they were aware of at that point. Even though I'd been in the middle of it all, I still felt shocked at the scope. In the space of just a few minutes, tables and exhibits burned to ash and rubber cords melted. In the mad rush to get out of the hall, hundreds of people got bumped and pushed around. EMTs bandaged dozens of scrapes and scratches. A few people got an ambulance ride to a hospital for broken bones or a concussion. And two very unfortunate people were dead. In a span of barely fifteen minutes, two people had gone from sampling thoughtfully handcrafted chocolates and artisan cheeses, savoring the delicate flavors of each bite, to lying limp on the floor, the zest knocked out of them permanently.

Helen raised a hand and asked if the rest of the conference would be canceled. The mayor muttered a polite "yes," but he looked as though he wanted to yell, "Of course it is, you dimwit! We had a fucking fire in the exhibit hall."

The police chief continued through the list of damages, but he didn't say anything about how the fire might have started. I wasn't going to let him off the hook.

"Excuse me, chief," I said, standing up and raising my voice above that of a reporter closer to the front who was trying to ask a question. I got the chief's attention, maybe because I was yelling so loud, or maybe because of the soot painted across my clothes. "I was inside the hall during the fire. Do you have any explanation for why it took the sprinkler system so long to turn on and why the side exit doors wouldn't open?" The reporter turned to look at me, as did Helen and the other two people sitting toward the front—reporters, I assumed. The mayor and the chief glanced at each other.

The chief looked flustered. "We heard that there might have been a few problems with the safety systems, but we haven't had a chance to confirm those stories just yet."

"I'll confirm them for you. I watched as a group of people tried and failed to push open several emergency exit doors. They just wouldn't open, even with a lot of people pushing on them." I could hear my voice getting louder, but I couldn't stop it. "We tried and failed to open two sets of doors. Also, the sprinklers didn't come on until after we'd tried to push open that second set. The fire burned and smoke filled the exhibition hall for several minutes before those sprinklers turned on." I had to pause to catch my breath, but I kept my eyes focused squarely on the chief. "Would you say the city government of Dubuque is incompetent or just negligent?"

The mayor pushed the chief aside and stepped back in front of the microphone. "We are going to do everything in our power to figure out what happened today," he said, that baby face phasing through several shades of red. "I pledge to move quickly to investigate what worked and what didn't work in that exhibit hall. If anyone was negligent, we'll find out who's responsible, and we'll hold them accountable. That's all we have to say for now."

With that, the major signaled the chief and the rest of his team to leave. I got up and started for the door, but before I could get out of the room, Helen came over to me.

"Frank, you look terrible, but I'm so relieved that you made it out of the fire OK."

"A little shaken, yes, but otherwise OK. I'm lucky."

"And your friends, how are they?"

"They're fine, too."

"Oh, what a relief!"

"You look like you did just before the fire," I said, looking her up and down. Her clothes still looked freshly pressed, and the only color on her face was a hint of rouge. "I guess you got out with no trouble."

"Yes, a minor miracle, I'd say." She looked around the room, then leaned in toward me and said, "Like my guardian angel was looking out for me. I left right after I talked to you. I got a call from an editor and had to step out of the hall. I was outside on the plaza talking on the phone when the fire started." She stepped back and put a hand over her mouth. "So many people in a panic! What a horrific sight!"

"I'm glad to hear you weren't affected," I said, with little conviction. "Too bad those two people who died didn't have a guardian angel as competent as yours." I took a step toward the door, but Helen put a hand on my shoulder to stop me.

"Frank," she said, "you really must watch your tone around here. I, of course, am accustomed to your generally dark demeanor, but folks around here might not be as accepting as I am. Especially under circumstances like this."

I thanked her for the unsolicited advice and took my generally dark demeanor out into the hallway. Before I got more than a few steps toward the outside exit, though, a young woman floated down the hallway to intercept me, the pin-thin heel of her pumps flying across the terrazzo tiles. She was slight and not much taller than a handrail, with aggressively blond hair that was tempered by a charcoal gray pantsuit. "Excuse me," she said and then caught her breath. "I'm Courtney Baker, the mayor's chief of staff. I know you must be anxious to get cleaned up, but could I have a word with you first? It'll just take a minute."

CHAPTER 5

Baker pulled me aside into a small alcove near the front entrance. "First, I am so sorry about what you, and all those other people at the convention center, went through. The mayor, all of us at City Hall are reeling. We're terribly shocked and sickened about what happened."

"Thank you. I'm still in shock myself."

"I bet you are." She paused and gave me a subtle look-over. "You're the travel writer Frank Dodge, right?"

"Yeah, that's me."

"I'm a fan of your work."

"Thank you," I said, pissed at myself for feeling so easily flattered.

"May I call you Frank?"

"Sure."

"Frank, I'm sure you can appreciate the position we're in here. We want to give our people a fair chance to do their job. They need time to figure out what happened."

"Which means you want me to shut up about the sprinklers and the doors."

"Oh, no. That's not what I'm saying." She moved closer and lowered her voice. "I would never tell you what to write about, and I certainly would never ask you to withhold information from anyone. I might suggest, however, that you carefully consider your criticisms of the city before we know exactly what happened. There will be plenty of time to skewer us later—if the facts justify it." She stepped back and found her voice again. "All I can do is suggest, though. It's your call about how to approach this."

"I understand. You're suggesting I shut up, but you don't want to say it directly." I knew her type. If only I had a buck for every time some publicity hack from the local tourism office asked me not to write about the muggings that had just happened on the riverfront or the recent food poisoning at the celebrity chef's restaurant.

"Look, Frank, it's just that everything is so preliminary right now, and we know how often the first impression of an event turns out to be false. Just ask CNN, right?" She chuckled. "But seriously, Frank. I'd like you to refrain from a rush to judgment." She paused and looked me right in the eyes. "I admire restraint."

What she meant was that she only worked with people she could trust to keep their mouths shut. But I was pretty sure she was also telling me that I could be rewarded if I walked into this story slowly, probably with a scoop about something unrelated. I wondered if playing her way, for now, would be such a bad thing. After all, I didn't have many good contacts in Dubuque, and being on good terms with the mayor's chief of staff could really come in handy.

"You know, I'm not a journalist, Ms. Baker."

"Please call me Courtney."

"Fine. Courtney, I'm not a journalist. I write about travel and the Mississippi River. That's what I do. I'm not an investigative reporter."

"Frank, don't sell yourself short. You write well, and you have solid instincts. You know a good story when you find one." She looked away, then back at me. "I read about the troubles you had in the Quad Cities recently. How the police suspected that you were involved in the murder of that poor young man. Your instincts were right about that—about his life being a good story, I mean—even if it didn't work out so well. Plus, you did a lot of investigating after he died to prove your innocence."

"I had a lot of help. And I was highly motivated to avoid long-term confinement." I couldn't tell if she was being sincere or if she was just flattering me, but it was working. I could feel my defenses crumbling.

"But you did it. You did the investigative work. That's all I'm saying. I don't understand why you haven't broken through into the national spotlight." She paused. "I sure hope it's not because more established writers are undermining you in some way. Writers like that woman you were just talking to... what's her name?... Helen Kraft?"

What did she know about Helen? If Courtney had done her homework on Helen as well as she had on me, maybe she had some dirt on her that I could use. Then again, maybe Courtney was thinking of working with Helen, too.

"Yes, that damn Kraft *is* part of the problem." I caught myself, wondering if it was a good idea to tell her about my history with Helen—but what the hell. "She's stolen my work twice, and I assume she's done the same to other writers. Don't trust her, Courtney. I sure don't," I said, my fists clenching. "And she gives lousy advice, too."

"That's what I was afraid of." She placed a hand on my shoulder. "If there's anything I can do to help you out," she continued, "please don't hesitate to ask. I have a few contacts who could be useful."

"Thanks, Courtney. I just might take you up on that, especially if it would piss off Kraft."

"Certainly. I'm glad to help."

We shook hands, and she took a step toward the door. Then she stopped and turned back to me. "There is one thing I can tell you—off the record, of course. We've had some concerns recently about our facilities management director, a man named Stan Mueller. If you hear anything about him while you're asking around, I'd be grateful if you'd let me know."

"No promises, Courtney, but I'll keep that in mind."

With that, she pivoted on those thin heels and marched away. Stan Mueller. I wonder if he is related to Stella Mueller, the owner of Cathedral Ice Cream.

Chapter 6

I drove back to my room to clean up. Then I called Stella Mueller to confirm our interview for the next morning. She asked to meet at her factory instead of the restaurant, which was fine with me. She promised me a tour of the whole ice-cream-making operation.

I still had some time before meeting Jefferson and Ruby, so I decided to call my brother, Mark. We didn't talk very often, hadn't talked regularly for years. I drove back to Dubuque and parked at the riverfront; then I walked around until I found an appealing bench to sit on.

The last time Mark and I had talked was right after my near incarceration in the Quad Cities. He was glad that I hadn't been killed, but he didn't express much sympathy for any of the other troubles. Like Jefferson, he tends to live by the creed "You made your own bed, so lie in it and shut up already."

We've never been all that close. Honestly, I pulled back after our sister, Tina, drowned. Mark was really young then, just in first grade, and I don't know that he blamed me for her death, but I blamed myself. I shouldn't have taken the canoe out in the storm with her. Even though I was just a child when it happened, I've never forgiven myself. Can't forgive myself. I assumed that Mark felt the same way, especially after Mom and Dad divorced. I figured that was my fault, too.

"Mark?" I said. "Hi, it's Frank."

"Frank. What a surprise! To what do I owe the honor of this call?"

"I had some time to kill, so I thought I'd see how you're doing."

"Not much new here, Frank. Jimmy and me just got back from a fishing trip. Went up to the Great Slave Lake, near Yellowknife. Up in Canada, you know."

"Yeah, I know," I said. "That's a long way to go for a fish."

"Not for us, Frank. Great fishing up there. Never caught so many northern in my life."

"How long were you there?"

"We stayed a week. It was our summer trip, you know. Since me and the ex split up, I usually only get him for a few days on weekends, but in summer it's easier to work out a deal with Sarah to have him for longer. He's becoming quite the sportsman, Frank. Might take him deer hunting this fall."

"Is he old enough for that?"

"Of course! He's fourteen now, Frank. That's plenty old enough to take him out. I went deer hunting with Dad when I was younger than that, you know."

"I guess I missed out on all that."

"You never seemed all that interested in hunting. We talked about inviting you along, but we figured you wouldn't want to."

"You were probably right. It wasn't so much that I had other interests. I liked being outside, but canoeing and hiking were more my style. There's too much sitting around waiting, with fishing and hunting. I wasn't that patient." I paused as a couple with three children walked in front of me. "Still, it would have been nice to be asked."

We talked about Jimmy awhile longer. Mark was a typical father; it was a lot easier for him to talk about his kid than about himself. The kid was growing up fast. He had his father's gift for fixing things. Mark had become an electrician, like our father—a damn good one apparently—and he'd done it without the alcoholism. I figured that's how he could afford those fishing trips to remote parts of Canada. Union electricians make good money, or so he'd told me, and he wasn't out blowing it all in bars. Mark was hoping that Jimmy would continue the family tradition and become an electrician, too. He had the aptitude for it, according to Mark. He picked up the basics quickly, and he'd helped out with a few service calls in the summer. But Jimmy was good at a lot of other things, too. He loved math and science and was already talking about going to college, maybe in a coastal city. The fishing trips had made Jimmy really curious about seeing more of the world, about traveling. I didn't think Mark was comforted by the fact that his son took after me in that way.

"So where you at now, Frank? You on some big trip again?"

"No. I'm just upriver in Dubuque. I have an assignment to write about some small food companies that might attract visitors up here."

"I guess that means you get to eat a lot of good stuff, huh?"

"Yeah, it does. Hey, do you remember that brisket Mom used to make? I got to thinking about that here."

"How could I forget? She gave me the recipe, you know, but I can never get it to taste as good as hers."

"She marinated it for a long time, right?"

"You bet. At least a full day. I think she must have put something in that marinade that she didn't tell me about." Mark seemed to drift away for a moment. "So what's next for you? A little steak and lobster today?"

"I wish. No. The food fair is done, canceled. There was a fire in the convention center."

"Geez, Frank. Trouble sticks to you like stench on a rotting fish. You OK?"

"Yeah, I'm fine. It was a pretty big mess, though. You'll probably hear about it in the news. Two people died."

"That's terrible. I'm glad one of 'em wasn't you. Stories like that—that's why I don't pay attention to the news. Too depressing, you know." I heard something clanking in the background. "Look, Frank, I hate to cut you off, but I gotta go. Still got a few things to get done tonight."

"Sure thing. Glad I caught you at home."

"You gonna be back in St. Louis anytime soon?"

"I think so. Maybe after I'm done here, if I don't have an assignment to go somewhere else."

"Let me know when you get home. We can go somewhere for beers. Nice talking to you, Frank."

"Sounds like a good idea to me. Talk to you soon, Mark."

After I hung up, I walked over to the Ice Harbor Inn to meet Jefferson and Ruby, a little more bounce in my step. Maybe Mark and I weren't as distant as I'd thought.

When I reached the hotel, Jefferson and Ruby were waiting for me in the lobby. "Are we well rested?" I asked.

"I can't speak for Brian, of course," Ruby said, looking over at Jefferson, "but I feel much better. I was so tired, I think I could have slept through another fire." She laughed. That was a good sign. I'd been worried about how she might feel after our brush with disaster. "After my nap," Ruby continued, "I looked through the articles that I brought with me. I wanted to be prepared for the conference, so I'd gone to the library back home and copied articles about some of the businesses that were listed in the program." She rummaged through her purse and pulled out a couple pieces of paper. "One of them was really interesting, Frank. It was about the women who run the chocolate shop and the ice cream factory, whose booths we visited just before the fire started." She handed me a copy of the article. "I think it might help explain how you ended up with ice cream on your face."

CHAPTER 7

The article, "Food Fight," had run in the *Chicago Tribune*. The first thing that caught my attention was the byline: Helen Kraft. How does she do it? Every time I get a story, she's already got a piece of it. This story was a pretty good one, though—better than that terrible title would indicate.

The owners of Cathedral Ice Cream and Post-Modern Chocolates—Stella Mueller and Ashley Johns, respectively—had been feuding for a while, the article stated, and it had only gotten nastier recently. It had started about two years before, when Ashley showed up in Galena and bought a building on Main Street—or, more likely, her parents bought the building. They were art dealers in Chicago, well-heeled art dealers. The storefront for Post-Modern Chocolates was just two doors up from Stella's shop.

Stella had a good thing going, with the old-fashioned made-to-order sodas, complete with the fizz, the flair, and the funky glassware. The real star, though, was her ice cream, all of it made from scratch using her own recipes. You could get a scoop in a bowl, on a house-made waffle cone, or in a float or sundae. According to the article, Stella's shop was always busy. Until Ashley moved in.

Ashley had come to town with a flourish. She ran full-color ads in magazines and local newspapers—the *Dubuque Register*, the *Galena Times*, and the *Rockford Daily Tribune*. Some of the ads included hunger-inducing photographs of small pieces of chocolate lined up, looking vulnerable but irresistible. Other ads appealed unapologetically to more primal instincts: long, elegant fingers with nails painted bright red, holding a truffle that was positioned in front of a mouth opened just wide enough for the chocolate to slip through a pair of alluring lips. If that didn't tempt you to commit at least two deadly sins, you needed to check your pulse.

The ads had generated quite a buzz, as you might imagine. On the first day Post-Modern Chocolates was scheduled to open, the first Friday in July, people began lining up two hours early. They just kept coming in after that. The business was so good that other food stores lost customers. After snacking on Ashley's chocolates—and buying a couple of boxes—most customers weren't in the mood to try raspberry jam, cranberry muffins, or spiced-apple ice cream.

Stella lost a lot of customers in those first few weeks. Galena's not that big a town, so her store needed the tourist traffic to do well. When those tourists no longer stopped in because they had filled up on Ashley's chocolates, Stella decided to act. She fired the first shot in the "Snack War" (Helen's words, not mine; she wasn't known for her imagination).

Stella began with a whisper campaign. She had grown up in nearby Dubuque, and she talked to a few trusted regulars about the gall of Ashley, a Chicago native, coming to town and stealing customers from local businesses. She apparently wanted to stir up a little anger among the resentment-prone. Then she took aim at the tourist crowd. She put up a new sign that had an American flag in the lower-right corner, just above the words "American owned." Ashley's family had been in Illinois for five generations, so she didn't think much of the new sign, but it worked, to some degree. The soda fountain rebounded slowly, attracting a few more passing tourists, especially the ones walking northeast along Main Street who passed the soda fountain before they saw Post-Modern Chocolates. Some of her regulars came back more often, too, shamed into supporting an old favorite owned by one of their own instead of patronizing the upstart business run by a transplant from the Big City.

Ashley noticed the trend and wasn't about to let it pass without a response. She reached out to many of the same locals and talked about how her family had been in Galena for twenty years. If pressed, she had to admit it was Galena Territory, a subdivision about ten miles out of town that was mostly made up of second homes for people with a lot of disposable income, many of them from Chicago. This wouldn't endear her to the real locals, the ones who had grown up on a farm in Jo Daviess County or the old-school artists who had bought the dilapidated buildings on Main Street and invested sweat equity in bringing them back to life. But it did help win a regular following from the Territory.

And that's how it was for a while: a stalemate, where locals from Galena and patriotic tourists spent their money at the soda fountain, while vacationing yuppies and foodie tourists spent their money at the chocolate shop. A stalemate is ultimately an unsatisfying state of affairs, however, so it was no surprise when a new front in the Snack War opened up.

Around the one-year anniversary of the debut of Post-Modern Chocolates, the walk-in freezer at the soda fountain malfunctioned—just before the Fourth of July holiday weekend, in fact. Stella's stockpile of artisan ice cream melted, flooding much of the freezer floor with liquid cream, berries, and nuts. To clean up the mess and to make more ice cream, Stella had to close the soda fountain for several days. She missed out on a lucrative weekend.

When one of Stella's employees, a guy in his twenties, started working at the chocolate shop a few weeks later, a lot of eyebrows got overworked. There was no proof that he was to blame for the freezer failure. In fact, it looked a lot more like a mechanical failure that was bound to happen, probably sooner rather than later. Most people thought Stella was to blame for not taking proper care of her equipment. A few people, though, marveled at the timing of the mechanical failure and wondered if it was more than a coincidence. Stella was one of them.

The soda fountain never really recovered from that lost weekend. By the end of August, with the summer tourism season winding down, Stella decided to close the store and focus on making ice cream for wholesale distribution. It was a good decision. Freed from the confines of the storefront, she moved into an old warehouse in Dubuque and turned it into an ice cream factory. As she found receptive retail outlets throughout the upper Midwest—except Chicago—her sales grew quickly. But she never let go of her suspicion that Ashley had somehow been responsible for the freezer failure.

That's where the article left off. Then Ruby showed me a second article, from the Dubuque paper, indicating that there was something of a truce after Stella had left Galena. The article recapped her difficulties in Galena but stated that her wholesale business was going well. Stella commented that all the conflicts were in the past. Unfortunately, however, the truce ended only days before, when an article appeared in *Chicago Magazine*, the third article that Ruby had with her. That article called Post-Modern Chocolates "the chocolate equivalent of a starving artist's sale, but less satisfying." I figured that the reviewer, someone named Steven Gold, must have eaten something different from what I was familiar with. I wondered if Stella had a hand in the article.

That article was still fresh when the boutique food fair opened. I wondered how, with so many booths set up in a big hall, that two hated rivals ended up within an easy toss of each other. It was almost as if someone hoped, or expected, that drama would break out.

One thing I was certain of: I was really looking forward to talking to Stella the next morning.

Chapter 8

Ruby, Jefferson, and I ate dinner at a restaurant near downtown, Maria's Italian Kitchen. We weren't alone. The typical Friday night crowd of families and retired couples filled most of the tables. If you grew up in Dubuque, you've probably had a lot of Friday night dinners at Maria's. You'd have no trouble recognizing the place, even if you hadn't been there in twenty years. The dining room looked like it hadn't been updated since *I Love Lucy* premiered. Light fixtures with colored plastic plates cast angular patterns of pastel light on faux wood paneling; a glowing newspaper review—from 1971—hung at the back of the bar.

The menu wasn't any more contemporary, but that was the point. Maria served the Italian food that she'd learned how to cook from her mother and grandmother in Tuscany. You wouldn't find squishy spaghetti with flavorless meatballs drowning in a sweet tomato sauce there. Maria served genuine *ribollita, pappardelle alla lepre,* and *bistecca alla fiorentina*; she just made sure that each dish came with an English translation (bean and vegetable soup, flat pasta noodles with a rabbit sauce, and Florentine-style T-bone steak).

We were seated near the bar, between a wall and a table of eight supersized Iowans. Jefferson pulled out a chair for Ruby and slid it back toward the table after she sat down. The server handed us each a menu; then he made the rounds pulling cloth napkins out of the water glasses, folding and placing each one atop the plate in front of us. In other cities, the waiter might put that napkin right in your lap, but that is too personal for Midwestern sensibilities.

"When you asked me to come along, Frank," Ruby began, picking up the napkin in front of her and placing it in her lap, "I knew something interesting would happen. I just didn't expect that it would involve running for my life."

"Frank has a real knack for landing in the middle of trouble, Ruby," Jefferson added. "At least this time I don't have to bail him out of jail."

"You didn't bail me out of jail," I said. "You kept me out of jail—well, after you got me thrown *in* jail for a night." While looking straight at Jefferson, I fought off a grimace. "Besides, the two of you would lead such ordinary lives if you didn't have me around."

"I've had enough excitement in my life lately," Jefferson said. "I came here to relax."

"Brian, you went to Hawaii to relax. You came to Dubuque to hang out with me because you were hoping for adventure." Jefferson grinned.

The server came back and took our orders as the big table next to us cleared out and another group took its place.

"We've been so busy, I haven't had a chance to ask how you're doing, Brian," Ruby said. "The divorce is final now, right?"

Jefferson's divorce had been final for a few months, and I thought he was handling it well. He and his ex-wife, Michelle, had sold their house and moved out, but they ended up renting apartments within a mile of each other. It wasn't a bitter split. They were still friends, and both were devoted to their daughters, so Jefferson and Michelle worked out a liberal joint custody arrangement that enabled them each to stay closely involved with the girls. After months of dividing up their possessions, reassuring the girls, and defending himself at work for killing a fellow law enforcement officer, Jefferson did something out of character: He took a vacation. He zipped off to Hawaii for a week by himself; then he came to Dubuque to spend a few days with me. When I'd mentioned the possibility of sampling good beer, whiskey, and sausage, he hadn't needed any other convincing.

A server brought out salads and drinks—*pinot grigio* for Ruby, *chianti classico* for me, and Beam and Coke for Jefferson. I was starving, so I didn't waste any time digging in.

"I'm so sorry that your marriage didn't work out, Brian," Ruby said. "I know how hard it can be. I got married when I was twenty-two. Matthew was a little bit older. We had a child right away, Paul, but the longer we were married, the meaner Matthew became. After seven years, I finally decided that I'd had enough, so I threw him out. I knew I wanted to divorce him, but in those days, it wasn't as easy to do as it is now. He was dead set against divorce." Jefferson and I worked on our salads as Ruby talked. "I think he knew I'd be a lot happier without him, so he did all he could to try to make me miserable. He was a terribly jealous man. I fought with him for three years before he finally signed the divorce papers."

"How did you convince him to change his mind?" Jefferson asked.

Ruby picked up the cloth napkin and patted around her mouth. "My ex-husband worked for the county government; he was an accountant. I noticed that he always deposited a little more money than he got paid. He didn't know I was watching our bank account, but that's something my mother taught me to do, to keep a close eye on our family's money. Money is just too important to trust to one person." Ruby shot me a stern look; Jefferson nodded in agreement.

"I expected to find out that he was squandering our money on himself," she went on, "so I was really surprised to see that we had *more* money than we should." Jefferson raised an eyebrow. "Well, it didn't take me long to figure out that he had to be stealing that extra money from the county. He thought he was being smart about it, I suppose, taking out just a little bit at a time and depositing the extra with each paycheck." She took a quick sip of water. "I kept my mouth shut for a long time, but when he kept fighting the divorce, I finally got fed up and threatened to turn him in. I told him I was going to make an anonymous call to the county and suggest they do a careful audit. It worked. He signed the papers and acted very nice to me, for a while." Ruby picked up a fork and looked down at the salad, poking a slice of tomato and sliding it around in the dressing. "About a year after the divorce was final, I turned him in anyway." Ruby looked up at us and smiled. We all started laughing.

"Ruby!" I said. "That's brilliant. And a little scary."

"I didn't trust him to behave," Ruby said. "I wanted him to stay away from us. It worked, too, for the most part. He served three years in prison. When he got out, we worked out a deal that gave him limited visitation with Paul, but, honestly, he didn't come by very often. He always made sure to visit on Paul's birthday, but not much otherwise. I think he was a little intimidated."

"I wonder why," Jefferson said.

When our main courses arrived, we stopped talking so we could admire the food placed in front of us, each entrée artfully arranged on bone white china, decorated with stems of leafy parsley and bright yellow lemon slices. Jefferson dived in first, slicing off a bite of steak and rushing it into his mouth. "Damn, that's good!" he said after swallowing that mouthful. "So, Ruby, you raised your son all by yourself after you kicked out Matthew?"

"Yes. I did," she responded. She chewed and swallowed a bite of pasta before continuing. "It wasn't easy, but we found a way. I got a job at John Deere in the accounting office. I guess they figured if I could catch my husband embezzling and turn him in, they could trust me with their books!"

Ruby was, as usual, being too modest. After the separation, she'd had a hard time finding work. She picked up a few odd jobs here and there to make ends meet, but she couldn't find anything steady. She filled in as a dishwasher at the grade school cafeteria, got temporary work cleaning the doctor's office, even spent a few weeks mailing out letters for a political campaign, not because she supported the candidate—she didn't—but because she was desperate for the money. She told me that she never once paid a bill late during those rough times, but she and her son got awfully tired of eating potatoes, carrots, onions, and noodles. Meat was a luxury they didn't get to enjoy very often.

After the news broke about her ex-husband, she got a call from someone she knew at John Deere. Not a good friend, but someone she was acquainted with because he used to work with her ex-husband at the county office. He had an opening for an entry-level position at the factory, and he asked her if she wanted it.

She was grateful for the work, but it came with its own hardships. She didn't own a car, and the bus trip to the north side of Dubuque took time, an hour trip each way. That meant she was away from home for nearly eleven hours a day, Monday through Friday. Paul was in school and played in the band, but there were a lot of hours in the day when he was home alone. I never asked, but I often wondered how she felt about being away from him so much when he was growing up, especially after his sudden death a few years ago.

The entrées were delicious and more than we could eat, but that didn't stop us from splitting a dessert, anyway. The tiramisu was too good to pass up. We walked back to the Ice Harbor Inn, where Ruby called it a night. Brian and I had work to do, though. It was time for a couple of drinks and a long chat to sort out what we knew about the fire.

Chapter 9

Jefferson and I walked down to Lonna's Livery, a neighborhood bar on Bluff Street, just a few blocks from the Ice Harbor Inn. Lonna had opened the place two husbands before, converting a walk-up townhouse into a bar. When she'd bought it, she decided to keep the layout intact; no walls were harmed when she turned it into a pub. She bought an antique oak bar at a salvage shop and put it in the front parlor; then she hung a couple of old gilt mirrors behind it. A couple dozen barstools from a nearby tavern that closed completed the setup. Everywhere else, though, she kept the house theme intact.

In one room, there were three pairs of armchairs, each with a maple end table between them. A wall of bookshelves was filled with old paperbacks that customers were encouraged to borrow. Another room had a couple of long, communal tables with an eclectic mix of metal folding chairs and plastic patio furniture, with bookshelves of board games, cribbage boards, and poker chips (for amusement purposes only, of course). Lonna took the doors off a couple of closets and put a beanbag chair in each—good spaces for the loners.

The real attraction, though, other than the cheap drinks and Lonna, was the patio. The backyard was narrow but deep. Lonna bricked over the crumbling parking pad that had been there and created a friendlier surface for tables and chairs. In the course of thirty years, her landscaping efforts had transformed the former barren space into a botanical garden. Climbing roses covered two arched trellises. Ivy and hostas grew around boxwood and Japanese yew in beds next to the privacy fence. Pots overflowed with annuals that bloomed without interruption from pansies to geraniums. A couple of fire pits extended the seasons a bit longer on either side of the condensed Dubuque summer, and a ceiling-mounted heater blew warm air down over the back door in winter to keep the icicles off the smokers.

The bar was starting to fill up when we got there. We squeezed between a couple of occupied stools and quickly caught Lonna's attention. She was short and slender, with rich caramel-colored skin, dressed in a loose-hanging Chicago Bears jersey and tight jeans. Her dark brown eyes, fine and endearing, concealed a fiery disposition that didn't suffer fools gladly. Treat her with respect and keep the noise down, and you'll get along fine with Lonna. Cause even a hint of trouble, though, and she'll personally throw your ass out the door.

As with most nights, Lonna was the only bartender, but after thirty years in the business, she had developed an efficient but friendly manner. I ordered a Snake Hollow IPA, from the Potosi Brewery across the river. "What'll you have, handsome?" she asked, looking at Jefferson. He looked starstruck and didn't answer right away, so she teased him a bit. "What's the matter, hon? Pussy got your tongue?" Jefferson cleared his throat, looked down, and said, "Beam and Coke, please, ma'am."

"Coming right up, but if you call me 'ma'am' again, I'm going to give you a good spanking." She filled a glass with ice and grabbed the bottle of Beam without looking down, then took a couple of steps to her right, reached in a cooler, and pulled out the IPA while chatting with another customer. From across the bar, her hands looked silky, but as she turned them over to collect our cash, I saw small calluses on her fingers and palms.

I was curious about Lonna's name, so I asked if it was a family name. "No," she told me. "My grandmother, Donna, died just before I was born, so my parents wanted to pay her respect, but they had a thing for names that began with the letter *L*—Larry, Louise, Leonard, and Leland; those are my siblings—so I had to be Lonna. What brings you and your handsome friend here?" she asked, looking at Jefferson.

"I'd heard there was a beautiful lady somewhere around here, but I didn't believe it until now," Jefferson replied, finding his tongue. I turned away and rolled my eyes.

"You're quite the sweet talker, once you open your mouth. What's your name?"

"Brian."

"Well, Brian, I hope you stick around for a while tonight. Most of the time I'm stuck talking to college boys. It's nice to have a real man around for a change."

Lonna slipped down to the end of the bar and popped open Stags for a couple of those college boys, so we went out to the patio and sat at a small table near a group of four college kids and a foursome who could have been their parents. There was no breeze, but the air had cooled. A couple of the kids sitting next to us were chain-smoking, but at least they were downwind.

"Looks like you made a new friend," I said.

"Ah, it's just a little flirting. It's no big deal."

"You're just as smooth as ever."

"Whatever, Frank. I was just being polite."

He wasn't going to talk any more about it, so I gave him a break and changed the subject. "So how was Hawaii?" I asked. "You haven't told me much about it yet."

"It was fucking awesome, Frank. Best decision I've made in a long time, taking that trip. It took a couple of days before I really let myself chill, but I can't remember when I last felt that relaxed."

"How was the Hilton? I'm sure you didn't mind staying on Waikiki Beach."

"Expensive, as you know, but it would have been worth every penny if I'd had to pay full price. Thanks for helping me get a deal."

"No problem."

"Honestly, they had everything I needed there. I relaxed on the beach every day, walked to a couple of restaurants for dinner, but most of the time I just stuck to the Hilton."

"You didn't mind being there alone?"

"Nah. It was a little strange at first. The first couple of days I had to remind myself I was single again, that it was OK if I wanted to look around and check out the women."

"Meet anyone?"

"Right to the gossip," he said. He took a sip of his Beam and Coke, then sat silently for a minute as he sorted out how much he wanted to tell me. "Yeah, I met someone. She was from Oakland. Cassie. She was vacationing with a few friends.

"I had a nice time hanging out with her, but I don't think we're going to keep in touch. That's all I'm going to say about her, Frank."

"So proper you are. Would you go there again, to that hotel?"

"Sure. I'm already thinking about setting aside some time next year for another week, maybe in the spring. I'm not like you, Frank. I'm happy going back to a place I like. I don't need to go somewhere new all the time."

"I'm glad you liked it. And glad you got some action."

"Knock it off."

"Fine. So what the hell do you think happened today in the convention center?" I asked.

"That's a damn good question. I'd like to know how that fire got started. I assume those places have all kinds of safety systems, but that was a clusterfuck: The sprinklers took too long to come on, and I don't understand why some of those exit doors were locked. I'm surprised only two people got killed."

"I was really worried about Ruby, if she'd be able to keep up."

"I think she showed us that we shouldn't be worrying about her. I hope I'm that plucky when I'm eighty-five."

"Me, too." I took a sip of beer. "Do you think someone tampered with the safety systems? The whole thing seems suspicious."

"Don't go looking for something sinister so fast, Frank. That's my job."

"The fact that a couple of key safety systems didn't work just when a fire happened to break out—that seems like more than a coincidence to me."

"It might be. Then again, maybe the sprinklers and doors have been that way for a while and no one noticed because there hadn't been a fire. I just think—"

"Were you guys at that fire today?" The voice came from a table next to us. Jefferson and I turned and looked. We said "Yes" at the same time.

The woman who asked the question was one of the college-age drinkers near us. "I just can't imagine what that was like. It must have been horrible, all that smoke and panic," she said, putting out her cigarette.

"It got pretty rough at times," I said.

"I heard on the news tonight they're trying to figure out if the city did anything wrong, but the mayor thinks it was just a terrible accident. Two people died, one of them about my age. I think they said he worked for a chocolate company."

Jefferson and I looked at each other. We hadn't heard any details about the people who'd died yet.

"Well, I'm glad you got out OK," she said, turning back to her friends.

"Thanks," I said. I scanned the group at her table and caught the eye of a guy with dark black hair and a full-sleeve tattoo on his left arm who looked a little older than his drinking pals. He returned my look, smiled, and nodded a hello. I nodded back.

I turned back to Jefferson. "So one of them worked for a chocolate company, huh?" I said. "The fire probably started near the booth for Post-Modern Chocolates. And it started not long after my face was mistaken for a waffle cone. Sure, there's nothing suspicious about that." I picked up my beer for another sip.

We finished our drinks and went back inside. Lonna smiled at Jefferson, but he pled fatigue. "It was a pleasure to meet you, Miss Lonna," he said after approaching the bar. "I look forward to coming back another night when I'm over this jet lag."

She grabbed a pen and scratched something on a napkin. "You're welcome here anytime, Mr. Brian. And feel free to give me a call while you're in town—just never before ten in the morning." She handed him the napkin and scooted to the other end of the bar.

"You ready?" Jefferson asked me, folding the napkin and sliding it into his shirt pocket.

"I think I'm going to stick around a little longer," I said, turning to look toward the end of the bar. The guy from the patio had moved inside and was sitting alone now. "I'm going to say hi," I said, pointing toward him. "Maybe he's heard a little more news about the fire. Might be worth checking out."

"Whatever, Frank," Jefferson said. "Just be careful. I'll find my way back."

I walked over to an open barstool next to the guy. "Mind if I join you?" I asked.

"Not at all," he said.

"I'm Frank." We shook hands, and I looked directly at him, into eyes glowing translucent green. The intensity of his gaze startled me, embarrassed me, so I looked away.

"Adam," he responded.

"Looks like you could use another drink, Adam. Let me get a round. What would you like?"

"A beer is fine, whatever you're having."

Lonna slid a couple more Snake Hollow IPAs down our way. "So tell me, Adam. What do you do for excitement around here?"

CHAPTER 10

The next morning Adam and I stopped for breakfast at The Green Tomato in Dubuque, a place that is beloved by local foodies for the fresh, locally sourced produce and meats. The restaurant was a typical Saturday-morning busy, even though we got there late enough to miss the early birds. I felt comfortable with Adam, and I was pretty sure the feeling was mutual. We stared at each other, flirted, and chatted about nothing in particular.

As we were about to leave, I saw Helen walk in and scan the restaurant. Before we could pay and slip out, she spotted me and came over.

"Hi, Frank. What a coincidence to see you here! We must have similar sources."

"Good morning, Helen. I've actually been here a couple of times before. What brings you here?"

"I've heard that they do an amazing breakfast, so I skipped, reluctantly, the glorious offerings at my B&B to try this. What do you like here?"

"I'm a big fan of the biscuits and mushroom gravy. Adam," I asked, barely hiding a smile, "what's your favorite dish here?" I turned back to Helen. "By the way, Helen, this is my friend Adam."

"Lovely to meet you, Adam. Frank is such a people person. Every time I see him, I get to meet some new friend of his." She flipped her hair back. "Frank, I bet you never have to eat breakfast alone when you're on the road."

Adam looked confused for a minute, then told her that he couldn't get enough of the corned beef hash.

"Nice to see you again, Helen, but we were just on our way out. I'm sure you'll love the food here."

"Of course," she responded, her eyes darting between me and Adam. She took a couple of steps toward the front of the restaurant, then turned back toward us. "Sorry. I almost forgot to ask. How are things back home, Frank, in St. Louis? Such a tragic situation!"

"Nothing new to report," I said, standing up and sifting through my wallet for cash. "Let's go," I said to Adam, dropping thirty bucks on the table and pushing past Helen and out of the restaurant.

"What was that about?" Adam asked when we got outside.

"My enemy. Or my rival, anyway," I said. "Just ignore her. She says a lot of things just to goad me."

"What did she mean about a tragic situation in St. Louis?"

"I had to move recently. She considers my new living quarters to be beyond dreadful." There was enough truth in that to make me feel like I hadn't told Adam a complete lie. "We have different standards about a lot of things."

Adam lived just around the corner from The Green Tomato, so I walked him to his loft. I told him I'd had a great time hanging out with him, and I promised to get in touch again before I left town. He seemed OK with that. After a quick hug and kiss goodbye, I walked back to my car.

I had to get to Stella Mueller's ice cream factory in the North End neighborhood of Dubuque—a short drive from where I was, like everything in Dubuque. After Stella had closed her soda fountain in Galena, she leased space in the old Dubuque Malting and Brewing Company complex, a regal but neglected nineteenth-century industrial building, seven stories of Victorian splendor sprawling over an entire city block at Thirtieth and Jackson.

The underused red brick edifice rose high above the neighborhood like a forgotten medieval castle, complete with crenellated towers, boarded-up Gothic windows, and chunks of eroded brick and stone that occasionally fell to the ground—hardly a place where one would expect to find someone churning out modest-sized batches of gourmet ice cream. On the other hand, the name "Cathedral Ice Cream" worked well.

Stella had renovated a ten-thousand-square-foot section of the first floor, part of the old dock, cleaning it up and installing mixers and freezers. Trucks could back right up to the doors and carry her ice cream to retail outlets around the region. It was an impressive operation.

Stella's office was tucked into a corner, set off from the production area by two ten-foot walls, the upper halves of which were clear single-pane windows. The ceiling inside the warehouse was at least twenty feet tall, though, so those office walls provided little buffer from the noise of the mixers that bounced off the brick walls. If it got too loud, Stella would tell me, she just took her cell phone and walked outside.

After I stepped through the foyer, Stella spotted me and quickly turned her back. I thought I saw her run a tissue across her eyes, but I wasn't sure. After a brief pause, she turned back around, stiffened up, and walked over to greet me, her long brown hair swaying from side to side as the industrial mixers whirled and churned behind her. She was dressed in blue jeans and a light gray shirt, with "Cathedral Ice Cream" emblazoned on the left side. She had a full figure but not as full as one might expect from someone who owned an ice cream factory—more Marilyn Monroe than Chris Christie. As soon as she reached me, she apologized again for her bad aim at the convention center.

"I get a little impulsive sometimes," she told me. "And I was just so angry at the way that woman was insulting me from her table. I lost my temper and, without thinking, I scooped out some ice cream and threw it." She reenacted the event in mime as she spoke, capping it off with an especially forceful toss.

"Rocky road," I said. "With walnuts, right? I'm sure it's very tasty when you get a chance to put it in your mouth."

"I hope you can forgive me, Mr. Dodge."

"Frank," I said. "I'm not that formal." I looked her over to make sure she wasn't packing another ice cream scoop. "Don't worry about it. But if you're consumed with guilt, I would declare your conscience clean for a quart of that rocky road."

"Whew! What a relief to have that burden removed!" she said, grinning and running the back of her hand across her forehead for effect. "I know you'll like it—the rocky road—as well as my other flavors. I take traditional ice cream flavors and reinterpret them, give them a personal twist. I'm impressed that you noticed the walnuts, given the circumstances. Rocky road is usually made with almonds, but the original version was probably made with walnuts. They're meatier; I prefer that."

With the apologies over, I asked for her back story. Stella was a proud Dubuquer, the fourth generation born in the city. Her family traced its roots back to Germany, immigrating to the States in the 1850s. In the ensuing century and a half, few of her family members had moved on to other places. They were happy in Dubuque, so they had no reason to look for anything else. Her father had worked at the John Deere factory most of his life. Her mother had taught at a Catholic grade school in their neighborhood. Stella's two older brothers lived barely a mile from the house where they'd grown up, one working quality control at John Deere and another as an engineer for a construction company.

She'd made her first batch of ice cream when she was eight years old, and she kept playing around with recipes into adulthood, but it'd just been a hobby. She became a teacher, like her mother, and got a job at a Catholic grade school, also like her mother. But after suffering through a couple years of headaches and temper tantrums—including her own—she realized that she just didn't like spending that much time with small children.

About twenty-five years before, she'd taken the plunge into the ice cream world and opened a small storefront in the North End, a few blocks from where she'd grown up. It was a hit—not a big one, but she made enough to hire a couple of part-time employees and upgrade her equipment so she could make bigger batches of ice cream.

After ten years of serving the neighborhood, she had ambitions to grow. That's when she moved her operation to Galena. It was a risk. Leasing a storefront on Galena's Main Street was a lot more expensive than renting space on a quiet neighborhood street in Dubuque, but she hoped that all the foot traffic on Main Street would make up the difference. She was right, and then some. Her soda fountain thrived. All those tourists, a million every year, sure liked ice cream, and she didn't disappoint them. It helped that she didn't really have any competition—at least in the beginning.

She immersed herself in the community, volunteering for the Galena Country Fair and sponsoring a softball team. She joined the downtown business association and volunteered for a couple of committees. All those activities helped her build a local following, a strong base that gave her steady, predictable sales, which came in handy when the seasonal tourist business slowed down.

Eventually the competition picked up, however. Someone else opened an ice cream shop, but they weren't from the area and their ice cream was mass-produced by a big company. It closed after a year. Other shops opened up, though, and each time someone came in to sell hand-crafted food, Stella saw her business dip a little. Cathy's Crazee Cupcakes took away a few customers, as did Pete's Perfect Pistachios. And then, two years before, Ashley Johns and her Post-Modern Chocolates showed up, moving into a storefront just two doors up from Stella. "I knew I was in for a fight," Stella told me. It didn't take long for open warfare to break out.

"Did you know her family name is actually Johnson?" Stella asked me. "Here. Try this," she said as she handed me a paper cup with a small scoop of ice cream in it. "It's cherry vanilla. We use only Madagascar vanilla beans in our ice cream. This one is mixed with dried cherries that we buy directly from an orchard in Door County, Wisconsin."

"It's rich. The flavors really pop," I said. "So you were saying that Ashley's family name used to be Johnson?"

"Yes. They dropped the 'on' because they thought Johns sounded classier. That should tell you something about them right there."

"I hadn't heard that," I said. "Maybe they just know their market. Her parents are art dealers, right?"

"Sure, they sell expensive art, but that's not enough for them. They want to be just like their holier-than-thou rich customers, pretentiousness and all. Maybe that seems OK to you, but I think it's disgusting, trying to be something you're not. Just a couple of snob wannabes."

"I wish you'd just tell me what you think."

"I have no respect for Ashley and her family." Her face turned bright red. "And I don't care for most rich people. Most of them lie and steal to get what they have, then turn around and act like they're morally superior to everyone else. It pisses me off, and I'll say that to anyone.

"Try this one now," she said, handing me another small cup. "This one is wild blueberry. We get the blueberries from suppliers in northern Minnesota, like the Red Lake Ojibwe, who pick the berries from wild bushes in the forest. The flavors are so much brighter than those puny blueberries that are shipped across continents."

"Wow! The blueberry flavor just explodes..."

"And out of it, too," Stella said, handing me a napkin.

"Help me out a little more." I wiped my mouth. "I don't really understand what you have against Ashley and her family. What did they do to you?"

"They came into our community with no connection to it at all, no history, and tried to use their money to muscle out locally grown businesses. They're bullies out to make a buck. They don't care a lick for the people or for Galena. They will do anything to get people to empty their wallets.

"Here, I've got one more for you to taste," she said, handing me a third cup. "This one will give you a boost for the rest of the morning. It's chocolate espresso. I buy the chocolate from a great little shop down in Davenport. The espresso beans are roasted locally by friends of mine who own a coffee shop called The Wired Bean."

"Again, wow! It tastes like a shot of frozen cappuccino." I finished the rest of the ice cream in the cup and licked my lips. "The Johnses, they weren't exactly outsiders, though, right? They owned a house near Galena?"

"Oh, please," she sneered. "Galena Territory isn't Galena. It's barely a community, more a collection of vacation homes for people who want to escape Chicago for a weekend. Owning a vacation home fifteen miles away doesn't make you part of the community."

"Do you think it really matters to most people whether a business is locally owned? Those tourists walking down Main Street in Galena, for example. Do they know or even care about where the products in the stores came from?"

"Sure. Some do. And we're working on the rest."

"Why should they care?"

"Look, when I open a business in my hometown, I live and spend my money there. I get to know my customers and their tastes, so when they come back, I can suggest something new for them to try, based on what I already know they like. I also have to behave myself, because they know me. If I get out of line, either personally or professionally, they'll let me know." She smacked her hands together, the sound echoing off the brick walls. "Not by literally slapping me, but by shopping somewhere else. These company stores, though. They pop up when a corporate CEO looks over data from their marketing department and sees a place where they think they can make enough money to please their stockholders. Then, as soon as the store performs below their financial expectations, they close it, with no consideration for the impact on the community. With my business"—she poked herself a couple of times—"I don't have stockholders to enrich; I have customers to keep happy."

"One thing that I wondered about, though. You grew up in Dubuque, then moved your store to Galena. Didn't you have trouble with that? You know, like being perceived as an outsider and maybe an opportunist by the folks who lived in Galena?"

"It's not that big a deal around here. Sure, there are people who insist that Galena and Dubuque are completely different places with different people, but that's bullshit. The people who grew up in Galena and Dubuque are cut from the same cloth. The people who moved into Galena in the 1960s, they did all right, especially after we realized that they were here to stay.

"The real problem, both here and in Galena, is these people with lots of money, most of them from big cities like Chicago, who want to use us as their playground and not contribute anything to the community. Like those people who own vacation homes in Galena Territory. Most of them couldn't care less about the well-being of the long-time residents.

"They aren't sensitive to how throwing all their money around makes it harder for a lot of folks. They come in and build big houses, for example, and want to have expensive meals. And gradually everything gets more costly for everyone. It's especially hard for the older folks who've lived here all their lives. It's just not right."

"But aren't those same people buying your ice cream? Don't they make up a big portion of your customer base?"

"Yes, I'll grant you that was true when I had the retail store. But I would have been just fine if my only customers were long-time residents and tourists. I didn't need the rest. Now that I do only wholesale, it doesn't matter so much. I sell all over the region."

"So what happened to you in Galena? You had the storefront there for a while but had to close it, I guess?" I knew what I'd read in the article Ruby copied, but I wanted to hear Stella's take on it.

"My freezer broke down just before the Fourth of July weekend. It wasn't so much the expense of the new freezer and the cleanup—much of that was covered by insurance—but I lost out on a lot of sales and just couldn't get back on track after that. I'd been thinking about wholesale distribution for a while, so I decided to close the store and take a chance."

"Looks like it worked out pretty well."

"Yes, it has."

"So the freezer. It was just old and destined to crap out?"

"That's what the insurance company decided. I had my doubts, though. The timing was suspicious. And when Jake left me..." Stella paused to clear her throat. "When Jake left me to go work for the chocolate diva, I felt certain that the freezer failure wasn't really an accident."

Jake had to be the young man mentioned in Helen's article. "You think he was responsible?"

"I think Ashley was responsible, but I think Jake sabotaged the freezer."

"Do you have any proof of that?"

Stella crossed her arms and looked hard at me. "No," she said. "But that doesn't mean I'm wrong."

"Jake... Is he the young man who died in the fire?"

Stella looked away from me and mumbled a soft "Yes."

"So now that he's dead—now that Jake is dead—I suppose it's going to be hard for you to prove anything."

"You might be right," she said, still barely audible. She cleared her throat a couple more times, which helped her find her voice again. "Ashley's still around, though," she said, her face hardening. "Jake's death is a horrible thing. I still can't accept that he's gone. I would never have wished that on him. Never. When he left my store, I was pissed off, but I moved on. I had to. I just feel so bad for his family. But I blame Ashley for it. For *all* of it."

"I'd probably feel the same way," I said.

Stella glanced at her phone—at the time, I assumed—and her mood returned to business casual. "I'm sorry, Frank, but I have an appointment I need to run off to soon. Do you have any other questions I can help you with?"

"Yes, one other thing I was wondering about. I'm sure you know that a Chicago paper recently printed an unflattering review of Post-Modern Chocolates."

"Just desserts, if you ask me," she said, with a hint of a smirk.

"Some people think you had a hand in it."

"People are going to think what they want to think; I can't change that." She turned around and walked toward a five-foot-long chest freezer. She lifted up the lid, pulled out a carton of ice cream, put it in a small Styrofoam cooler, covered it with ice, and handed it to me. "Feel free to call me if you have any other questions. I hope you enjoy the ice cream. Rocky road, just like you wanted."

"Thanks. I'm sure I'll enjoy it plenty. And then curse you when I step on a scale."

"So don't step on the scale!"

After listening to Stella all morning, I realized that I needed to get a broader perspective for this article. If I was going to be thorough and balanced, I needed to visit Ashley, to hear her views on boutique food in the region. Maybe it would also help me figure out if Ashley was a legitimate part of the boutique food world or, as Stella suggested, if she was just a culinary carpetbagger.

CHAPTER 11

I met Jefferson and Ruby for lunch at a place called The Gregarious Greek (their motto is "*Spanakopita* is Greek for 'smile'!"). "I'm not even that hungry," I told them, "after all that ice cream that Stella made me try. I was really blown away by the blueberry. How amazing the flavor was!"

"She didn't make you wear any of it this time, did she?" Jefferson asked, smirking.

"Not this time. But she gave me a quart of rocky road, so I could find out if it tastes any better in a bowl than it did sliding down my cheek."

Since the rest of the foodie conference had been canceled, Ruby took advantage of the free time by doing some sightseeing. She'd bought a ticket for the hop-on, hop-off tourist trolley and spent the morning jumping on and jumping off to her heart's content. "It was the most fun I've had in a long time," she told us. "So much to see. I had forgotten that Dubuque had so many beautiful buildings. It's been years since I looked at the city like a visitor might. Still, I nearly missed out on most of them, because I didn't want to leave the Methodist Church, St. Luke's." Ruby chuckled. "Those Tiffany windows are so stunning! I don't think I've seen them since before Paul went to college—that was a long time ago. They are every bit as captivating as I remembered. We are so lucky to have those windows here in Dubuque."

While Ruby had been hopping her way around town, Jefferson was doing his own sightseeing. "I don't want to say much yet," he told me, "but I went around and checked on a few things." Typical Jefferson. He was obviously up to something, almost certainly poking around in business related to the fire, but he wouldn't say anything about it until he'd gotten something good.

"I ate ice cream," I told them.

"We know!" Jefferson and Ruby said in unison. "What did you learn about her, the ice cream woman?" Jefferson asked.

"Stella? A few things. She doesn't care for rich folks. She really hates Ashley and her family, but we pretty much knew that already. She also told me that Ashley's family name was apparently Johnson, but her parents shortened it to Johns. Stella thinks they wanted their name to sound more high-class."

"Well, that's just silly," Ruby said. "It sounds like a story someone would invent to make someone else look bad."

"Shouldn't be too hard to figure that one out," Jefferson said. "At least whether or not they changed the spelling of their name. I'll get on that one."

"So you're investigating the fire now?" I asked.

"Don't know yet. I'm interested in finding out what's going on, but right now it just sounds like the kind of feud you'd find in a TV soap opera." Jefferson leaned back and locked his hands behind his head. "If that's all it turns out to be, I'll be packing up and heading home."

"Which is why you spent your morning investigating?" I asked.

Jefferson didn't flinch. "I wouldn't call it 'investigating.' I was just trying to get to know the major players a little better, that's all." He flashed a subtle grin. "What's next for you, Frank?"

"I'm heading over to Galena, to interview Ashley."

"You didn't waste any time."

"I have an assignment, remember? I'm supposed to be writing about the explosion of boutique food in the Midwest. Ashley is part of that, and she has time to talk to me this afternoon."

"Now, you keep an open mind, Frank," Ruby said. "Don't go prejudging her. After all, she really knows how to make chocolate, in spite of what that ignorant reviewer wrote."

As we were leaving the restaurant, Helen Kraft was just walking in. "We must stop meeting like this," she said.

"Fine by me," I mumbled.

"What was that, Frank?"

"I said we were just leaving. These are my friends, by the way. Ruby, who lives upriver at Friesburg, and Brian, who's from St. Louis. They were also caught in the fire."

"So nice to meet you," she said, placing her right hand over her heart. "And I'm so grateful that you all made it out of that fire without getting hurt." Ruby and Jefferson thanked Helen for her concern.

"What are you going to do now that the convention has been canceled?" I asked. "There must be bigger stories better suited to your talents."

"I don't have to be anywhere for a few days, so I thought I'd stick around Dubuque. See what turns up. I guess you still have the assignment for *Wandering Gourmet*? That must be why you had a chat with Stella Mueller this morning. She's a dear old friend of mine. I'm so glad the two of you had a chance to meet."

"I didn't know that the two of you were friends."

"Known each other for years. I was an early fan of her ice cream. I believe I wrote the first article about her, at least the first one that was in a national magazine. She had a gift from the beginning for creating amazing flavors. I didn't think she could get much better, but she has. It's remarkable."

"Practically a miracle."

"Indeed," she said, nodding.

"I'd love to read that piece you wrote some time."

"I don't even remember where it ran. I've written so many articles since then, for so many different publications, I can't keep track of them anymore. Someday you'll know what that's like, Frank." She did that damn hair flip again. "Maybe Stella has a copy of that original article. You could ask her. But then again, you're so resourceful, so doggedly determined, I'm sure you will find it." Helen turned to look around the restaurant and spotted the person she was looking for. She turned back to me. "It's so nice to bump into you again, Frank. And to meet your friends, too."

"Nice to see you, too, Helen," I lied again. She walked to the back of the restaurant and sat down at a table where another woman was sitting. I stepped back in the restaurant to see who was waiting for her. It was Courtney Baker, the mayor's chief of staff. Courtney must be in full damage control mode, working the press hard to discourage negative stories about Andelfinger's handling of the fire. Helen might have met her match.

Chapter 12

I left Dubuque and drove east. Ashley invited me to her home, which was about ten miles outside of Galena in a secluded hollow. At Galena, the highway passed by a few strip malls before descending into the valley of the Galena River and into the red brick architecture of the old city. I had plenty of time to check out the buildings as I crawled down Highway 20; on summer weekends, the road was clogged by packs of motorcycles, RVs, and confused tourists vying for parking spots.

I finally got across the river and turned onto Hanover Road, a narrow country lane that alternated between blacktop and gravel. The road snaked its way through, over, and around the hills that marked the southern end of the Driftless Region, an area of some twenty-four thousand square miles that the glaciers didn't have a chance to flatten during the last Ice Age. As I drove, tree canopies would stretch out over the road and then quickly disappear; I'd find myself surrounded by lush green fields with Victorian farmhouses, where horses were grazing next to white picket fences. I wasn't sure if I was driving through Illinois or a cliché.

I had the road to myself except for a silver pickup that was behind me most of the way from Galena to Ashley's place. Her house, a bright white, two-story Queen Anne farmhouse, was tucked into a hillside near the Mississippi River. The house was built several feet above the floodplain—high enough, I suspected, that when the river was up, the house stayed dry, even if you might need a boat to get to it.

Ashley met me at the door, wearing a white apron that was dotted with blotches of chocolate; she looked like she was wrapped in Dalmatian fur. Even with the dirty apron, she was the essence of elegance; the gold necklace she wore around her neck and the matching earrings helped. She was remarkably slender for someone who made her living selling calorie-laden sweets; I wondered how much of her own product she ate.

"Welcome, Mr. Dodge. Thank you for meeting me out here. Did you have any trouble finding the house?" Her handshake was limp, her hands cold, but at least she looked me in the eye. She struck me as formal and reserved, so I figured it was best to call her Ms. Johns for the time being.

"Not at all," I replied. "You have a beautiful house." I looked around the foyer and front parlor, both decorated sparingly but conspicuously with antiques.

"Thank you. I can't imagine ever living anywhere else." We followed a vapor trail of chocolate down a narrow hallway and into a spacious kitchen outfitted with high-end commercial appliances: a large Sub-Zero refrigerator and a Wolf double oven, both covered in stainless steel, stacked near an eight-burner stovetop, half of the burners covered by copper pots of various sizes. On one counter were boxes of cacao, fruits, and nuts, alongside bottles of liquid flavorings. On another counter, pans of chocolates that looked like they were fresh out of the oven were arranged in neat rows atop gray marble. Ashley noticed me looking around.

"This kitchen obviously isn't original," she said, her eyes scanning it from one side to the other. "I had it redone when I bought the house. It's where I test all my recipes and make some of the products we sell at the store." She rubbed the gold necklace around her neck. "I like the isolation. I can focus my creative energies completely, without the distraction of running a retail store."

"Speaking of your store, I'm so sorry to hear about the young man who worked for you, the one who died during the fire."

"Thank you," she said, leaning back against a counter. "I'm still in shock. I can't believe I lost him." For a minute, I thought Ashley was going to cry, but she blinked a couple of times and cut it off. "Jake was such a fine young man. A real dear, and a devoted employee."

"Had he worked for you for long?" I asked.

"Yes, several months, I believe. I'm not entirely sure how long it was, to be honest; it just seemed like he'd always been with me. I feel such a deep loss, but I can only imagine how painful it must be for his parents."

"Yes, I'm sure it's very tough for them."

"Well, you didn't come here to discuss my tragedies. I'll have plenty of time to process all that with my friends. I suppose you want to hear about my business, how I got started."

Ashley launched into her story as she turned around and walked to a countertop, where she prepared to make a new batch of bark, pulling items off the shelves that she carefully measured and added to a mixer bowl. She'd been an art history major at the University of Chicago and expected to join the family business as an art dealer. After she graduated, she traveled to Switzerland to look at a couple of paintings, but she kept getting distracted by the chocolate. At some point she realized she was spending more time in chocolate shops than in art galleries, and she figured there was some kind of message in that. When she got home, she told her parents that she wasn't interested in selling art, that she wanted to be a chocolatier. They weren't crazy about the idea at first, especially after they'd spent a couple hundred thousand bucks to get her a first-class education at the University of Chicago. But they loved her and wanted her to be happy, so they offered to help her out anyway.

Ashley went back to being a student, enrolling in the French Pastry School in Chicago, then traveling to Switzerland again to study *in situ* with one of the masters. When she returned home, her parents rented a small storefront in Lincoln Park to get her started. Chicago was a tough market, though, with a lot of well-established competition. Her chocolates weren't radically different from what other chocolatiers made, so she had a hard time breaking out beyond her neighborhood customer base. She wanted to be a bigger fish in the chocolate world, so that's when she decided to move the store to Galena. "We've had a home around here for over twenty years, so I knew the area well."

"Twenty years?" I asked. "Interesting. The articles I've read about your store all described you as a newcomer."

"I'm so tired of that." She put her hands on her hips and turned to look at me. "My family owns a house in Galena Territory. Has owned a house there for those twenty years. To some people, that's a greater sin than being a thief. We're always treated as if we did something wrong by buying a house in the Territory."

"What do you say to people who accuse you of trying to drive out locally owned businesses?"

"I *am* a locally owned business. One hundred percent. That's what I tell them. It's a ridiculous double standard." She rubbed the necklace again. "After all, Stella Mueller wasn't exactly local, either. She lived—and still lives—in Dubuque."

"I imagine that must have been galling. To open a shop in a place you've been connected to for so long but to still be considered an outsider by some people."

"You can't please everyone, Mr. Dodge," she said, smiling faintly as she gave me a quick look. "I don't spend much time worrying about those people. I have plenty of others on my side."

"Right. You already knew a lot of people here, so that must have been encouraging."

"Of course. That was another reason I moved the store from Chicago. I assumed I had a head start building a customer base, even if I knew to expect trouble from certain people."

"Who did you think would give you the hardest time? The old-timers?"

"Sure. I knew I'd have trouble winning some of them over. Some folks just don't like anything new. I assumed, though, that I'd get the most trouble from Stella Mueller."

"Why Stella? Was she head of the local chamber of commerce at that time?"

Ashley lowered the bowl from the mixer and turned to look at me. "Stella and my family have a long history, Mr. Dodge. Didn't you know that?"

"No. That hasn't come up in conversation yet."

"Mr. Dodge, I'm beginning to wonder if you've done any background work for this story. You wouldn't have to talk to many people to find out about our history."

"You're right, of course, Ms. Johns. Perhaps I should have done more digging before I called you. But I'm here now, so tell me about your relationship with Stella." Ashley added a few almonds to the batter she was working on and told me how a pleasant friendship turned into a bitter feud.

When Stella first opened her ice cream store in Galena, the Johnses had been enthusiastic supporters, according to Ashley. They got ice cream several times a week and told everyone they knew to go there. Over time, they visited so often that they became friends with Stella, even invited her and her husband over to their house in Galena Territory for drinks and dinner.

"My parents believed they had become good friends with Stella and started confiding details about their work to her. They're trusting people, Mr. Dodge. Too trusting, if you ask me." She gave the chocolate mix an especially aggressive fold.

"Let me guess: Stella and your parents had a falling out."

"You're right. That woman betrayed my parents' trust. She revealed confidential details about a business deal they were working on. Not only did it kill the sale, but it took a long time for my parents to regain the trust of people in the art world."

"What exactly did she do?"

"The details don't matter now. But we'll never forget, much less forgive her."

"Why would she do it? Why sabotage someone who's been a big supporter?"

"You'd have to ask Stella, Mr. Dodge. My parents certainly asked the same question, many times."

Ashley glanced over at a clock. "I don't mean to be rude, but I have so much to get done today. I should get back to work."

"Of course. You've been generous with your time. Can I follow up by phone if I have any additional questions?"

"Yes, of course. Feel free to call me," she said, escorting me to the front door. When we reached the door, she surprised me with an invitation. "I know this is short notice, but tomorrow I'll be celebrating the two-year anniversary of Post-Modern Chocolates in Galena. I'm hosting a three-hour cruise on the *Princess Potosa*, complete with music and food. I'd be delighted if you could join us."

"That sounds like fun. I'd be honored. Do you mind if I bring a couple of guests? My friends Brian and Ruby would love it."

"Not at all. I'll put your name on the list, with a note that you'll be bringing up to three guests, in case you think of someone else you'd like to invite. We begin boarding at Ice Harbor at three thirty and will leave the port promptly at four. Dress code is business casual," she said, glancing down at my pants. "No jeans, please." She looked back up at me, turning a frown into a slight grin. "See you then."

I pulled out of the long driveway, feeling disappointed that I'd left Ashley's country retreat without having tasted any chocolate—not a truffle or a single-source bar or even a cup of hot cocoa. I had a whole new perspective on Stella and Ashley, though. As I drove away, I felt more certain than ever that the fire had been no accident. It had started near Ashley's booth. Had she been the target? Had someone, maybe Stella, been trying to hurt or kill her?

As I was reviewing the details of what I'd learned, I heard a loud roar that forced me to shift my attention back to the road. In my rearview mirror I saw a pickup kicking up a trail of dust and gaining on me very quickly. "Asshole," I thought to myself.

I looked around for a place to pull over, but there was no shoulder on either side of the road—just a drainage ditch that ran a couple of feet below grade. As the truck closed in on me, it swerved to the left as though it were going to pass me. I felt increasingly annoyed, so I slowed down a little and drifted to the left, too, to piss off the driver. When the truck nearly bumped into the rear end of my car, though, I reacted quickly—panicked, honestly—and steered to the right to get out of the way. As I lost control and careened into the ditch, the pickup zoomed right by me without slowing down.

Chapter 13

My car came to rest right side up in the drainage ditch, the airbag shooting out and crushing me between the steering wheel and the seat. My hands were shaking, and I felt stunned—at least until I thought about what had just happened; then I was just pissed off. Who the fuck was that? They didn't even stop to see if I was OK.

I moved a few body parts to make sure nothing was broken, slowly flexing my arms and legs. I was bruised, but everything was in working order, so I cut the engine, opened the door, and climbed out of my car. It was in much worse shape than I was. The car was pointing down into the ditch, the left rear wheel still spinning in the air. The front axle looked bent, and the windshield had a long crack in it—and that was just the damage that I could see. One thing was obvious: I wasn't going to be driving anywhere soon, much less back to town.

I didn't see much around except cornfields and trees. It was getting late in the afternoon, and I didn't have a cell signal, so I just started walking, hoping that the gravel road would lead me to a house or someone with a phone that worked. The air was dense and still; just the thought of walking was enough to soak the hair on the back of my head. No one drove past me, but it turned out that civilization wasn't so far away after all. I walked only about half an hour before I came to an old roadhouse.

I wasn't sure what to make of the place. In the gravel parking lot, there were a few motorcycles parked next to a couple of pickups, a Prius, and a couple of '80s-era Escorts. The building was a simple four-square with a tin roof; the patio had been covered and enclosed, probably to make sure that the customers who smoked didn't freeze in the winter. Panels of white vinyl siding were hanging at odd angles, some ready to fall off completely. Up front, an Old Style neon sign flickered next to a window that was boarded up.

I opened the screen door, nearly pulling it off the single hinge that it hung on, and passed through the patio to a cluttered but clean bar. Once inside, I was greeted by a blast of cold air laden with the smell of hot grease and cheap beer, with just a hint of lavender beneath it all. A few people turned in my direction, but I didn't hold their attention; they went back to working on their drinks.

I sat down in the middle of the bar, near the taps labeled Natural Light, Bud Light, Miller Lite, and Miller Genuine Draft, that last one obviously meant for the beer connoisseurs. The bartender was a thin woman, probably in her fifties, with well-weathered, dark brown skin, much of which was visible, thanks to the Van Halen–themed halter top around her chest.

When she came over, I told her I'd been in an accident and asked if I could use their phone. "Sure thing, dear," she said as she handed me her cell phone. I called AAA for a tow, then called Jefferson and filled him in on my wreck. After I assured him I was fine, he agreed to meet me in Galena in a little while.

With time to kill, at least a half-hour wait for the tow, I ordered a gin and tonic and chatted with the bartender, Stacy. She'd lived in the area her entire life, and she liked cats, drinking cold beer on the river, and hot men on Harleys, probably in that order. The bar, The Landing Roadhouse, had been around a long time, founded when Craigs Landing was still an actual town.

"There's been a bar here since the 1850s," Stacy told me. "You can see part of the original tavern over there." She pointed across the room to a front corner where a hole had been cut through the plaster. "We did that a couple of years ago to show off the original timbers." And here I'd just assumed that a drunk biker had punched a hole in the wall.

Stacy reached down to a countertop below her and pulled out a small bottle and spritzed a couple of mist clouds in my general direction. "It's lavender, hon. It'll help calm you down after the accident." She put the bottle back down under the bar. "So what brings you out to this neck of the woods?"

"I'm a writer. I was just driving back from an interview when I got run off the road."

"You gotta watch yourself on these roads. Some people drive like it's their private street."

"So I learned."

"Who was you talking to?" Stacy asked.

"Ashley Johns."

"Oh, the one that makes the fancy chocolates, right?"

"Yeah, that's her. She come down here much?"

"Doubt it. I never seen her here anyway. From what I hear, she pretty much keeps to herself." She put her arms on the bar and leaned forward. "I don't think she gets outs much." She slowly articulated each word, as if English were my second language.

"I suppose she's not that popular around here, seeing as she didn't grow up here," I said.

Stacy leaned back and moved a few glasses from the bar to a dishpan out of my view. "I wouldn't say that. People around here aren't that particular. Sure, we got some cliques, like anyplace else, but we're good people. All you gotta do is hang out with us, you know? Drink a beer or two with us. Just try. It ain't that big a deal." She looked down and ran a sponge over one of the glasses, then set it on the rack to dry. "So she's not exactly popular around here, sure, but I wouldn't say she's unpopular, either. She just don't try. Enough about her, though," she said, drying off her hands and looking up. "Tell me about you. You married? Got yourself a wife or girlfriend back home?"

"No, I don't have a wife or girlfriend back home."

"So I guess that ring don't mean nothing."

"Not anymore."

"Such a shame! A fine-looking man like you running around unclaimed. You better look out around here. There's lots of single women about your age who will be very eager to meet you."

Stacy had to run down to the end of the bar to serve a couple of other customers, leaving me to stare at the odd collection of license plates, deer antlers, and fishing lures that dressed up the bar. I got up and walked around to check out some of the objects more closely, sipping my drink so slowly that the ice melted and watered down the gin beyond recognition. Before I could draw any firm conclusions about the decorating decisions, the tow truck showed up. I thanked Stacy, left a couple bucks for a tip, and then rode with the truck into Galena.

I left the car at a repair shop on Highway 20, just east of downtown Galena. While the station and my insurance company negotiated a repair plan, I figured I had plenty of time to check out what was happening in town before I met Jefferson at the D & G Brewery.

It was a beautiful July evening, even with the humidity, so I walked from the repair shop down to Main Street to see what was going on. Galena gets a lot of attention from professional list makers like Inane Traveler (for example, their *Best Small Towns with Names That End in Vowels*), and while most of those lists are pure bullshit, Galena deserves the recognition it gets.

After I crossed the bridge over the Galena River, I turned right onto Main Street, the picture-postcard-perfect road that is lined with two- and three-story stone and red brick buildings, many built before the Civil War. Downtown Galena has no traditional grid; the roads bend along the gentle curve of the Galena River and have few cross streets. Most of the buildings went up with the profits of lead mining. The town's name even comes from a word for lead sulfide and replaced sexier names like Bean River Settlement and Fever River Diggings. All that lead combined with a growing steamboat trade transformed a quiet, isolated place into a boom town. Galena didn't have much industry after the lead was tapped out, though, so lots of people moved on—nearly two-thirds of the population, in fact. But they left those gorgeous buildings behind, and absent the prosperity to raze any of them to follow the latest trends in architecture and urban redevelopment, the buildings survived. A couple of generations later, those buildings defined Galena.

I took my time on Main Street so I could get in some quality people watching. Every parking place was full, as were the restaurants and gift shops. The sidewalks were packed with the usual assortment of tourists: families with young children, yuppie bikers, history buffs on walking tours, retired people sitting on benches, men pacing the sidewalks while their wives were sorting through stacks of scented candles, women waiting impatiently while their husbands were trying to pick out a T-shirt with the right fart joke.

When I finally got to the D & G Brewery, I pushed open the heavy wood doors and entered the cavernous restaurant. As servers scurried between tables and the kitchen, the sounds of voices, chairs sliding around, and clanking glasses ricocheted off the brick walls. I walked past the host's station and the packed tables to the bar, where Jefferson was sitting. "What'd you do this time, Frank?" he started.

"Nice to see you, too. I'm feeling fine, by the way, just a little bruised."

"I know; you told me that already. So tell me what happened."

"I wish I knew. I had just finished interviewing Ashley—feeling disappointed that she didn't let me sample anything—and was driving back toward Galena when a pickup came out of nowhere, driving fast and tailgating me. I looked for a place to pull over, to get out of the way, but the road was narrow and didn't have a shoulder. The truck got real close, like it was about to hit me, so I made a quick turn to avoid it, but I ended up losing control and landed in a ditch. Whoever was driving that truck didn't even stop to see if I was OK."

"So you didn't do anything to piss him off? Didn't flip him off for driving too fast? Or slow down to irritate him? Nothing like that?"

"That's right, blame the victim here."

"I'm not blaming the victim," Jefferson said. "I'm blaming *you*. I know you."

It pissed me off that Jefferson guessed that I might have slowed down to annoy the driver of the pickup, so I didn't feel like sharing that detail with him. "I didn't do anything to that driver," I said. "You know, sometimes things happen to me that aren't my fault."

"I suppose that's possible. Just like it's possible that someday when I hail a cab, it'll actually stop for me. It's just a safer bet that it won't happen."

"Thanks for the vote of confidence." I told Jefferson about my conversation with Ashley, about Ashley's accusation that Stella had sabotaged the art deal that Ashley's parents had been negotiating. Jefferson was intrigued but thought it still sounded more like a soap opera than a crime. When I told him about Ashley's invitation to go on the cruise, he got excited and asked if he could invite Lonna. I didn't object. "So what have you been up to?" I asked.

"Get yourself a beer, and I'll fill you in."

I started with a big beer, the Lead Poisoning double IPA, a beer about as subtle as it sounds. While I had been interviewing Stella and Ashley and while Ruby had been sightseeing, Jefferson was busy digging into Dubuque. He'd paid a visit to the Dubuque Police Department, where he made a couple of new friends who filled him in on the investigation.

The fire had started at an overloaded electrical outlet next to the booth for Post-Modern Chocolates. They hadn't decided yet if it was an accident or if it was intentional. It spread quickly, because the outlet was next to a box of packaging material that the vendor had brought in, which in turn ignited paper and cardboard near it. They confirmed the stories about the delay in the sprinklers and the locked exit doors, but they didn't yet know what happened with either one of them. Both of the fatalities apparently resulted from head injuries. One, a man in his seventies, probably got pushed down when the panic set in; his body was bruised, too, like he had been kicked or stepped on a couple of times after he fell. The other fatality was Jake, the young man—twenty-four years old—who worked for Post-Modern Chocolates. He'd fallen and hit his head, too, probably during the same panic. The police thought his head had smacked into a table.

"He's the employee who switched sides," I said. "Helen's article mentioned him."

"Yeah," Jefferson answered. "That's what I heard, too."

"Another interesting coincidence, don't you think?"

"Yes, Frank, but it still doesn't prove that there's anything criminal going on. The only hint I got of a conspiracy is from a couple of cops who told me they're worried that the appointed panel is going to try to whitewash the investigation to protect the mayor. The mayor has ambitions for much higher office, and one of the people being investigated is a long-time friend and ally of the mayor, the director of facilities management, a guy named Stan Mueller."

"I've heard that name before. I think Courtney Baker, the mayor's chief of staff, mentioned him. Is he related to Stella Mueller?"

"You could say that," Jefferson said. "They're married."

Chapter 14

"Stella's husband runs the convention center?" I asked.

"That's right," Jefferson said. "He's in charge of all the maintenance operations for the city, but right now he's on leave while the city investigates what happened."

"Why am I always a step behind everyone else on this assignment?" I threw up my hands as I sat back, then leaned forward again and looked over at Jefferson. "Did you know that Stella used to be friends with Ashley's parents?"

"No. I sure didn't," Jefferson said.

"They had quite a falling out," someone said behind us. Jefferson and I turned around to see who had just spoken. It was the mayor of Galena, Melissa Potts. I hadn't realized we were talking loudly enough for someone to hear our conversation. At least it was someone I recognized.

"Hi, mayor," I said. "I guess I shouldn't be surprised to bump into you here."

"Please, call me Melissa. We're not very formal here." Standing in front of me in jeans and a burgundy polo shirt with "Galena" embroidered on the left chest pocket, she proved the point. "I remember you from the press conference after the fire. You're Dodge, one of the journalists, right?"

"Yeah. Call me Frank. I don't really think of myself as a journalist, though. I write about travel. This is my friend Brian Jefferson."

"Hello, ma'am," Jefferson said, extending his hand.

"Please," she said, shaking his hand. "Just Melissa." She caught the eye of the bartender, who greeted her with a big smile. "This is my favorite place in town," she whispered. "I know a politician isn't supposed to have favorites, but the hell with it. I love this place. Come here all the time."

"I promise not to quote you on that," I said. "We were just talking about the falling out between Stella Mueller and Ashley Johns's parents. You know anything about that?"

The mayor glanced around the room. "Let's go sit at that table over there," she said, pointing to a remote corner in back. "It'll be easier to have a frank conversation there."

She got a beer, a Fever River Oatmeal Stout, and we made our way to the back. It took a while to get there, as nearly every table had someone who wanted to thank the mayor for this or ask her about that. If you took a poll of the patrons in the brewpub that night, the mayor would have been the most popular person in town.

After we sat down, she gave us a quick rundown on her bio. She'd moved to Galena in the 1960s, from Indiana. She was starting a new business making hand-woven tapestries and was looking for a cheap place to live. She'd heard about Galena, that it had a lot of inexpensive buildings, so she came up for a weekend and fell in love with the place. On her second day, she bought a three-story brick building at the far end of Main Street, not realizing at the time that she would be putting in three decades of sweat equity to rehab it. She lived in the two upper floors and turned the first floor into her studio. A year later, she opened a retail store.

She and like-minded neighbors formed the backbone of a generational effort that had transformed Main Street from a row of derelict buildings into a collection of art galleries and gift shops, all with local owners, not a Subway or a GAP or a Crate&Barrel to be found. In 1970 the group staged an open rebellion against a city plan to raze twenty-two buildings on Main Street for parking and a strip mall. They weren't going to tolerate any plans to change the essential character of Main Street. "We weren't looking to create a tourist Mecca," she told us. "And we didn't want to emulate the suburbs. We just wanted to live cheaply where we worked, to keep our historic core intact." That group was eventually so influential that it had elected most of the mayors, and most Galenians by then would be considered preservationists, even if they didn't always embrace the label.

"You've been here quite a while now," I said. "You must've seen a lot happen in that time. Like the fight we were talking about, between Stella Mueller and the Johnses."

"My, that was a doozy!" She looked around the bar, casually. Then she turned back to Jefferson and me and talked in a lower voice. "A few years ago, Richard and Lynn, Ashley's parents, told Stella about a painting that they were trying to sell. It was a… sensitive deal, one where a lot of money was at stake. Richard had a problem, though. The painting's provenance was in question."

"What do you mean by 'provenance'?" I asked.

"There were whispers that the painting might have been stolen from its owners during World War II by the Nazis. The Johnses claimed that they had thoroughly vetted the issue but couldn't definitively prove that the painting had been acquired through wholly legitimate means. In fact, that was almost their exact words," the mayor said, pausing to sip her beer. "Nevertheless, they had a buyer who was very interested in that particular piece, who was willing to take the risk and purchase it anyway. He just wanted to keep the deal very quiet. No publicity."

"It sounds like the Johnses were willing to take a risk, too," I said. "Presumably for a big payday."

"Yes, they were. I heard that they were going to make a couple hundred thousand dollars on the deal. I don't know if that's true, but that's what I heard. It never happened, though. A couple of weeks after Richard and Lynn told Stella about the painting, an article appeared in the *Chicago Tribune* about art plundered by the Nazis. Many of those pieces were never recovered. One of the examples cited in the article was the very painting that the Johnses were about to sell. Not only did the writer mention it by name, but she gave the names of the Jewish couple who were believed to own it at the time the Nazis stole it."

"Ouch," I said.

"That's an understatement, Frank. Having the painting mentioned by name in an article about Nazis wasn't too good for business. The buyer was scared off, and not only did the Johnses lose a big commission, but I heard that their reputation suffered for a while. I guess it's not good business for an art dealer to be associated with illegitimately acquired pieces."

"Or to be *publicly* associated with them, anyway," I said. "So I guess the Johnses blamed Stella for the article?"

"I don't know that they blamed Stella for the article per se, but they blamed her for the fact that the article just happened to mention a painting that they were trying to sell."

"And one that they had told Stella about at that," Jefferson said. "That would be a pretty big coincidence."

"Right. You know, some in town thought that Stella might just have been doing a favor for an old friend, passing along an extra tidbit to spice up the article."

"An old friend?" I asked.

"Yes, Helen Kraft. She's the one who wrote the article on stolen art."

Helen, again. She and Stella had one hell of a good working relationship. "I should have guessed that, I suppose," I said.

"Yeah," Jefferson said. "I suppose you should have."

I ignored his comment. "One other thing, Melissa. I know we were all in a state of shock after the fire, but you looked really distraught at the press conference. If you don't mind me saying so."

"I don't mind you saying so," the mayor said. "Or noticing it. It was a horrible turn of events. We had high hopes for the food fair, with all that potential for national exposure. I believe that Galena could really benefit from the interest in supporting smaller, noncorporate stores. That's what we've been about for a long time. So to go from that, with all the positive media buzz, to a fire in which two people died—it was deflating and horrifying. I just couldn't stop thinking about those two people who were dead."

She looked down and grasped her glass, but she just held onto it. "I didn't want to go up on that podium, but Mike—Mayor Andelfinger—insisted that we show a unified front. He wanted to assure everyone that we were in control and would stop at nothing to find out what happened. I really felt like it was his problem to deal with, but that wasn't the time to say so."

"What have you heard about the investigation so far?" I asked.

"I know they have a group in Dubuque looking into it. But, off the record, I wouldn't expect much."

"What do you mean?" Jefferson asked.

"I don't expect the investigation to go very deep. Mayor Andelfinger has big ambitions—he's running for Congress, you know—so I expect he's going to insist on a quick turnaround for the report. They'll probably put the responsibility on some lackey who works at the convention center, claiming negligence or incompetence. That'll give Mike a scapegoat he can publicly blame and then fire."

"Like Stan Mueller?" I asked.

"No, not Stan," the mayor said, nodding her head. "Stan is a big fish, not a little one. He's too close to Mike to take the fall for this."

"Just how tight are they?" Jefferson asked.

"Very. They grew up together, I hear. In some rural area south of Dubuque. On the river, I think. From what I understand, they've been best friends pretty much their entire lives. I don't see any way that Mike would try to pin this on Stan."

CHAPTER 15

The mayor finished her beer and left. I talked Jefferson into heading a few blocks down Main Street to listen to a band at a corner bar called The Bean River Settlement House; the name of the place was a play on one of the early names for Galena. We entered through a door at the corner of the building and pushed through a tight group of people to get to the bar. Up front, I spotted a man wearing a brown vest and matching bowler and a woman dressed in a plaid skirt and gray leg warmers. They were standing in a corner surrounded by stringed instruments, where they chatted with a few fans, each holding a bottle of beer that they sipped from as often as they could. We took advantage of the break between sets to get drinks and find an open space next to a wall where we could stand. The room was narrow but deep, running nearly a half block long. The crowd was a pretty good mix of older and less-old patrons, with a few twenty-somethings mixed in with a fondness for plaid unifying the generations.

"If anyone in that band pulls out a banjo, I'm leaving," Jefferson said.

While we were waiting for the band to start playing again, we talked about our next steps investigating the fire.

"You having fun yet, Brian?" I asked.

"I'm getting there, I admit. Some things are starting to get my curiosity going."

"What do you want to do next?"

"Good question. We're going to need to find out more about that Dubuque mayor and his friend Stan Mueller. I don't think we're going to get that done tonight, though. Maybe I can find out some more about that guy tomorrow. And you should use your journalist credentials to set up an interview with somebody."

"I can do that. I have a number for the mayor's assistant, Courtney."

"I'd like to find out more about the kid who died, too. Jake. I have a feeling there's a lot more to his story."

We talked for a few more minutes, until the band started to play and the sound ping-ponged off the stone walls and around the bar, making it hard to hear each other. When one of the musicians put down a guitar and picked up a banjo, Jefferson quickly grabbed my arm and ushered me out of the bar and back onto Main Street.

"I really don't understand what you have against banjos," I said, stumbling off the stoop and onto the sidewalk.

"Like I said, I can't stand them. Let's just leave it at that."

"You have more issues to work out than I realized."

"You're one to talk."

We walked down a couple more blocks to a larger pub, Uncorked, which was a lot less crowded. We scanned the bar, trying to decide which of the leopard-skin-covered barstools we wanted to sit on.

"This is cool," Jefferson said, smiling. "If I ever set up a bar in my house, I'm going to find barstools just like these."

"Like I said, you have issues to work out."

The bartender was in front of us before our asses hit the black spots on the fabric, handing us each a drink menu. Uncorked had a long list of fancy cocktails, including their specialty, the Nine Generals, a blend of nine ingredients (just four liquors, thankfully, not nine) named in honor of the city's Civil War generals. Since I didn't have to drive, I ordered one. Jefferson got another Beam and Coke.

"Don't you want to try something different?" I asked him.

"Don't need to. That'll be good enough for me right now."

"But they have a list of more than forty different cocktails. Aren't you curious to try something new?"

"Why you bugging me about my drink choice? I don't always need to try something different, like you do. I like Beam and Coke, so I drink what I like."

The bartender came back with our drinks and set them in front of us. The Nine Generals was poured into a small stein, with a slice of lemon as garnish. We paid in cash, tipping a couple of bucks per drink. When the bartender came back down to check on us, we asked him if he'd heard about the kid who'd died in the fire in Dubuque.

"Jake Horgan? Sure," the bartender said. "This isn't a big city. Most people who live here knew Jake."

"I imagine everyone is in shock about it," I said.

"Of course. Jake was a good kid, really popular. Everyone liked him. Terrible tragedy."

"Did he grow up around here?" I asked.

"Yeah. His family's been here a long time. They have a farm up in Wisconsin. By Sinsinawa, near the monastery."

"Seems like he got caught in the middle of a big feud," Jefferson said.

"You mean that mess between Stella Mueller and Ashley Johns?"

"Yes," Jefferson said. "That's what I was thinking of."

"Yeah, that was a pretty big mess. I don't really understand what happened there. Jake was such a nice guy, but some folks thought he was double-dealing."

"What do you mean?" I asked.

"He went to work in that ice cream shop when he was a senior in high school, I think. Even after he started college, he kept some hours there. Of course, he was just up the road in Dubuque, so he didn't have far to drive. Seemed like he got along really well with Stella, the owner. Then that accident happened."

"You mean the freezer that broke down?" I asked.

"Yeah. That seemed to change everything. The ice cream store had to close over a busy weekend. Then Jake suddenly changed jobs and went to work at the chocolate shop, for Ashley. I think he burned a bridge with that move."

"If I was Stella, I imagine I'd be pretty pissed," Jefferson said. "And I'd be looking over my shoulder, too."

"There was plenty of suspicion going around, that's for sure. Even though the official story was that the freezer failure was an accident—maybe even the owner's fault for not taking proper care of it—when Jake switched sides in the middle of the fight, it made folks wonder if he might have had something to do with it after all. I'd say those folks felt even more strongly that something was up when other... rumors went around."

"What were people saying?" Jefferson asked.

The bartender gave us a look-over before continuing. "I hate to be spreading rumors about a nice guy like Jake—especially with his passing—but, honestly, this was more than just a rumor; it was pretty much common knowledge around here. Ashley has a house in the country, about twenty minutes from here. She says she uses it to experiment, to create and test new recipes. That's all fine. Got no reason to question her. But she had Jake out to that house a lot. Claimed he was helping her create and test new chocolates." He leaned forward and put an elbow on the bar. "When he worked at the ice cream store, he was, you know, a clerk. He scooped up ice cream and took customers' money. I don't know what suddenly qualified him to be a chocolate maker. Not long after he started with Ashley, he was pretty much managing the store. That's some pretty rapid advancement."

"Are you saying that he had something more going on with Ashley?" Jefferson asked.

"Like I said, I don't want to be spreading gossip, but this was an open secret around here. Her house is near a boat ramp, near the Mississippi. Lots of people who know Jake saw his car parked at her house early in the morning when they were on the way to go fishing. I hear he told his friends that he was in love with her but that she insisted on keeping their relationship very quiet. She didn't think folks around here would be too approving, given how much they liked Jake and how little they liked her."

"Ashley's not very popular?" I asked.

"That's an understatement. We love her chocolates but not her. I think that's the real reason she does so much work at her house. She knows she's really unpopular and doesn't want to ruin her business by being around customers too often. I figured that's part of the reason she had Jake around, too, to improve her image and jack up sales at the store."

The bartender had to run off and make a few fancy cocktails, giving us a chance to bat about his revelations. Jake hadn't been quite the innocent bystander I'd thought he might be. He was right in the middle of the dustup, maybe even kicking up some wind by choosing sides for the most personal of reasons. I wondered just when Jake's affair with Ashley had started. Were they sleeping together when the freezer broke down? Did Ashley flirt with him to lure him from Stella, then keep him around by sleeping with him? When I'd interviewed Ashley that morning, I hadn't picked up any hint that she'd been having a relationship with him. And Stella—what had been her reaction when Jake switched sides? I had a lot of work to do.

Our new buddy, the bartender, got busier as a few more people walked in, so we decided to call it a night and head back to Dubuque. We waved goodbye to him and exited back to Main Street, where we were among just a handful of people walking around. Galena is known for a lot of things, but late-night entertainment isn't one of them.

We climbed the stone steps of Washington Street up to Bench Street, where Jefferson had parked. The air was still and comfortable, the sky clear. The laughter of the few remaining partiers echoed faintly through the streets. Light pooled around the bases of the streetlamps, replicas of the ones that lined the streets a hundred years before. I felt like I was jumping from island to island as we moved from light to darkness and back to light again. I was calm, the most relaxed I'd been all day, maybe in weeks. I turned to Jefferson to see if he was relaxed or on edge, but it was hard to make out his facial expressions.

As we got to his truck and opened the door, a foul smell emptied out with a blast. "What the fuck is that?" Jefferson asked.

"Geez. What'd you have for lunch?" I asked.

"Just shut up and look around."

I held my nose as we searched inside. In the back, on the floor behind the driver's seat, I spotted a pile of dead fish—or, rather, a pile of fish parts: guts, heads, and tails, mostly.

"I didn't know you went fishing today," I said.

"I didn't," Jefferson said, his face and fists tightening. "I don't fish."

"So where did the fish parts come from? A souvenir for your daughters?"

"I didn't buy them, didn't put them there. If this is some kind of sick joke on your part, you're paying to clean it up."

"It wasn't me," I said, trying not to laugh. "So if neither one of us put them in your truck, who did?"

"Don't fuck with me, Frank. Did you put this shit in my truck?"

"Absolutely not," I said. As it started to sink in that neither one of us was responsible for the pile of fish remains, I didn't feel so calm anymore.

"I guess someone is trying to tell me something," Jefferson said.

We scooped out the fish remains and headed out of Galena, with all the windows down. Jefferson dropped me off at my motel and went back to his room in Dubuque.

It had been one hell of a day. I got forced off a country road, and someone served notice to Jefferson in a highly aromatic way. I had assumed that my accident was just that, an accident. Maybe that person just thought I was a lousy driver. And it's possible that someone else was just suggesting that Jefferson should make a pot of fish stock. Then again, maybe someone had taken exception to all the questions we were asking.

We'd been working this from the bottom up, checking on the people we thought were the main players in the feud, Stella and Ashley. Maybe it was time to think a little bigger. Maybe it was time to rattle a few cages higher up the food chain.

CHAPTER 16

Jefferson picked me up at the Clear Lake Inn the next morning and took me to get a rental car. We met back up at the Ice Harbor Inn, by the fountain in the middle of the lobby.

"What a beautiful church that is!" Ruby said, fresh from attending mass at the Cathedral of St. Raphael. "I tried to listen to the priest and to follow along with the mass, but it wasn't easy. I kept looking at those beautiful stained-glass windows, trying to understand what they represent." I didn't know that Ruby had such a fondness for fancy windows.

"Did you get down to the mortuary in the basement?" I asked.

"Yes. I went down right after mass." Then she chuckled. "I've never seen a room that white."

"You haven't been in the rooms I've been in," Jefferson said.

"I suppose I haven't," Ruby said. "But this room, the mortuary—with all that Italian marble covering everything, even the floor and ceiling—will always be white."

"I've seen rooms like that, too," Jefferson added, this time with a smile.

Jefferson dropped off his truck at a car wash for a thorough cleaning—it was still carrying more than a hint of fish stink—so the three of us got into my rental car and drove to the Parthenon Bistro, a cozy neighborhood place near Loras College that hosted a popular Sunday brunch. It was the kind of place that ambitious politicians can't resist, like ribbon-cuttings on highway bridges and back rooms with check-writing millionaires.

We got there just as the rest of the post-church crowd was arriving, so we put our names on the waiting list and went inside the bar, staking out standing room in front of a large mirror framed by plastic Corinthian columns and next to a bust of Athena. I went up to the bar and ordered two Bloody Marys and a ginger ale.

"I'm so surprised at what happened yesterday," Ruby said. "Someone wants you to go away, I think."

"Looks that way," I said, but I didn't want to dwell on it. "So what else did you do yesterday, besides admiring those Tiffany windows?"

"I had the most interesting time, and no one tried to run me off the street. I rode the trolley out to Eagle Point Park. I have always loved that place. I wish I had spent more time there over the years. Every time I've gone to the park, I've looked at those buildings and thought that there was something familiar about them. This time it hit me: They remind me of some of the Frank Lloyd Wright houses I've seen pictures of."

"You have a good eye, Ruby," I said. "They were designed by a man named Alfred Caldwell, who studied under Wright."

"Well, the park is so beautiful! And the views of the river from on top of that bluff—well, it just makes you appreciate the river in a whole new way. If you look hard enough, you can almost see Marquette and Joliet paddling right by," she said with a laugh. I joked that I was going to steal that line the next time I wrote about the seventeenth-century French explorers.

"You see things that I'm pretty sure no one else can," Jefferson said.

"Yes, people have told me that before." She laughed again. "After my walk around the park, I rode the trolley back to the library." She put her hand on my shoulder. "You know how I love libraries."

"Was there something you were trying to find out?" I asked. "Or did you go just to make sure they knew what they were doing?"

"They don't need my help, at least not here. Back home in Friesburg, they do pretty well with the library, but sometimes they need a little push. They can get too..."

"Safe?" I asked.

"Predictable, I'd say. I like to request books that will get someone a little upset." Ruby took a sip of her ginger ale. "But I don't need to do that in Dubuque. They have plenty of other patrons like me to take care of that."

"What did you look up?" I asked, signaling that we should keep our voices down.

"That Helen Kraft keeps coming up, so I thought I'd look up some of her articles. I sat down with a reference librarian, who helped me search on the Internet. Goodness, that Kraft is prolific! We found a dozen articles she had written just this year—and for good magazines, too, like *Condé Nast Traveler*, *Travel and Leisure*, and *AARP The Magazine*."

"Were they all about travel?" I asked.

"Most of them were, Frank, but she had a couple about food as well. As we researched further back, we found more variety in what she wrote: articles about art, history—even a couple about fashion."

"Did you find the article about Nazi stolen art?" I asked.

"Yes, we did. We also found the article she wrote about Stella's ice cream, when she first started selling it on Main Street in Galena. I copied them, of course."

"Do you have them with you?" I asked.

"No, sorry. I didn't think to grab them when we left the hotel. I'll show them to you after we eat."

Just as our Bloody Marys were getting low, the host called our names and we were escorted to a table. The restaurant filled a long room that was split into two sections by a half wall with a flimsy screen on top of it. Embedded in the screen were images from Greek art—two-dimensional cutouts of disc tossers, javelin throwers, Aphrodite and Zeus, the standard Greek American chic.

In the back end of the room, where the half wall ended, tables were lined up against a wall; they were covered with about a dozen silver chafing dishes. It was an impressive spread. On one end, the usual breakfast options were laid out—scrambled eggs, sausage, bacon, hash browns—but a few surprises, too, like eggs benedict with gyro meat and ricotta-stuffed waffles. On the other side, chafing dishes were filled with traditional Greek dishes: chicken *souvlaki*, stuffed eggplant, *spanakopita*. Between the breakfast and lunch tables were two stations with chefs preparing made-to-order dishes, one making omelets and the other carving slices off a prime rib roast. Jefferson and I ordered another round of Bloody Marys; then the three of us hit the buffet and filled up our plates.

We had barely chewed our first couple of bites when a quiet buzz began near the front door and slowly spread from the bar to the dining room. Conversations quieted to a whisper, and some of the diners tried to check out the scene by looking out of the corners of their eyes. Midwestern etiquette doesn't prohibit staring, after all; you're just not supposed to get caught doing it.

Two men were at the center of the buzz: Dubuque Mayor Andelfinger and a man I didn't recognize. Courtney Baker, the mayor's chief of staff, trailed a step or two behind, occasionally stepping forward to whisper in the mayor's ear, probably telling him what to say.

"I wonder who that man is with the mayor?" I asked.

"That's Congressman Geiger," Ruby said. "He's the one who is retiring. The mayor wants his job."

The two of them took their time working the room, stopping at nearly every table to say a few platitudes and to beg for support. The congressman was going out on top. He'd been the area's rep for some thirty years but finally decided it was time to slow down. "I hear he just got tired of fundraising," Ruby said. "It's not like when he first ran for Congress. Now it seems they never stop asking for money."

"That's because there used to be a time when they'd stop campaigning for a while and do some actual governing," I said. "Now they just campaign all the time, especially when they're in session."

As the entourage approached our table, the mayor frowned when he recognized me, but I think he realized that he would look bad if he didn't stop at our table. He gave a subtle wave to Courtney, almost as if he were asking her to step up and serve as a buffer. Before she could get around him, though, I jumped up and shook the hand of the congressman.

"It's nice to meet you, congressman," I said. "Thank you for representing the area so well for so long." I had no idea if he really did represent the area well. I was just looking to score a couple of quick points, so I could corner the mayor for a minute.

"Thank you," the congressman said. "I'm glad we have someone as talented and ambitious as Mayor Andelfinger to carry the torch forward." The congressman turned to the mayor, who reluctantly stepped forward. He didn't reach out to shake my hand.

"I believe we've met before, haven't we?" the mayor asked. "You're a journalist, right?"

"Not exactly. I'm a writer, not a journalist." I noticed that Courtney slipped a little closer, inching up next to the mayor. "I write mostly about travel, especially travel along the Mississippi River."

"That's great," the mayor said, taking a step toward the next table. "Nice to see you again."

Before he could take another step away from me, I slid over and blocked his path. "How's the investigation of the convention center fire coming along, mayor? I imagine it's not easy to investigate a disaster that happened on your watch when you're running for higher office, especially when your best friend might be culpable."

The mayor turned bright red, and his jaw clenched before he responded. "We're doing all we can," he replied. "But this isn't the time for questions about that."

"I understand. It's naive to assume that public officials should actually be accountable to the public, especially during a campaign."

The mayor didn't flinch. "I promise you, and everyone in this city, that we won't rest until we know exactly what happened on Friday. We're going to do it right, and we'll find who's responsible, regardless of who that turns out to be."

With that, Courtney pushed between me and the mayor. The congressman looked around the room, back at me, then said something about needing to rush off to an appointment. The mayor followed quickly behind him. Courtney stood in front of me long enough to ensure that the two politicians could make an easy exit, racing to the door without any further trouble and never once turning around to look at me.

"That went well, I think," I said to Jefferson and Ruby as I sat back down.

Before I could get back to eating, though, my phone buzzed with a new text message. It was from Courtney. "Ambush journalism won't work here. Not impressed. Maybe Kraft not the prob; maybe its u." I expected that from Courtney, but she had no idea how much of a problem I was willing to be.

We finished eating brunch amid sideward stares, most of them curious but a few hostile.

"Just how did the mayor get to be the anointed one, anyway?" Jefferson asked.

"I'm not sure," Ruby said. "But I read in the paper that he has a lot of connections, and he's very good at raising money."

"That figures," Jefferson said.

"He should have changed his name when he went into politics," I said. "Andelfinger. It sounds depraved. Either he's a thief or a pervert. A politician may be both of those things, but they usually prefer not to advertise it."

As we walked up front to pay, a woman sidled up to me at the bar. "You're not from around here, are you?"

"What gave me away?" I asked.

"The way you talked to the mayor, for one. No one from Dubuque would do that to him, at least not in public."

"Why not? He's a public servant. He needs to be held accountable."

"Of course. It's just that Dubuque isn't that big a city. Everyone knows everyone. If you want to get along, you have to be careful about the fights you start."

"I get that," I said. "But what about the local journalists. Don't they hound the mayor and other public officials, to hold them accountable?"

"Not really. The paper and the mayor's office are pretty cozy, I hear. I guess they figure it's better for everyone if they get along and show a united front."

"Unified against whom?" I asked. "Is Dubuque at war with someone?"

"It's not war, exactly. It's just that folks around here tend to rally around one of their own when they are being attacked by someone who isn't from here. It's probably like that in a lot of places. But here, you get to be one of them only if you're born in Dubuque."

"Why are you telling me all this? Shouldn't you be pulling your wagon into the circle with everyone else?"

"I suppose, but I never bought into all that. Besides, there's something really shady about that man, the mayor. I don't trust him, never have. I'd like to see you catch him up to no good. You won't do it, though, by making people around here mad."

I resolved to be a little less confrontational—or less so in public, anyway—and left a nice tip with our bill. Jefferson, Ruby, and I went back to our respective rooms to change into something less comfortable, the business casual clothes required for the riverboat cruise celebrating Post-Modern Chocolate's second anniversary. It was going to be a tough place to roll out my friendlier public face.

CHAPTER 17

I convinced Jefferson and Ruby to head down to the harbor early, so we could take a quick tour of the Mississippi River Museum and Aquarium. I wanted them to know what was swimming beneath us—blue catfish, sauger, walleye, sturgeon, drum, snapping turtles—while we enjoyed our rich chocolates and fine wine.

When we got to the dock at three thirty, people were already lined up, waiting to board the *Princess Potosa* for the party. Our group had grown to four; Jefferson had invited barkeep Lonna, who hadn't needed any convincing to accept. The boat, a replica of a nineteenth-century steamboat, had been built to twenty-first-century standards: fresh paint on blind nostalgia. The foundation was an old barge hull; the paddlewheel was just for show, since diesel engines provided the real power; the resident band played the same Dixieland songs they'd played forty years before; the cook was pretty good with a microwave but not much else. Good thing I wasn't there for a standard tourist cruise.

When the cord across the gangplank was lifted, we filed onboard and wandered around for a few minutes. The handrails on each deck were wrapped with chocolate-colored streamers. On the second and third decks, congratulatory signs in hand-drawn calligraphy covered the interior walls, and flowers—roses and daisies mostly—were placed in vases on every table and in tall urns in each corner. On the second deck, a brass quartet in matching tuxedos, obviously not the house band, was blowing out some swinging tunes. Chocolate truffles and sheets of chocolate bark had been placed on glass plates covered with plastic wrap, off-limits until we got underway. Ashley (or her parents) had obviously spent some serious money on this party.

We climbed to the top deck to check out the views and to find the bar, working our way around large coolers aligned in a row on one side and the pilot house that spread across the front of the deck. It was another warm, bright day, but a light breeze occasionally drifted off the river, refreshing the air and my mood.

I recognized a few of the other guests. In one corner, Melissa Potts, the mayor of Galena, was talking with the bartender from the D & G Brewery and the musicians from the band Jefferson and I had walked out on the previous night. I caught a glimpse of Stella Mueller boarding, Helen Kraft at her side; I couldn't imagine any reason that Stella would want to be part of this. Courtney Baker was working the crowd, shaking hands and smiling at people, but Mayor Andelfinger was nowhere in sight. I felt increasingly confident that this was going to be a very entertaining cruise. One person I didn't see anywhere was Ashley. Maybe she was hiding in the green room, waiting to make a grand entrance.

At four o'clock, the boat's whistle blew, the gangplank was raised and swung around, and the engine engaged to move us out into the river. The floor vibrated and the smell of diesel fuel wafted past us as we slowly drifted away from Ice Harbor and under the graceful arch of the Julien Dubuque Bridge. We found a seat for Ruby, and the rest of us went to get drinks. "You think I'm gonna trust you to pick out a drink for me?" Lonna teased Jefferson.

The bar was stocked with the good stuff: craft beer and fancy booze, top-shelf vodka and single-malt Scotch, nothing younger than twelve years.

Lonna and I each got the eighteen-year Highland Park Scotch; Jefferson got a vodka martini.

"No Beam and Coke this time?" I asked.

"I'm not paying for it, so why not get the good stuff?"

"What kind of vodka's in it?"

"Belvedere something, in a black bottle. They had a couple of others, but I couldn't figure out how to pronounce any of the names," he responded, raising his glass to mine and Lonna's to toast.

The bar didn't have any strawberry or apple wine, so we ordered a glass of Alsatian Riesling for Ruby. Courtney walked toward the bar, but when she saw me, she turned around and went back to mingling on deck. I wished Helen had done the same.

When we got back to Ruby, Helen sauntered over to our table. "Frank, surprised to see you here," she said, with a half flip of her bangs. "I'm also surprised that you found something appropriate to wear. I assumed you'd be hunched over your computer somewhere working on your feature article, trying to write an edgy story about fine food from your unique perspective." She pretended to type, shoulders rounded down for effect. "I'm sure you'll figure something out."

"I'm nearly done with it already," I lied. I've learned that Helen doesn't need to know everything I'm up to.

"Good for you, Frank." Helen turned her attention to the table. "And you have your lovely friends with you, too. How special it must be for you, Dolly," she said, looking at Ruby, "to come from such a humble background and yet, here you are, on an elegant cruise like this."

"It's Ruby, not Dolly," Ruby said, looking right at Helen. "Yes, I'm thrilled to be here. And I feel so lucky that we found a place to tie up our wagon at the port." I don't think Helen heard Ruby's comments, but Stella did. She slid a hand over her mouth to hide a big grin, stepping around Helen and next to me.

"Hi, Ruby. It's nice to meet you. I'm Stella."

Ruby and Stella shook hands, then Stella turned to me. "Frank. Nice to see you again."

"Nice to see you, too," I said. I introduced her to Jefferson and Lonna and thanked her for the factory tour and the free ice cream. "I can't stop thinking about how delicious it was," I said.

"Thank you. I appreciate it."

"I'm surprised to see *you* here, though," I said.

"I'm surprised to *be* here. I got a handwritten invitation from Ashley, virtually begging me to attend. She wrote something about making a fresh start, putting old disputes to rest."

"Huh. That's a nice gesture, but it hardly sounds like the woman everyone has described to me."

"That's what I thought," Stella said. "I could hardly believe it came from her."

"But we figured there couldn't be any harm in showing up," Helen said, jumping in.

"I suppose not," I said.

"We should move on," Helen said. "Let these people enjoy their cruise."

"You're right," Stella said. "I'm sure we'll see you later. Nice to meet you all." Helen and Stella walked off to explore. I shot a look at Jefferson.

"I don't know anything about your history with that woman," Lonna said, "but I can't imagine anyone anywhere that I'd let talk to me like that and get away with it. You need to stand up for yourself better, Frank."

"What she said," Jefferson added.

"And what exactly did she mean, that Helen, that this cruise must be a special treat for me?" Ruby asked. "Just because I live in a small town doesn't mean my cultural experiences are limited to barn dances and pig calls. No, I don't like her one bit."

Before I could defend myself for feeling defenseless with Helen, Galena's Mayor Potts came over to say hi. "Hello, Frank, Brian. Nice to see you again. I didn't know you'd be here today."

"I got a last-minute invitation from Ashley," I said. "Mayor Potts, this is our friend Ruby. She lives just upriver in Friesburg."

"Ruby, nice to meet you. And please, call me Melissa." The mayor reached out to shake Ruby's hand.

"It's so nice to meet you, too, mayor... Melissa," Ruby said. "Galena is such a beautiful city. All those handsome brick buildings on Main Street. And the mansions! I have some very good memories from trips to Galena."

"Thank you, Ruby. We're lucky that so much of our city has been preserved. I haven't been to Friesburg in a while, but from what I remember, it has a very nice riverfront park. Is that right?"

"Yes, that's right. It's been cleaned up a lot in the last ten years. A lot of people take a daily walk along that riverfront path now. I don't get down there as much as I should, though."

"That's something we don't have in Galena. While we have a nice walking path along the levee next to the Galena River, it's not quite like taking a stroll along the Mississippi, is it?" The mayor turned to Jefferson's date. "And who is this?"

"This is Lonna, owner of Lonna's Livery," I said.

"I believe we've met before," the mayor said. "I've had drinks at your place several times. I love that patio!"

"Thank you," Lonna said. "I don't tolerate many politicians in my bar, but you don't seem much like one to me. I hope you'll come back sometime soon. The first round will be on me."

"Believe me, I understand. Politicians are a shady bunch. I will be back, for sure, and I'll be happy to take you up on that offer." The mayor turned to face me. "Did you see Stella Mueller here?"

"Yeah. I saw her walk on board. With Helen Kraft."

"Hmm. That surprises me. I wouldn't have expected to see Stella at this party, given the circumstances."

"You mean with her husband under investigation?" Jefferson asked. "Or just the general hatred between her and Ashley?"

"Oh, no. It's not that. Sorry," she said, catching herself. "I'd better not say any more. It'll become obvious soon enough." She smiled, then scanned the room. "I should get back to the friends I came here with. Nice to see you again, and to meet your friends." She shook our hands and disappeared up the stairs, leaving us to wonder what the hell she knew that we didn't.

Right after she walked away, the music stopped playing, and an announcement came over the PA system inviting all the guests to the second deck for a toast. "I have a feeling that something more entertaining than a simple toast is about to happen," Lonna said.

CHAPTER 18

We went back down to the second deck, where we squeezed into a spot in a corner, close enough to see what was happening up front and just a couple people removed from Stella and Helen. Ashley was standing to the side of the small stage next to two people that I assumed were her parents, Richard and Lynn Johns. Ashley was wearing a black dress—did she own anything but?—with a silver necklace hanging down the front and diamond studs in her ears. Her father was dressed in a suit, pin stripes, her mother in a stunning red dress that would have looked more appropriate on a New York runway than on a Mississippi River tourist boat.

Richard Johns walked up to the microphone, tapped it several times, and said a quick "Testing." Satisfied that it was working, he waved his hands to signal for the crowd to shut up. When that didn't quiet anyone, Lynn Johns stepped up the microphone and said a full-throated "Please. We're about to begin." That worked. Richard stepped back to the microphone and pulled out a piece of paper that he unfolded without looking at it, his hands trembling just enough to notice.

"I'm so thrilled to be here with you today, to celebrate the second anniversary of my daughter's business, Post-Modern Chocolates. We," he said, looking at his wife, "couldn't be more proud of Ashley, of her success, of those incredible, those artful chocolates that she creates. We had no idea that she was so creative, that she had such an exceptional palate." He quickly glanced down at the paper, then back up at the crowd. "We're humbled that you came here today to celebrate with us."

"I'd celebrate just about anything with anyone for free top-shelf booze," Jefferson whispered to me.

"Amen," I whispered back.

"I could go on all day praising Ashley, but I know she's anxious to get up here and speak for herself... And to make an exciting announcement. So please, let's give a cheer for my... our daughter, Ashley Johns. Congratulations, Ashley!" He gave her a quick half hug and a pat on the shoulder.

As Richard stepped back from the microphone, I looked around the room. A few people clapped with enthusiasm for Ashley, but most of the guests seemed more interested in their drinks or in whispering something to their friends.

Ashley turned to face the crowd and cleared her throat, but as she spoke, her voice was so soft that no one could make out what she was saying. After a couple of shouts from the crowd—"Speak louder!"—Ashley cleared her throat again and started over.

"Thank you, all of you, for coming here and celebrating with me. I'm humbled. It means so much to me to have you here, to feel your support, whether you're one of the people I've known since I was little or a new friend."

The crowd didn't seem any more interested in Ashley than they were in her father. The noise level was beginning to pick up a little when she cleared her throat for a third time and found a voice that finally carried above the crowd.

"As you know, I've strived from the beginning to serve you nothing but the best chocolates, while keeping the prices affordable enough that you can enjoy them regularly. I'm lucky to have a kitchen where I can experiment, so I can continually bring you new flavors to try. On the tables around the boat, you'll find some of my latest experiments. I hope you'll let me know what you think of them."

The hint of free chocolate was enough to hush the crowd and focus their attention back on Ashley.

"There's one truffle I'm especially proud of: creamy milk chocolate with wild blueberries. I can't take all the credit for it. It was really Jake's idea." She paused, tearing up after mentioning his name. "I still can't believe he's gone," she said, softly, while wiping away a tear. "I've decided to call this new truffle Sweet and Wild, in his honor."

A collective blush rippled through the crowd. Stella groaned, "Oh, please."

"I'm so lucky I have the good fortune to pursue my dreams," Ashley continued. "Ever since I began crafting chocolates, I've known that there was something else I could create that would be their perfect match, the perfect frame for the canvas of my chocolate creations. I'm finally making that vision a reality. Next month, I'll be introducing my own brand of ice cream. I'm calling it Frozen Expressions!"

"What the hell? She's going to make ice cream?" was the first reaction I heard from the crowd. Followed quickly by "'Fresh start,' my ass!" I don't know if Ashley heard Stella's outburst, but I certainly did. I watched as Helen put an arm around Stella and whispered into her ear, before leading her out of the room and down the stairs. Stella stared down Ashley the whole way out; she was burning hot enough to melt all the ice cream on the boat. I swear that Ashley saw Stella leaving the deck and reacted with a barely visible smirk.

"As I speak," Ashley continued, "the staff is setting up tasting stations on the deck above us and another on this deck. Please sample all you'd like. I just know you're going to love it." She rubbed on her necklace as she looked around at the crowd. "Within a few weeks, you'll find it in my new store in Galena, and soon I hope to have it in grocery stores all around the area. Thank you again for sharing this with me today." She stepped back from the mic, and her parents walked up and framed her: Richard on one side and Lynn on the other.

"I guess Stella's got some competition," Jefferson said.

"I'd say so," Ruby said.

"Hell of a way to announce it," I said, "with Stella, your main competitor, just a few feet away. It's a good thing Stella wasn't armed with an ice cream scoop."

"But it would be rude of us not to taste it, right?" Lonna asked. "After all, we're guests on her cruise."

"I suppose I should find out how it compares to Stella's ice cream," I said. "For research purposes."

We followed a crowd upstairs and got in line. Four servers were stationed on one side of the deck, each standing behind a large cooler. As we got closer, I saw that each cooler had eight gallons of ice cream, eight different flavors for us to sample. Most flavors used chocolate in one way or another, but a couple were chocolate-free.

"I wonder where she's making it," I said. "I don't remember seeing any ice-cream-making equipment at her home, and I doubt she's making it at her retail store."

"Then she's probably got a partner she didn't mention," Jefferson said. "Someone who has the space and equipment."

"Right. That would make sense." We moved a couple of steps closer to the coolers. "Who could that be? Who else in the area has the capacity to help her out?"

"I'm not an expert in ice cream manufacturing," Lonna said, "but Dubuque is a big enough city to have at least a couple of places that could do it for her. Besides, who said the partner had to be local? Her family's from Chicago, right?"

"Right. There are dozens of places in Chicago that she could work with, I suppose."

As our turn in line came, we pledged to each try a different flavor. I love good chocolate, but I'm not a huge fan of chocolate ice cream, so I volunteered to try the cherry vanilla. Lonna jumped on the Mexican chocolate, Jefferson chose mint chocolate, and Ruby, without hesitation, chose triple chocolate explosion.

We walked to the side of the deck and compared notes. "I like it," I said, "but it's not the best I've ever had. I'd say Stella's is creamier, the flavors more intense. What do the rest of you think?"

Lonna thought it was as good as Ben & Jerry's. Jefferson might buy some ice cream once in a while, but he thought the cheap ice cream was as good as the expensive stuff, and Ashley's samples didn't entice him to change his mind. Ruby thought it was delicious but not as good as the chocolate by itself. The consensus opinion was that no one was about to leave any of the ice cream uneaten—that would be wasteful—but we'd wait to see the price before deciding to buy it. And we were surprised that the flavors were, for the most part, conventional.

Before we had a chance to go down to the second deck and sample the chocolates, we heard a commotion from below, a couple of screams followed by a loud splash. Jefferson and I raced down the stairs to the passageway around the second deck and found Stella in Ashley's face, screaming things like "This means war!" and "You picked the wrong person to fuck with!" and "Your ice cream is just like your personality—bland and forgettable!" At least Stella had found time to taste it for herself, so she could make an informed insult.

I looked over the side of the boat and saw a couple of gallons of Frozen Expressions Ice Cream floating in the Mississippi, the dark chocolate color distinguishable from the muddy river water more by a glossy sheen than by its color. Ashley's father came running down the stairs, followed closely by two rather large men who looked like they weren't much into joking around. They pushed their way between Stella and Ashley. Richard Johns faced Stella directly and warned her to step back or she'd spend the rest of the cruise locked in a closet, emphasizing his threat by poking at her shoulder again and again. When the boat shuddered for a second, he grabbed a handrail to steady himself; then he turned to say something to Ashley: "I told you this was a bad idea. She'd have found out soon enough. We didn't need to do it this way." Ashley looked unfazed by her father's comments.

I watched as Stella's face turned bright red and she took a few steps backward. Then, as Richard and Ashley argued, she pointed herself toward Ashley and raced forward. She might have connected with her intended target if not for the pool of ice cream on the deck. Instead, she slipped, lost her balance, crashed into a wall sideways, then bounced off it right into Richard, pushing against him to steady herself but with enough force to send him tumbling over the handrail. She grabbed that same handrail to steady herself as Richard splashed into the Mississippi, some fifteen feet below us and just upstream of the floating cartons of Frozen Expressions Ice Cream.

Ashley screamed, as did a couple of other people. Someone yelled, "Man overboard!" One of the bullies that had come with Richard grabbed Stella, while the other ran down to the lowest deck. I looked down to see Richard splashing around, trying to keep his head above water. A life preserver landed just in front of him, but he was too disoriented—or panicked—to notice it and kept splashing away. The guard who'd run down the stairs jumped over a handrail and into the water; he grabbed the life preserver and Richard in one smooth motion. Richard held on to him tightly, like a cub hanging on to momma bear. They swam in place for a minute or two until a deckhand threw out a rope and pulled them in.

"You were right," I said to Lonna. "That was a lot more entertaining than a toast."

Chapter 19

I don't know how much longer the cruise was supposed to last, but after Richard Johns was pulled out of the water, the boat turned around, and we went right back to port. The Johns family made a quick exit, their two thugs clearing a path for them, with Courtney Baker close behind. I tried to catch up with Stella before she got off the boat, but she was too quick and disappeared into a parking lot near the Mississippi River Museum.

With the action over and no more cruising to be had, we took our time leaving the boat, making sure that no truffle went uneaten. There were a lot of confused passengers, as most had no idea that Richard Johns's dip in the Mississippi River wasn't exactly accidental.

"Frank," Ruby said. "I'm a little confused about what just happened."

"You aren't alone," I assured her.

"Did that woman, Ashley, the chocolate maker, invite the other woman, Stella, just to show her up?"

"Yeah, it looks like she did."

"I guess that's one way to put to rest an old conflict: pick a fight over something new."

"What now?" I asked as we got off the boat. Jefferson looked at Lonna, who gave a subtle head nod. Jefferson said they were going to find a place for dinner, on their own.

"Don't stay out too late," I said to Jefferson. "We've got an early start tomorrow. I'm taking you down south of town, to Aquoqua, to check out where Mayor Andelfinger grew up."

"I'll be there," he said, then turning to look at Lonna. "I guess I'm taking a few more days off." He turned back to me. "Call me when you're ready, Frank."

Ruby said she'd had enough excitement for the day and wanted to catch up on some reading, so I took her back to her room. I had some free time that I hadn't expected, so I figured I would see what Adam was doing. I sent him a text and heard back right away; he said he could meet me at the Trophy Room in an hour.

I grabbed a quick sandwich from a downtown café and walked over to the Trophy Room, one of my favorite bars in Dubuque. The downtown building had housed a general store for about a hundred years before it was converted to a pub. There was a lot packed into that space. One side of the tavern was lined with a row of beat-up plastic booths that looked like they'd been salvaged from an old A&W Root Beer restaurant. The bartenders roamed behind a long bar carved from old-growth white pine that was topped with a worn slab of soft white marble. Bartenders pulled beer from shiny brass taps advertising the standard cheap beers that their customers demanded, except for one tap that now dispensed Good Old Potosi, a local beer.

All that was pretty cool but not nearly as impressive as what was hanging on the walls. Every space on the upper half of the walls was covered with glass cabinets stuffed with dead animals: beavers, minks, otters, muskrats, snapping turtles, bobcats, a couple of deer heads, owls, songbirds, even a fisher. The Trophy Room had enough dead critters in glass cases to qualify as a natural history museum, and enough cheap beer to make it seem more kitschy than creepy.

I sat at the end of the bar away from the front door and made a few notes in my journal about the people on the cruise. I played word association, coming up with one or two words to describe the main characters in the drama on the riverboat:

Ashley: Hubris (underlined twice)

Richard Johns: Smug + Asshole

Helen: Calculating

Stella: Driven + Competitive

Lonna: Heartbreaker

Before I could get any further, Adam showed up. He strode into the bar with his head up, walking slowly and confidently toward me in baggy khaki shorts and a black tank top that clung tightly to his slender trunk, the tattoos that ran the length of his left arm and around his right bicep on full display. I didn't understand what he saw in me, but I wasn't in the mood to question him about it. He sat on the barstool next to me and said, "What's up?"

"Just catching up on some notes from the day. Hell of a day."

"Tell me about it."

I got a beer for him and told him about the cruise, about the rivalry between Stella and Ashley and how Richard Johns ended up going for an unexpected swim in the Mississippi.

"Sounds like your days are a lot more interesting than mine," he said. "With the luxury cruises, feuds, and people getting killed in fires at food conventions."

"Yeah. My life is like that all the time. How about you? What'd you do today?"

"Jammed with my band," he said. "I play drums, but it's mostly just for fun."

"What kind of music?"

"Swing. Today's band, anyway. I play in a rock band, too, but the swing band gets more gigs."

"Where do you play around here?"

"Bars, mostly, but we've played at a few weddings and even a bar mitzvah once. Looks like we're gonna hit the road this fall and tour for a couple of weeks."

"Is that what you do for a living?"

"No," he said, grinning, "not at all. We make enough to pay for everything, like our equipment and travel, but not much more than that." He looked right at me, and those green eyes made me forget that I doubted that he could like me. "Don't get me wrong. It'd be nice, but I know better. Not many people make a living from playing music, especially in Dubuque. And being a poor artist sounds a lot more romantic when you're a teenager."

Then I remembered that he'd said something about a day job when we met on Friday. "You told me Friday night that you work for a marketing company, right?"

"Yeah. I do the artwork for ads." He picked up his phone and showed me a couple of pictures of his work. Then he glanced at my hands. "So what's the deal with the ring?" he asked. "You married?"

"No," I answered. "I'm not married. The ring... it's just a reminder." I forced a smile. "Tell me about your artwork. What exactly do you make?" Adam didn't look totally convinced by my answer, but he didn't press me about it.

"I'm a visual artist," he said. "I love playing with color. I really wanted to be a professional painter, but my practical side took over when I went to college, so I studied graphic art. I was pretty sure that would give me a better shot at a job than a degree in art would. I was right. I got hired right out of college a few years ago. By a company in Dubuque, even." He sighed and looked away. "I wonder if that was a mistake."

"What do you mean?"

"Maybe I should have lived somewhere else for a while." He leaned toward me and put a hand on my shoulder. "Don't get me wrong. I love Dubuque, love being close to my family. But I've lived my whole life here. Grew up in the West End, went to the University of Dubuque, then went to work for a local company. I've traveled some, but I've never lived anywhere else. Might be good for me to do that before it's too late, before I'm too settled down," he said. "After all, bodies at rest tend to stay at rest..."

"And bodies in motion tend to stay in motion," I added. We talked for a while longer about his painting, then I invited him back to my motel.

"I'd love to, but I can't stay all night this time," he said. "Gotta be up early tomorrow and to my cube. If you want, you can come over to my loft for a while, though. Save some driving time."

Chapter 20

I woke up early on Monday morning after a short night. (I'd left Adam's loft around midnight, and I'd driven back to my motel.) I put on a small pot of coffee and called Jefferson. "How was your night?" I asked.

"Fine, I suppose," he said. "You ready to go?"

"Sure. Let's take that truck of yours. I can be at your hotel in about twenty minutes."

"Just text me when you get here."

Aquoqua, where we were headed, was an enclave south of Dubuque that was once home to a colony of river rats. Now it was more of a summer nesting site for snowbirds, but a handful of river rats still lived there year-round. It was also the place where Mayor Andelfinger and his pal Stan Mueller had grown up.

On the way to meet Jefferson, I got a call from the editor at *Wandering Gourmet*, Gordon Harper. He'd heard about the fire at the convention center and called to find out if I was OK—or at least that's what he said.

Truthfully, he was more worried that I'd miss my deadline for the boutique foods story than he was about my health. I assured him that I was making good progress and would have the story to him on time. He probably read about the fire in the news; then again, maybe Helen had called him to make sure he heard about it.

When I got to the hotel parking lot, I texted Jefferson, and we were soon on our way out of the city.

"You don't seem all that happy," I said.

"Don't really want to get into it right now," he said. "So what's our plan for today?"

"I don't really have a plan. I just want to poke around the nest and see what takes flight."

"Jesus, I hate it when you talk like that. So exactly whose fucking nest are we going to be poking in?"

"The mayor's. We're going to start by having breakfast in his old 'hood."

"At least there's food involved," Jefferson said. "Where are we eating?"

"At a bar and grill at a marina."

"Great. At least I can get a Bloody Mary with my eggs."

"If you wish," I said. "Just don't overdo it. I need you sharp this morning. We're going to try to get information from folks who may not want to share their stories with us, and you're going to stand out more than I will."

"I don't know about that, Frank. I don't think anyone at the marina is going to be wearing a fedora, but a lot of folks will have the same camo ball cap like that one I have in back," he said, pointing behind him. "Hand it to me... please. I'm not going in that place without it on my head."

After a short drive south, we turned onto Aquoqua Road from the top of a ridge and began the gradual descent toward the river. Aquoqua Road snakes down through a narrow valley, dropping some three hundred feet in elevation to reach the bottoms, passing through groves of tall oak trees, by a small farm with a decrepit red barn and an old log cabin, and down to the thickly wooded bottoms. At the top of the hill, we passed a few modern ranch houses, but as we dropped deeper into the valley, older houses were more common, many of them simple four-squares constructed from local limestone. When we reached the floodplain, we passed compact subdivisions of frame houses. The houses in the lowest spots were elevated several feet above the ground on tall poles or concrete pillars.

We pulled into a gravel lot next to the marina office and found a parking spot between a couple of trucks with empty trailers attached. We walked a few feet to the Hungry Point Bar and Grill, a boxy frame building with rustic wood siding that sat on four thick wooden posts that lifted the building about twenty feet above the ground, high enough to stay dry except during the highest of high water. On one side of the building, a staircase rose up and ended at a large deck that extended out from the main entrance. Near the front door we spotted a line cut in the siding about halfway up that was marked with the words "High water mark, 1965." We pulled open the screen door and walked past the lures, the refrigerator full of bait, and the '70s-era posters of fishing boats, through another door and into a small room with a bar and the aroma of fried potatoes. We claimed a couple of barstools at the front, after navigating through a few curious stares.

"Can I get you fellas something to drink?" the bartender asked, sliding a couple of menus in front of us, the laminated covers cracking at the corners and peeling back. He looked older than us, with dry brown skin that puckered up on his cheeks. He wore a baseball cap that matched the color scheme of Jefferson's. I stuck to coffee, with extra sugar and cream in case it was as stale and bitter as I expected, which it was; Jefferson asked for a Bloody Mary.

We stuck to the basics for breakfast—eggs with bacon, toast, and hash browns—then looked around the bar to size up the place. There wasn't much to set it apart from any other riverfront bar. It had the usual posters of local fish species—pretty pictures of walleye and sauger. The decor was boat salvage chic, the tables and walls spiced up with anchors, old props, and life jackets. We were the only customers sitting at the bar, so we had the bartender's attention for a while, long enough to ask him about Aquoqua and nearby parts. His name was Rick, and he'd lived in the area a long time.

"Pretty quiet down here most of the time," Rick said. "A lot of sportsmen come down on weekends—guys, mostly—and their boats, just looking to fish. We get some campers, too, though most of them park their trailers on a site for the season but use it only on weekends. It's a vacation home for people short of money."

"What about the houses we saw scattered around here? Who lives in those?" I asked.

"That's a mix. Some of 'em are summer houses, people with more money to burn than those campers I just told you about. Others are year-round homes for families who've lived here a long time, though there's fewer and fewer of them."

"What's happening to those old-timers?"

"Moved away, mostly. A lot of the kids from those families want a nicer life than what Aquoqua offers: a bigger house, nice cars, fewer mosquitoes and floods." He leaned back, took off his cap, and scratched his head. "It's a pretty good life down here, but it's not for everyone. I guess a lot of people today just want to be here for the good stuff and not have to deal with the headaches. Can't say I blame them, not completely. It's a lot of work to live here all year. Get tired of it myself sometimes."

"How long have you lived here?" Jefferson asked.

"About fifty-seven years, which is all my life. Got no need to live anywhere else. Aquoqua suits me fine, and Dubuque is a short drive away if I need anything from the city, which I don't very often." He put the cap back on, using both hands to get it sitting just right on his head. "How about you two? Where you from?"

"St. Louis," I said.

"St. Louis, huh? We get a few people up here from St. Louis who visit us. You here to fish?"

"Nah," I said. "I'm a reporter. Supposed to write a fluff piece about the mayor, now that he's running for Congress. I thought I should find out more about where he grew up."

"I figured you weren't from here," Rick said, looking at me. "No one wears a hat like yours in these parts." Jefferson pretended to cough, trying not to laugh.

"I suppose the mayor is pretty popular around here," I said.

"I wouldn't exactly say 'popular,' but he's all right, I suppose. Done a lot to get us some help out here, like getting money to lift this building above the high water mark and to pave the road from the highway to here."

Another person walked into the bar, and Rick called out, "Hey, Joe." Then he reached into a cooler and pulled out a can of beer.

Joe took a seat near me, and Rick popped open the can and slid it in front of Joe. "These two fellas are reporters," Rick said to Joe.

"Not me," Jefferson jumped in. "I'm on vacation." He pointed at me. "He's the one who's working."

"Yeah, I guessed there was something different about you," Joe said to me. "I've never seen a hat like yours before, at least outside of church." He took a long sip from the beer, a Miller Lite.

"He's writing about the mayor and his roots down here. What do you think of him, Joe?" Rick asked.

"The reporter?" he said, looking my way. "Seems OK, but I just met him."

"No, Joe. The mayor."

"Right. Don't think about the mayor that much."

"Did you know him when he was younger?" I asked.

"Sure," Joe said. "Practically grew up with him. He's a few years younger than me, but we know each other."

"What was he like when he was a kid?" I asked.

"A lot like he is now, I suppose, except shorter," Joe said. "I knew back then that he wasn't going to stay in Aquoqua. Wanted bigger things for himself. Looks like he still does. None of that surprised me." Joe emptied the rest of the Miller Lite; Rick slid another one in front of him. "Now when Stan left Aquoqua to go to work for him, that surprised me. I figured Stan was like me, a real river rat."

"You mean Stan Mueller, I guess?" I asked.

"Yes, that's the one. Heck of a guy. Dependable as anyone I've ever known. His family still lives down here, the ones that are still alive."

"He still has a house himself in Aquoqua, Stan does," Rick said.

"I guess that's so," Joe said, "but I don't see him very often. I hope he's doing all right up there in the city. River rats like us do real well down here, in the bottoms, but we have a tough time when we get out of our element. Maybe Stan's doing better than most river rats who leave."

"You probably heard about the fire up in Dubuque, at the convention center?" I asked.

"Sure," Joe responded. "I suppose everyone around here heard about that."

"I heard that Stan was given some extra time off. Sounds like they might hold him responsible for the fire, like maybe he didn't stay on top of things the way he was supposed to," I said. "Does that sound like something the Stan you know would have done?"

"No, it sure don't," Joe said. "Look, I sure don't know what went on up there, but I just can't believe that Stan did anything wrong, especially something that would kill two people. He's damn good at what he does, and he takes too much pride to let something like that happen."

Our food came out, and Joe finished his beer and stood up. "Got me an appointment with a couple of walleye. Can't be late." He wished us luck on our story and walked out of the bar.

As we finished up, Rick came back over to us.

"You know, if you really want to learn more about what the mayor was like growing up, you should talk with Big Dan, Stan's uncle."

"He knows the mayor well, too?"

"Sure thing. Practically raised both those boys."

I looked at Jefferson for any hint of objection but didn't see any. "That sounds like a good idea," I said. "I'd like to talk to Big Dan. How do we find him?"

"He's not too hard to find. He lives just downriver, in a cabin by himself. You'll probably want a boat to get there."

"That might be a problem," I said. "We aren't well equipped in that department."

"I've got a canoe you can borrow if you'd like," Rick offered. "You ever paddle before?" I could see Jefferson's eyes open wide with that "what the hell are you getting me into" look taking over his face.

"Yeah," I said. "I've spent a lot of time in canoes. How far downriver is his cabin?"

"Not far. You could paddle there in about fifteen or twenty minutes. There's just not a road to get you there."

"How will we know which cabin is his?"

"Oh, you'll know. It's the one with the driftwood fence, the barking dogs, and the dozen or so 'No Trespassing' signs. Don't let any of that bother you, though. He's real nice and not as good a shot as he used to be."

CHAPTER 21

Rick walked us outside, unchained the canoe from the post, and handed us each a paddle and a life preserver. "There's some extra boots over there," he said, pointing to the opposite corner. "You'll want those, too. Good luck, boys. Let me know when you're back."

After he left us, Jefferson threw down his equipment. "Frank, you know how I feel about this. I don't go in boats that don't have a motor. Period."

"Well, this is a good time to start. We can't get to Uncle Dan's place in your truck. We have to go by boat."

"That's fine. I don't have a problem going there in a boat, but I want a boat with a fucking motor!"

"That's not an option. It's this or nothing, and we didn't come down here for nothing." I was getting pissed, but I didn't want to fight with Jefferson over this, so I lowered my voice and picked up a paddle. "Don't sweat it, Brian, seriously. We don't have far to go. All you have to do is sit up front and let me paddle. I'll do all the work."

"I don't have a problem with doing my part. I have a problem knowing all the things that can go wrong. I don't like small boats. I'm not a small guy. Little boats weren't built with me in mind."

"Damn it, Brian, shut up already. We don't have a choice. It's this or we miss our chance to talk to someone who knows both the mayor and Stan Mueller well. I'm not ready to give up and turn back. Are you?"

"You know I don't quit. Damn it, Frank. How do I let you talk me into this crazy shit?" He bent down and picked up the life preserver and put it on. "Fine. I'll do it. I'm not gonna like it, but I'll ride in it."

"That's the spirit. Let's get this in the water." We carried the canoe to the boat landing and slid it into the water. I told Jefferson to step gently as he got in and to keep his center of gravity in the middle of the canoe.

"I got it, Frank," he said. "Now stop with the instructions."

He was right. He got in the canoe and sat down with hardly a ripple. I pushed off and climbed into the stern.

"If you want to practice your paddling skills, feel free," I said. "I might need your help to get us back up here."

"You said you'd do all the work, Frank, so I'm going to let you keep your word. I'm just going to sit here, keep my hands inside the boat, and let you do your thing." Jefferson didn't budge after he sat down, and he kept his hands down around his knees. He looked around the backwater channel with the same wariness he exercised when pursuing a suspect. "God only knows what's in this water. I'm not putting my hands anywhere near it."

I paddled us out of sight of the marina and around a bend, past islands thick with silver maples and swamp white oak. The pleasant July weather we had over the weekend was giving way to higher humidity and more heat; the air had turned hazy and thick. I could feel sweat sticking to my eyebrows and mustache before I'd paddled five minutes. I tried to narrate the tour, pointing out a beaver house and a hornet's nest, but Jefferson wasn't too interested.

"Keep your eyes on the shore, Frank. I don't want to miss that cabin we're looking for," he said. Then he mumbled just loud enough for me to hear: "I don't want to spend one more minute in this damn boat than I have to."

After a few minutes, we left behind the cluster of elevated houses on the mainland side of the channel for a shoreline of trees and mud. "Did we miss it already?" Jefferson asked.

"No. I think we've got a little ways to go yet."

"Can't believe you talked me into this. And what was that crack about him not being as good a shot as he used to be? I don't want some old white guy firing a shotgun at me as soon as we get out of this boat."

"I'm sure we'll be fine. Otherwise, Rick wouldn't have sent us down this way."

"You sure are an optimist when it's convenient."

We had paddled for about fifteen minutes when Jefferson spotted a small log cabin on the shore. It was just as Rick had described. The front yard was set off by a low fence built of driftwood stacked on top of driftwood with the occasional vertical post for structural support. Every couple of feet was a "No Trespassing" sign nailed to a post. As soon as we got close to shore, a couple of dogs near the cabin barked out our presence, but to my surprise, they didn't run at us.

We pulled up to shore and looked around, but we didn't see anyone. "Hang tight," I told Jefferson. As soon as I stepped out of the canoe and onto the shore, a single gunshot rang out. "Get down, Frank," Jefferson whispered.

"It's OK," I said. "I think he shot straight up, not at us. Let me handle this."

"Let you handle this? When did you become Samuel L. Jackson?"

"I grew up in an area like this, remember? I hung out with guys like him when I was a kid."

I took a couple of steps away from the canoe and toward the cabin. "I'm looking for Big Dan," I yelled. "Rick from the marina sent us."

"What do you want?" I heard him before I saw him; he was standing next to the front door of the cabin, a shotgun resting against his shoulder.

"I'm writing a story about Mike Andelfinger, the mayor of Dubuque."

"Yea, I heard of him. What's he got to do with me?"

"Rick said you're Stan Mueller's uncle and that you knew the mayor well when he was growing up. I'd like to hear more about what he was like as a kid."

"You're a reporter or something?"

"Yes, sir. I promise not to take up a lot of your time. My friend and I..." I said, pointing toward Jefferson in the canoe. "We're just interested in hearing a few stories."

Big Dan set down the shotgun and walked toward us, the dogs following him a couple steps behind. When he reached the fence, he gave us a good look-over, then said, "You can tie up to that tree over there." I turned to Jefferson and asked if he needed a hand getting out of the canoe, but he just glared at me with his "fuck off" eyes.

"I'm fine," he said, as he stood up slowly and took a tentative step toward shore. He was less confident getting out of the canoe than he'd been getting into it. I held the side to keep it steady as he made his way out. When he was safely ashore, instead of "thank you," I got another "I'm fine."

Big Dan lived up to his nickname. He was tall, about six-feet-five, and wide; he wore a leather cowboy hat up top and muddy rubber boots down below. In between were the largest pair of overalls that I had ever seen, enough denim to clothe a small village.

He opened the gate by moving a couple of pieces of driftwood aside, giving us just enough room to sidle through. "Don't worry about the dogs," he said. "They bite only when I tell 'em to."

We walked up a gentle slope and past a small garden. He nudged a wooden rocking chair to the side and held the screen door open for us; it was a simple wood frame with chicken wire strung over it, a screen fine enough to keep the coyotes out but hardly enough to stop the mosquitoes.

His cabin was a single room, about twenty feet long by twenty feet wide, with a loft built out over one end. On the far wall, deer antlers hung over a fireplace built from irregularly shaped limestone blocks. A turtle shell was placed atop driftwood to form a small table. A couple of beaver pelts hung on another wall, near a rocking chair and above an old camelback trunk. "That trunk was my mother's," he told us.

Near his bed, a mattress resting on a frame carved from cottonwood, Big Dan had hung old prints of Keokuk and Blackhawk, two men who'd had a big impact on the lives of their Sauk and Meskwaki brethren at the time Europeans were moving in and stealing their land. In a nearby window, I spotted a dream catcher, those once sacred, snowshoe-shaped ornaments that were appropriated by New Age spiritualists and are now sold at every art fair and rendezvous in the country.

Dream catchers had traditionally been made from thin pieces of wood that were bent into a curve and held together with woven strands of plants or sometimes muscle from a deer. They were hung to protect children, to make sure their good dreams filtered through, while snagging the bad dreams and bad influences in the webbing until the morning sun could burn them off. They probably had their origin in Ojibwe culture, but with the rise of the American Indian Movement in the 1960s, many other Native American nations adopted the dream catcher as one of the symbols of a new, unified American Indian identity.

Many of the dream catchers being sold at fairs today, especially the ones from non–Native American artists, have a kitschy quality, like a sixth-grade craft project destined to hang on your parents' refrigerator for a week before it's thrown away. Big Dan's, though, looked skillfully handcrafted, like he'd put it together himself with great care. Big Dan noticed that I was checking it out. "I made that there dream catcher out of willow from these woods and strands of reed grass," he said. "The feathers came from a red-tailed hawk.

I didn't kill anything to make it. I found all of that in the woods and saved 'em until I had enough to make a dream catcher." Then he looked squarely at the two of us. "Where you fellas from?"

We gave him the same rundown we'd given Rick, adding that we'd been friends since we were kids. "How about you?" I asked. "You ever lived anywhere else?"

"Other than my two years in the army, no. Born and raised here. Lived in this cabin 'bout forty years. Built most of it with these," he said, showing off two mud-stained, bear-paw-size hands.

He gave us a quick tour of his home. The wood had been salvaged from construction sites or cut from dead trees. The stones for the fireplace were rejects from a nearby quarry. Many of the treasures that decorated his cabin had come from the river or the woods: beaver he'd trapped, deer he'd shot, wood that had floated by. He lived off what he could get from the land and water around him, mostly. He hunted and fished for meat, harvested berries and plants from the woods. He also worked odd jobs here and there, various fix-it and construction jobs, to get money to buy what he couldn't harvest himself, such as milk, butter, and beer.

"Your cabin isn't on stilts like the other places around here," Jefferson said. "Don't you get flooded?"

"Sure do. Even with this little rise I'm on, I get wet about every other year. The cabin's been completely swamped three times."

"That must be pretty rough, having to clean up and rebuild so often."

"It ain't ideal, but I deal with it. I open up the windows on the upstream and downstream sides of the cabin to let the water flow through, so that helps keep the cabin from washing away. The only thing I have that I'd hate to lose is that trunk from my mother. Everything else I can replace. Because of that loft up there, I can stay in the cabin during some floods. Even built a hatch in the roof above my bed so I could get out during the big floods without having to swim through the front door."

"Clever," Jefferson said.

Big Dan walked over to the rocking chair and sat down. "Make yourselves comfortable," he said. "I don't get much company, but there's a couple of places to sit over there." Jefferson and I each found a seat next to an end table and sat down.

"Hope I didn't scare you too much when you showed up," Big Dan said. "A lot of people think they're entitled to hunt and walk wherever they want. I get a lot of folks who don't respect the idea of private property. Some of them are just ignorant; they're OK. They'll learn to stay away." He sat back, planted his feet, and made full use of the armrests; the chair began to slowly rock back and forth. "Others, though, are pure trouble, like the ones out to hunt when it's not season and who think they can use my land as cover. Or worse, people who see my cabin and figure it's abandoned, so they just walk in and make themselves at home. I used to be polite to everyone, but I don't have the patience for it no more."

"I'm just glad you don't have a shoot-first policy," I said, "although Rick swears you aren't as good a shot as you used to be."

Big Dan picked up a tub of chewing tobacco and put a pinch in his mouth. "You can tell Rick to try sneaking around here at night; we'll see just how good a shot I really am. Then again, don't have to be a great shot with this baby," he said, petting his shotgun. He smiled a wide smile, exposing a wad of chew and teeth the color of faded newspaper. "So what is it you want to know about the little sprout?"

"Is that what you call the mayor?"

"I call him a lot of things. Most of 'em aren't worth repeating to strangers."

"What was he like when he was a kid? He grew up down here, right?"

"Sure, this is where he's from, but he don't come down this way too often no more. I guess he's too busy moving up in the world."

"Were you close to him when he was a kid?"

"Sure was. Back when he was little, this was a real community. Not like today, where it's mostly just a place for weekenders. We knew each other and looked out for each other. That's the world he grew up knowing. I'd like to think he remembers what he learned from those years." He picked up a tin can and spat into it. "He was always an ambitious one, though. Life down here was never gonna be good enough for him. Of course, that was true of a lot of folks. His generation wants different things than mine did, like nice things to own. I never cared what I owned. I cared how I lived."

"I suppose Mike was really into the outdoors and good with his hands when he was a kid," I said.

"Hell, no!" Big Dan roared. "I've never seen someone who was so clumsy. He couldn't figure out how to tie a simple knot. Couldn't paddle his way out of a washtub. Beside that, that boy just didn't have much common sense. Good thing he had my nephew Stan looking after him, or else he might never have gotten out of here alive."

"He and Stan have been friends that long?" I asked.

"Friends? Hell, they're practically brothers. They lived next door to each other from the day they was born. Spent practically every day together when they was growing up."

"I guess that qualifies as close," Jefferson said.

Big Dan got up and walked over to an old icebox and pulled out a beer. "You fellas want one?" We accepted, never ones to insult a man's generosity. He sat back down in the rocking chair and continued: "Stan was a completely different breed. That guy could find his way out of a swamp at night blindfolded. He was always the generous type, too. One time he loant his canoe to some strangers who needed help; he walked all the way back deep in the night so they could get safely back to their campsite."

"Did he ever have to bail out the mayor?" I asked.

"I know you're fishing for a good story or two to write about, but I don't mind. It's no secret that Mike needed bailing out damn near every day down here," Big Dan said. "Like I said, the little sprout wasn't cut out for life in the bottoms. Getting in a mess came as easy to him as field dressing a deer is to me. A couple of times he dug a real deep hole, almost too deep even for Stan."

"What happened?" I asked.

"Well, I don't know if I really should say. He don't need all his embarrassing stories ending up in the papers." He picked up the beer, drank about half of it, sat quietly for a minute, deep in thought, then slammed the rest of the beer. He got up and walked over to the fridge to get another beer, then turned to us and said, "Then again, it don't hurt to be reminded of where you come from."

"I hear that," Jefferson said.

"I don't remember exactly how old he was, but I'm gonna guess about thirteen or fourteen. He took a canoe out by himself, which was mistake enough, for him. Said he wanted to get away from his family for a little while, to escape to an island and think. It was fall, real warm for that time of year, but he hadn't paid no attention to the weather. He'd been out a couple of hours when the winds turned to the north and brought in a nasty storm. Temperature fell 'bout thirty degrees in an hour. Happened so sudden he didn't have time to paddle back home."

"Did he get stranded?" Jefferson asked.

"He woulda if Stan hadn't gone out and got him. When Stan saw that the canoe was missing, he took his daddy's jon boat and went looking for Mike. Found him at one of their favorite hideaways, at the far end of Nine-Mile

Island, not far from this here cabin, in fact. He'd turned the canoe over and was hiding under it. He hadn't brought a coat or nothing with him. Coulda froze to death out there if Stan hadn't rescued him. Fool kid got in over his head."

"Was that the only time Stan rescued him?" I asked.

"Hardly. Like I said, Stan rescued him all the time. Just mostly in little ways, like getting him out of fights or reminding him to get home on time."

Big Dan got up, walked over to the window, and looked outside. "Well, fellas, as much as I'd like to sit in here and gossip all day, I've got my chores to finish before the day's over." He turned back to face us. "I gotta send you on your way back to the marina and wherever you're heading next." He moved toward the door. "You know where to find me if you have more questions. I won't even fire another warning shot if you come visit again."

We thanked him for the time, stories, and beer and went back to our canoe.

"Damn!" Jefferson said. "I forgot that we're still stuck riding in that little boat."

"It's a canoe," I said. "A canoe."

"Boat, canoe—same damn thing."

"You sure have been grumpy today," I snapped.

"I know, I know. Sorry, Frank," he said. "I let Lonna get to me.

"What happened?"

"I like her, Frank. Damn it, I really like her. I didn't want to get involved with another woman so soon after the divorce, but it feels like fate put her right in front of me. I could see myself with her for a long time, so I decided to go for it."

"So what's the problem, then? You two have been spending a lot of time together, so it must be going well."

"I don't know. I can't tell. I mean, I know she wants to sleep with me, but I want something more than that. I don't want to just roll from bed to bed. I want commitment."

"She seems pretty good at that. She's already been married a couple of times, after all."

"If that's supposed to be funny..."

"Sorry. Are you saying that she's not looking to make another go at it?"

"Like I said, I can't tell. I feel creepy, like some clingy momma's boy, if I bring up marriage right after meeting her, but she's dropping hints that she doesn't think much of the institution. If that's true, I'd like to know that now. I guess I'm just not used to having to play this game again. I didn't expect to ever be single again."

"Sorry, Brian. I know it hasn't been easy for you. But at least you and Michelle are still friendly, and you get to see your girls all the time, right?"

"Yeah, those are good things. But it's not anywhere near as good as still being married and all of us living together. Anyway, let's get this boat—canoe—out of here and back to my truck."

We pushed off, and I paddled back upriver. I got to work coaxing Jefferson to use his paddle. "Between the weight of the two of us and the current, it's a lot to handle for a single paddler." I chose not to mention that there really wasn't much current in that backwater channel; I just wanted to see him paddle.

After a few minutes of prodding, he gave in. I showed him how to grip the paddle and demonstrated a couple of strokes. When his first stroke hit the water, though, the paddle slipped right out of his hands and into the river.

"Son of a bitch!" he screamed. Before I could tell him not to worry about it, he leaned over to grab it, but he leaned too far and flipped us over, sending us both into the water. When I hit the water, I panicked. My heart pounded, and I felt like I had just killed my best friend. My arms flopped around with a flurry as I tried to regain my orientation—which didn't take very long after my feet found the bottom. I stood up in the waist-deep water and looked around for Jefferson. He was standing a few feet away from me, in water about the same depth.

I put my hands on my waist, bent over, and caught my breath. "Guess I should have known better," I said, my feet sinking deeper in the mud as I took a couple of steps to fish my hat out of the water.

"That's what I get for listening to you and trying something new," Jefferson said, wiping water from his eyes. "Good thing I didn't wear anything nice today. Too bad about your hat," he said, watching as I tried to shake out the waterlogged fedora. "Now you have an excuse to go buy a new one."

"It'll dry," I said.

We flipped the canoe right-side up, but before we could push it ashore and get back in, a guy in a jon boat came around a corner and over toward us. "I shoulda guessed I'd find you two like this," he said. "I hear you've been asking around about me and the mayor. I'm Stan Mueller. If you can get yourselves back to the marina, I might tolerate a question or two. I'll be in the bar, but I won't wait all day."

With that, he turned the jon boat around and sped away from us.

Chapter 22

We walked ourselves and the canoe to shore and tried as best as we could to wipe off the mud.

"So that's, Stan, huh?" Jefferson asked.

"Seems so," I responded.

"So much for him being a stand-up guy. He could have offered to help us."

"Let's get ourselves back to the marina," I said.

We got in the canoe and paddled back to where we'd begun. Or, I paddled anyway. Jefferson wasn't eager to give it another go.

Rick must have heard us sloshing to shore. He came down from the bar to greet us. "Sure didn't see that coming," Rick said, looking at our dirty, wet clothes. He pointed to a hose at the end of the building. "You can wash off the mud over there," he said, tossing us a couple of large rags that doubled as towels. "I'll be up at the bar, with Stan. He's waiting for you."

We rinsed off our pants and boots, toweled off as best we could, then grabbed a few minutes of sun to help speed the drying. "This should be fun," I said. "You ready?"

"Hell, yes," Jefferson said. "Let's see what this guy has to say for himself. I just wish we were more presentable."

We climbed up the stairs and walked to the bar, where Stan was sitting and talking to bartender Rick.

"Don't ask me anything about the fire, 'cause I can't talk about that," Stan said as soon as we sat down next to him.

He wasn't what I'd expected. He was rather plain, dressed in jeans and a red plaid shirt, a Cabela's ball cap covering brown hair. He had a common-looking face, the kind you forget just a few minutes after meeting him. A thick mustache of coarse brown and gray hair was the only thing that distinguished his look—no scars, no double chin, no tribal tattoos, just a mustache.

"Thanks for waiting for us," I said. I wanted to start slow, to see if I could put him at ease before we got to the more delicate topics.

"Sure," he said. He didn't bother to look at either of us as he spoke.

"Is it OK if I ask you a few questions?"

"Like I said, don't ask about the fire. Otherwise, I'll do my best to help you with your story about the mayor."

"I'm Frank, by the way. This is my friend Brian."

"I know who you are," Stan said, still without turning to look at us. "I know you've been trying to show up the mayor, confronting him about the fire at a press conference and ambushing him at a restaurant."

I shouldn't have been surprised that he'd heard about my earlier interactions with the mayor, but I was. "I have a big mouth sometimes," I said. "Even my mother had trouble shutting me up."

"I bet she did. I've known people like that, but I generally don't have much to do with them. What do you want to know, Mr. Dodge?"

"Please call me Frank." Stan didn't respond, so I continued. "We've had a chance to look around the area a little bit. Tell me what it was like growing up here in Aquoqua."

"It was great." Stan wasn't going to make it easy.

"How much time did you spend on the river?"

"I was on the water almost every day, fishing or swimming or just floating in a boat with no purpose." Stan picked up his beer, Miller Lite, and took a sip.

"Sounds like fun." I pulled a moleskin notebook out of my shirt pocket; the cover was wet, but I found a couple of dry pages to jot down a few notes. "You and the mayor—Mike—how did you meet?"

"We grew up practically next door to each other, so I couldn't tell you how we met. We were just always around each other, from as far back as I can remember."

"So his family has deep roots here, too?" I fixed my eyes on Stan, watching him as he worked hard to avoid looking at me or Jefferson. He was composed—indifferent, at least to us—but he gripped the beer bottle with purpose, holding on tight as if letting go might send him cascading out of control.

"I'd say so. I think it was his dad's parents who first settled down here, so he'd be the third generation, about the same as mine."

"What was the mayor like when he was younger? Was he a sportsman like you?"

"What would you say, Rick?" Stan said, looking over at the bartender, who was busy rinsing pint glasses. Rick just smiled and shook his head without looking up. "No," Stan said, "the mayor's not much of a sportsman. Never was. He wasn't much for getting his hands dirty," he said, finally looking at me, then quickly turning away.

"I heard you rescued him once. Saved his life, even."

"I've had to rescue him more than once. You'll have to be more specific."

"There was a time, maybe when he was about thirteen, that he took a canoe out by himself and got caught in a storm. You took a boat out to search for him and found him under his canoe. Does that sound familiar?"

"I suppose Uncle Dan told you about that one," he said, pausing to take a long sip from the bottle. "There's some truth to it, but people around here always make too much of it. Mike was fine and never really in danger. He'd pulled the canoe out of the water and flipped it over for shelter. Not a bad idea, really, considering how bad the storm was in places around here. I saw how dark the sky was getting and felt the wind picking up, so when I figured out that he'd gone out on the river alone, I hopped in my dad's jon boat and went right to the spot where we liked to hang out. Found him right away and got him and the canoe back home before the worst of the storm hit us. It wasn't that big a deal."

"You have a gift for understatement," I said. Stan, again, didn't respond. "So when else have you had to rescue him?" I asked.

"When you grow up around a place like this, there's always an opportunity to get in trouble. Just about every day, you need a helping hand from someone. Mike got himself in his fair share of scrapes where he needed a hand, but truth is, so did I. He's helped me out plenty of times, too."

"How'd he help you?" I asked.

"I didn't do too good in school, especially English and social studies. Mike helped me get through those classes, helped me pass 'em."

"When did you figure out that he was interested in politics?"

"When wasn't he?" Stan said, almost letting himself smile. "If he coulda been president of his kindergarten class, he woulda run. It was in his blood, I guess. He was in student government in high school. Seems like he's been campaigning for something ever since." He picked up the bottle and gave it a gentle twirl, sloshing around the beer that was left. "It was real important to him to make a life for himself away from Aquoqua. He wanted more from life than this place could offer."

"But you stuck around."

"Sure, mostly. Aquoqua suits me just fine. But since I work for Mike, I have to live in his world, too. I just figured I could keep one foot in the city and the other here in Aquoqua. It works out pretty good, most of the time."

"The mayor seems like the favorite to replace Congressman Geiger. If he wins, will you move to Washington with him?"

"I'll do whatever he needs me to do. Whatever office he's in, there's more work than he can do himself. I'll help him however I can, wherever he decides is best. If I have to move to Washington for a while, I'll do it, but I won't be giving up my house down here in Aquoqua." Stan finished off his beer. "What else can I tell ya, Mr. Dodge?"

I didn't want to push my luck right away. I figured we'd have another chance to talk, another time when I could go after him more directly. I wanted to leave him with a good impression, make him think that maybe I wasn't his enemy, after all, so I kept it short. "I can't think of much more to ask right now," I said. We all stood up, ready to leave. "I'm a big fan of your wife's ice cream, by the way," I told Stan.

"Yeah, she's good at that. Made quite a name for herself."

"You probably get to taste-test her newest creations, huh?"

"Not as often as you might think. Mostly she just goes ahead with her own judgment. She seems to know what she's doing."

"That's what I thought, too," I said. "Well thanks for talking to us, Mr. Mueller, for tolerating all my questions. We should probably get ourselves back to Dubuque and changed into dry clothes," I said, turning to Jefferson.

"You took it awful easy on me," Stan said. "I assumed you'd be tougher than that."

"Thanks, I guess," I said. "If I think of a few more questions, how can I reach you?"

"It's not hard. Just come down here to Aquoqua and tell Rick. He knows how to find me."

We paid our tab with Rick and left down the front stairs. As we walked around to the back of the building, I saw a silver Chevy pickup parked near the boat ramp. "That looks a lot like the truck that ran me off the road near Galena the other day," I told Jefferson. After throwing towels on the seats, we got in Jefferson's truck and sat and waited a few minutes, long enough to see Stan get in the truck and drive away.

"Should we follow him?" I asked Jefferson.

"No," he said. "We'd be too obvious. He'd spot us right away." He put the truck in gear and slowly drove out of the parking lot. "You'll just have something else to ask him about the next time we see him."

Chapter 23

By the time we got back to Dubuque, it was late in the afternoon, and we hadn't eaten since breakfast. Jefferson dropped me off at the parking lot of the Ice Harbor Inn. We needed to clean up and put on some fresh clothes, so we agreed to regroup for dinner at six. Jefferson tossed me the towel I'd been sitting on, so I could throw it on the seat of the rental car for the drive back to my motel.

After I showered and changed, I called Ruby. We'd missed some big news, she told me.

"The city released a report on the fire," she said. "I believe it's on the Internet, so you might want to go there and read it all. I'm surprised by what they concluded. They said it was just an accident, a mistake—the fire, the deaths—although the city's maintenance director is being blamed."

"Stan Mueller?" I asked.

"Yes, I believe that was his name," Ruby said. "There was also a short story in the *Chicago Tribune* about that ice cream, Frozen Expressions, from the cruise we went on," she continued. "It said that some experts are skeptical about it; they said that the market is already too crowded for expensive ice cream. They also quoted someone in Galena who is worried that the owner is extending herself too much, worried that it might hurt her chocolate making. The article was written by Helen Kraft, of course."

While I'd been hanging out with Adam the previous night, Helen Kraft had been busy writing a quick article for the *Trib*. She had to have a friend on the editorial board there, too.

"There was a little more in Kraft's story, too," Ruby said.

"Go on."

"At the very end, the article mentioned that… Wait, let me find it and read it to you. Here it is: 'Ashley Johns is the daughter of Richard and Lynn Johns of Chicago, art dealers and Democratic Party activists. They are major contributors to Dubuque Mayor Michael Andelfinger's campaign to replace George Geiger in Iowa's First Congressional District '"

"Contributors to the mayor's campaign? Why would they care about an Iowa congressional race?" I asked.

"I have no idea," Ruby said, "but I thought you might like to know about it. Maybe it'll fit in with something else you've learned."

"Not yet, but thanks, Ruby. I'm sure we'll figure it out. By the way, I told Jefferson to meet us for dinner at six. I hope that time works for you."

"Oh, yes, that will be nice. I'm glad we can all get together one more time before I go home tomorrow."

"Great. We'll look for you in the lobby."

I had a little time to kill before meeting Ruby and Jefferson for dinner, so, after a quick nap, I looked up the city's preliminary findings on the disaster at the convention center. The fire had begun when a cupcake baker's portable oven overheated the circuit it was plugged into. If I remembered right, the cupcake booth had been right next to Ashley's Post-Modern Chocolates. The report stated there'd been a lot of combustible material near the circuit—cardboard boxes, paper wrappers, curtains hiding makeshift plywood walls—which apparently caught fire when sparks shot out from the circuit. The whole area around the booths had stacks of similar material, so when the cupcake maker's booth went up in flames, the fire spread quickly down the line.

There were a couple dozen confirmed injuries, mostly bruises and a few cracked bones. One person, who'd swallowed too much smoke, was still in the hospital. Then there were those two deaths, both from head injuries. The older man who died had fallen to the floor and banged his head on the tile. The report didn't say this, but I'd bet he was shoved around by the crowd during the panic and pushed down. He'd been buried that afternoon.

The other death was, of course, Jake Horgan, the twenty-four-year old who worked for Post-Modern Chocolates and who, according to that bartender in Galena, was also apparently quite intimate with its owner, Ashley. He'd also died from a head injury that he suffered during the fire-induced chaos, but the report didn't indicate how it happened. His funeral would be Tuesday morning.

The report confirmed that the sprinkler system hadn't engaged as quickly as it should have and blamed the problem on a technician who had set the sensitivity too high. There was no mention of the locked exit doors, however. The report put most of the blame on Stan Mueller, the city's director of facilities, for failing to provide proper oversight. The mayor had suspended Stan for four weeks without pay. The article said that the city was waiting on the results of a few additional tests, but they didn't expect it to change the conclusions in the report.

So that was it. The fire was just an accident. No one was responsible, but the mayor's buddy, Mueller, was getting a token spank. The two guys who died were just unlucky. Case closed. Nothing to see here. No need to ask any other questions. Please move on to the next crisis.

I didn't buy it. I'd been there. I knew there was more to the story than the report addressed. There had to be. If the whole event had just been a fire in a convention center hall, I would probably have moved on to something else myself. But two people were dead, died needlessly because someone had fucked up, and I wasn't about to let those deaths go without someone being held to account.

CHAPTER 24

Refreshed after the nap and shower, I drove back into Dubuque to meet Ruby and Jefferson for dinner. I took them away from downtown, to an old neighborhood place on the north side that had been serving German food without pretension for decades, the Bavarian Inn. I imagine there'd been a time when Dubuque had had a place like that on nearly every corner, a home away from home for the city's thousands of German-born citizens.

The outside of the building was nondescript, if not a little decrepit; it looked like any neighborhood pub from the 1960s. Inside, though, was a different story. The wainscoting that lined the walls was an eye-catcher—maple panels decorated with squares outlined in mahogany. Above the wainscoting the walls were plastered with color prints depicting the German countryside and the crests of old Dubuque families; in between them, brass instruments hung like ornaments. It was dark inside, the windows covered by thick shades hidden behind tan cotton curtains fraying around the edges. The inside hadn't changed much since the 1960s, except for the ATM in one corner and a digital jukebox on a wall.

We sat near the bar at a small table with a red-checkered tablecloth. The bartender looked up from the dull brass taps where he was filling a pint glass with Hacker-Pschorr and another with Bud Light. "*Willkommen!*" he bellowed at us. "Be with you in just a minute." His freshly polished head acted like a beacon in the dark room. He had a thick mustache that drooped down the middle of his face, hiding his lips; the tips of his mustache were heavily greased and turned up 180 degrees to lead your eyes straight up to his bald head.

The bartender slid the two full glasses down the bar to a couple sitting a few stools from the taps, then skirted around the end of the bar and over to our table, handing us each a menu like a calling card. He was dressed in lederhosen and suspenders, with white stockings stretching up to his knees. He introduced himself, Ben, and took our drink orders. Back behind the bar, he poured our beers while singing a few lines from an opera—Wagner, I guessed.

"How do you find these places?" Jefferson asked.

"Good detective work," I said.

We watched Ben for a few minutes, mesmerized, before we turned our attention to the menus. "They make a great schnitzel," I told Jefferson and Ruby. We made our decisions—sauerbraten for me, Wiener Schnitzel for the other two—and shifted our attention away from the entertainment.

"So where are we at?" I asked.

"Did you have a chance to read the full report, Frank?" Ruby asked.

"Yeah, I did. I didn't find it very convincing." Jefferson looked confused. "While we were out for a swim yesterday, the city released a preliminary report about the fire," I told him. "They said it was just an unfortunate accident, that the sprinkler system wasn't set to the right sensitivity. They've suspended Stan Mueller for four weeks without pay for failing to provide proper supervision."

"How did they explain the locked exit doors?" Jefferson asked.

"They didn't," I replied. "The report didn't include any mention of that at all."

"I shouldn't be surprised," Jefferson said. "I guess my buddies at the PD knew what they were talking about. This is a report meant to give a quick answer and pick a scapegoat, so everyone will feel like they got their answer and move on."

"That's what I thought," I said.

"So are we moving on?" Jefferson asked.

"What do you think?" I said as Ben the bartender broke out into another chorus.

"I don't mind helping you out some more, Frank, but we need a plan this time. No more making it up as we go along. If this is a cover-up, then we need to be careful. We don't want to attract attention to ourselves."

"We might be beyond that already, Brian," I said. "Stan certainly knows we're up to something, and I'm sure the mayor's assistant, Courtney, is keeping an eye on us—or on me—too."

"That's true, but we can still go about our business carefully. Let's go over what we already know."

We started with what we remembered during the fire itself. "I don't dispute the report's conclusions about where the fire started," Jefferson said. "That cupcake booth seems plausible as the source."

"The report didn't say anything about how quickly the smoke spread," I noted. "or note the confusion when the exit doors didn't open. What do you make of that, Brian?"

"Either they have no explanation, or they're trying to protect someone."

Stan Mueller was getting the public blame, but he was nicked just for negligence, not for sabotage. Did he know something about the locked exit doors? Was the report covering up a more serious mistake on his part? And what was his role in the Stella-Ashley dispute? Did he stay out of it all, or was he doing something to help Stella out in very subtle ways? Was the location of the booths just a coincidence, or was someone hoping for fireworks from Stella and Ashley?

We still had a lot of questions to answer and didn't know if the Dubuque police, or anyone else, was still investigating, or if the mayor's political ambitions trumped a closer look at a fire that had led to two preventable deaths.

I was also getting tired of Helen popping up at the wrong time and scooping stories that I was working on. I wanted to find a way to scoop her for a change, or maybe I could send her down the wrong path after a false lead. It was the least I could do for her.

"Did you tell Brian about the campaign contributions?" Ruby asked me.

"Sorry, no I haven't." I turned to Jefferson. "Ashley's parents contributed big bucks to the mayor's congressional campaign."

"Why would they do that? They live in Chicago, right?"

"Right," I said.

"So why would they care about politicians in Iowa?" He paused to take a long drink of his beer. "Something feels wrong about that. We better put that on our list of shit to look into."

By the time our food arrived, Jefferson was ready to lay out a plan. "There are a few things we need to figure out soon," he said. "We need to find out the status of the police investigation, make sure we don't make them cranky as we continue to poke around. I can take care of that. We also need to find out more about that kid who worked for both Stella and Ashley. That's your job, Frank, but you have to do it quietly; don't upset his family." He cut off a piece of schnitzel and put it in his mouth.

"I can do that. His funeral is tomorrow morning. I'd like to go, to see who shows up."

"Damn, this schnitzel is really good, Frank," Jefferson said, cutting into the schnitzel again. "At least you have good judgment when it comes to food," he said, in between chews. "Go to the funeral, but just remember to lay low. We don't want to alienate anyone who can help us." Jefferson wiped a napkin across his mouth. "We're going to need to learn more about Stan Mueller, too."

I assured Jefferson that I would behave, and I offered to bring Ruby along as my chaperone. I also got assigned the job of continuing to poke at the Stella-Ashley rivalry, to see what else might be hiding beneath the surface. Jefferson was going to check with the police to try to find out why the report hadn't mentioned the locked exit doors. Ruby wanted to read more about the mayor and his campaign, hoping to find something that might illuminate the Johns family's interest in Iowa politics.

With our plans in hand and our bellies full, I drove Ruby and Jefferson back to the Ice Harbor Inn. Ruby went to her room. Jefferson said he was tired and was probably going to stay in for the night. I was pretty sure he was going to see Lonna, though; he just didn't want me giving him shit about it. I thought about dropping into Lonna's Livery and maybe catching him there, but instead I called Adam and spent the rest of the evening forgetting about canoe accidents, locked exit doors, and Helen Kraft.

Chapter 25

I picked up Ruby at eight thirty on Tuesday morning, and we drove to the Church of St. Mary for Jake Horgan's funeral. It was hazy and warm, not a cloud in the sky, the kind of day that begs for floating on the river, not mourning in a church.

"I'm glad I found something to wear," Ruby said. She was wearing an ankle-length dress, a gray cotton blend over white lace. "I wasn't sure I'd packed anything that would be appropriate for a funeral."

"You always dress well, Ruby," I said. "Me, though—I was lucky that I'd grabbed a sports coat and slacks when I packed. I don't usually do that."

"Yes, that was lucky," she said, "if you consider 'needing them for a funeral' lucky, I suppose." She dropped down the visor on the passenger side and used the mirror to make sure everything was in its proper place. "What do you know about his family? His parents must be so distraught."

"I don't know much about him yet. Been too busy with the bigger fish. I think he grew up on a farm in southern Wisconsin, but that's about all I know."

I parked on Fifteenth Street, and we walked the remaining block to the church. It wasn't hard to miss. The Gothic Revival building had a 252-foot steeple that stretched up toward heaven, the tallest in town and a decades-long maintenance headache. Inside, it was dark but hardly oppressive. The ceiling was painted deep red, the two halves separated by a long row of gilt vaulting. Underneath us, velvet carpeting in a similar red covered the floor from the nave to the choir. A hand-carved statue of Mary stood watch over the congregation, staring down at the rows of oak pews, most of which were empty when we entered.

Along each wall, rows of art-glass windows depicted scenes from the life of Mary, the creation of Bavarian artisan F. X. Zettler, who'd managed to ship the windows out of Germany just before World War I. We sat near the front, and Ruby lost herself admiring the decorative details of the church—those windows, mostly—while I scanned the growing crowd, looking for familiar faces. I saw just one, Ashley Johns, sitting in the second row behind an older couple—Jake's parents, I assumed. Next to Ashley sat a couple of people I assumed were employees at the Post-Modern Chocolates shop. As a few more people arrived, Ruby and I found ourselves seated amid a group of folks who were in their twenties—friends of Jake, no doubt.

The service began promptly at nine. There was nothing remarkable about it, nothing that spoke to anything in particular about Jake. The eulogy was so generic that I swore the priest must have just downloaded text from EulogyInAHurry.com. When we filed past the open coffin at the end of the service, I got my first good look at the deceased, at Jake. Sure, I'd gotten a piece of chocolate from him at the craft-food fair, but I'd barely noticed him then, much less looked at him. Now I could see that he was an attractive young man, and not just because of the blond hair and blue eyes. He looked affable and trustworthy, like someone you wanted to bump into on an empty train platform late at night, a face to put you at ease.

After the service, we followed the group to Mount Calvary Cemetery for the burial. Two dozen or so mourners gathered around the grave for a few more parting words and one more good cry, most of them squeezing together under a blue canopy to hide from the summer sun. The family—Jake's parents and a sister—sat in folding chairs near the coffin; Ashley stood near them.

The priest said a few more words but kept it brief; then Jake's sister got up to express the family's shock and grief at losing the youngest member of the family. "We can't get over the fact that Jake has been taken from us already, but we feel so blessed that he was part of our lives for twenty-four years."

"Blessed," my ass! They got cheated. At twenty-four, Jake was just starting to live, but here he was instead, lying in a coffin for eternity. I understood that the family was just doing what families are supposed to do in the face of tragedy, but if I'd been in their shoes, I'd have felt bitter and pissed and wouldn't have been shy about letting people know.

While his sister was speaking, I glanced to my right and caught sight of a woman standing near the road. It was Stella. I watched as she said a brief prayer, then made the sign of the cross. As the coffin was being lowered into the ground, I looked back to see her get into a car and drive away.

After the service broke up, I walked over to Jake's parents and expressed my sympathies. I told them that I was working on a story about Post-Modern Chocolates and would like to include a brief profile of Jake, as a tribute. They were flattered and offered to meet with me the next day at their house. I gave them my card, and they promised to call me later.

"Are you ready?" I asked Ruby.

"Yes," she replied, patting a handkerchief around her eyes.

We started driving back to Friesburg; Ruby was ready to be home. "I hope that didn't bring back bad memories for you," I said.

"Not at all," she said, "It doesn't do any good to hide from the past. It doesn't help anything. I see what they're going through, and I feel bad for them, because I know exactly how they feel. And I know how they will be feeling from now on."

"How long ago did Paul die?"

Ruby didn't answer right away. "It was seventeen years ago. Seventeen years. It's hard to believe he's been gone that long already."

"How did you not break down after that?"

"Who said I didn't? I felt crippled by it for a while. Paul had never been sick a day in his life, I swear, then just like that a heart attack took him away from us. He was only forty-five, but at least I had him a lot longer than the Horgans had Jake." Ruby turned her head and looked out the passenger window, then looked back at me. "It was a long time before I could talk about his death, Frank, because I tried to look strong, for his children. I wanted my two grandchildren to see me moving on, so they could too. I wanted them to understand that it was OK to feel sad and to cry, but our lives didn't have to end because his did. It was important that they understood that."

"That sounds easy to say but not so easy to do."

"Of course. That's why I said I *tried* to keep up appearances, because inside I didn't feel that way at all. Part of me felt like my life really was over. I'd put so much of my life into his, after all." She reached into her purse and pulled out a Kleenex, keeping it in her hand as if she thought she might need it. "But sometimes, if you act a certain way for a while, the feelings catch up. That's what happened, at least for me. After some time, and a lot of prayer, I realized that Paul wasn't my whole life, that I had more to live for, even if he wasn't around. As the loss felt a little less intense, I began to see how lucky I was to have had a son like Paul. He was smart and caring and one heck of a good artist, too. I felt like that boy's family: hurt by the loss, but so grateful to have known someone like him." She rested a hand on my shoulder. "You can feel both, you know. Which is good, because the pain never really goes away."

"But how can you—and they—not be bitter? You'd put your life into raising Paul, sacrificed so much for him, so he could have a good life of his own. And the Horgans, they lose their son before he even had a chance to get out in the world and create a life for himself. How does that not make you bitter?" I gripped the steering wheel a little tighter, so Ruby wouldn't see my hands shaking.

"It can, Frank," Ruby said, turning to look at me and resting a hand on my shoulder. "I can't help but feel like we're talking about you here and what you've been through, first with your sister drowning and now with Greg. But look at me. I'm not bitter about losing my son. Yes, it hurts, and I miss him so terribly much, but there's more to my life than being a mother." She lifted a hand up to the middle of her chest. "I'm also an amateur sleuth who helps a travel writer solve crimes!" We both cracked up.

Ruby turned back to look at the road. "We have to move on, Frank. We can't go back in time and edit out the bad parts. And standing still hurts too much. No. There's only one way to go, and that's to keep pushing ahead, no matter what."

We pulled into Friesburg on Elm Street and drove past the museum, where Ruby volunteered. I dropped her off at her house, a bungalow near the downtown strip that she was sure was the oldest house in town, even if its origins had been buried under layers of vinyl siding and drywall. She promised to get started researching more about the mayor's political history as soon as she unpacked and to let me know what she learned.

On the drive back to Dubuque, I turned on the radio just in time to hear a political ad for the mayor's campaign in the Democratic primary. Under normal circumstances, that would provoke me to switch to something else, but I was curious to hear the mayor's talking points. In the ad, Mike Andelfinger was described as a "doer," honest and hardworking—the usual blather. He had deep roots in Iowa and Dubuque, so I figured his opponent must be a transplant; the mayor was appealing to his tribe. He had come up through the city's political system and knew how to get things done—more blather. His opponent, Laura Adler, was inexperienced and "too liberal for Iowa"; again, she was not one of us.

An ad for Adler's campaign came on right after the mayor's, and she hit just as hard: Mayor Andelfinger was an apologist for the city's elite business interests, unable and unwilling to fight for Iowa's working people. I could tell that she was probably appealing to the same tribe but looking for a different way to connect with them. The mayor was a political insider out to feed his political ambitions, she averred; he was trying to climb the political ladder as high as possible. He was a dreaded Career Politician, who was owned by wealthy backers. The rich already had enough politicians looking out for them, but the mayor would just be one more lackey for their interests. Adler, though, was a fighter, she'd been fighting all her adult life for working people. If ever there was a time to elect someone to fight for working people, it was today, she argued. I lost track of the number of times the word *fight* was used in her ad.

I drove back to Dubuque along the Great River Road, through Sherrill and past its four nineteenth-century churches, through Sageville and into the north side of town, thinking about Jake's death and Ruby's experiences. Life is short and time precious. I began to feel impatient, like I'd been wasting too much time trying to figure out what had happened with the fire, had been too passive about following up on leads. As I drove back into the city, I knew it was time to cut through the bullshit. I knew where I wanted to start, so I headed right to Thirtieth Street, ready to grill Stella until I got the truth out of her.

Chapter 26

I didn't bother to call Stella in advance this time; I just showed up at the Cathedral Ice Cream factory. I'd accumulated a long list of questions and didn't feel like giving her a chance to prepare this time. I wanted to see more of the real Stella, unvarnished and off balance.

As soon as I walked in, Stella spotted me from behind her office window. She ended a call and slipped her phone into a pocket before walking over to greet me.

"What a nice surprise, Frank!" she said. "I wish you would have called first, though. I have to run off to meet with one of my retailers shortly."

"I'm sorry to drop in unannounced," I said, reaching out to shake her hand, "but I was in the area and realized I had a couple of follow-up questions. Can I steal a few minutes of your time?"

"Of course. Let's grab a seat over there," she said, pointing to a tall café table near the front entrance. "What can I help you with?" she asked after we sat down.

"I wanted to find out how you're doing since the cruise. That was an especially nasty move on Ashley's part to invite you under the pretense of a truce." I pulled out a notebook and opened it to a blank page.

"I should have known better, I suppose." She glanced down at my notebook. "I guess this is on the record, Frank?"

"If you don't mind. I thought I'd take a few notes. I might need them later."

"OK. I don't mind. Well, let's see… I'm doing OK. I think my chances of breaking into the Chicago market will probably be harder now, but it's too soon to know anything else." She glanced back down at my notebook. "I think the Chicago market is her real target, anyway, not any place around here. She'd like to be big in Chicago. We're too small for her ambitions."

"That's good to know, but it's not exactly what I was getting at. You put on quite a show at the end of the cruise. Seemed like you were really upset."

"Of course, I was upset. Wouldn't you be?" I watched her closely, zeroing in on her eyes and hands, but to her credit, she didn't show any hint of being nervous.

"After the cruise," she continued, "they threatened to sue me, but I know they won't follow through. I know how they think. The image of Richard Johns floating in the Mississippi at his daughter's party isn't one they want shown over and over. I can still see him flailing around helplessly." Stella laughed, reaching over to slap me on the knee. "The guy apparently can't even doggie paddle! No, he won't want to relive that experience. That's not the image a high-end art dealer wants to project."

"You didn't tell me that you had your own history with Ashley's parents."

Stella didn't flinch. "It didn't seem relevant to your story." She tilted her head slightly. "Why?" She leaned forward. "What have you heard?"

"I heard that you used to be friends—you and Ashley's parents—that they were big supporters of your ice cream shop, that they invited you over to their house regularly."

"Ha! Of course, they would say that. I was never a regular guest at their house. It was more like two or three times they had me over. And I wouldn't say they were big supporters of my ice cream shop. Sure, maybe they stopped in for ice cream a couple of times a week. It probably made them feel good, to drop ten bucks a week in my store. They might have been impressed with themselves, but it didn't impress me."

"So they didn't invite you to any parties? Or maybe confide anything in you?"

Stella turned her head slightly to the right and gave me a good look-over. "Are you talking about the Nazi art they were trying to sell? The sale they bragged about but that ultimately fell apart?"

"Yeah. A couple of people thought you might have been responsible for the demise of that sale, that you tipped off a reporter to get back at them for something."

"And what was I supposed to be getting revenge for? That they didn't spend fifteen bucks a week on my ice cream instead of ten? No one has ever been able to tell me exactly why I would try to undermine them. Am I supposed to be so petty, so small, that I would mess with someone's livelihood just because?" She leaned back and crossed her arms. "I'm not, Frank. That's not who I am."

"So even though the story was written by Helen Kraft..."

"Oh, that was just a coincidence, nothing more." She made a *pfft* sound and waved dismissively. "Just because Helen and I had been friends for a while, that doesn't mean I passed on any information to her. I mean, I didn't even know she'd been working on that topic. She told me later that she'd been researching it for months. In fact, she was very apologetic about the trouble it caused me. The Johnses, of course, refused to believe any of that, which is fine. I don't need their approval or their friendship."

"So you're saying that you absolutely did not tell Helen that the Johnses were trying to sell a painting that might have been stolen by the Nazis?"

"Of course, that's what I'm saying." She looked right at me and paused. "Where are you going with this, Frank? I thought you were here to write about ice cream."

"That's what I thought, too, but the story has gotten more complicated." I scratched down a couple of notes before continuing. "About Helen Kraft, it would have been... considerate if you'd told me up front that the two of you were friends."

"Oh, Frank. I'm sorry if I hurt your feelings. I thought about telling you, but I was afraid it might start us off on the wrong foot. I was concerned that it might influence how you write about me. I know that the two of you haven't always seen eye to eye."

I felt my blood boiling but tried to control my temper. "We don't have a simple difference of opinion, Stella," I said, straining to keep my voice from getting too loud. "She stole my work."

"Oh, no, I didn't mean to imply anything. I don't know what happened between the two of you. It's none of my business. And she hasn't talked to me about it, other than to alert me that you two had some kind of trouble in the past. Like I said, I just didn't want any of that history influencing what you might write about my ice cream."

I took a deep breath and, to mute my anger, I tried to think about the delicious blueberry ice cream that I'd tasted during my last visit. "You're right. It's not your problem. It just would have been nice to know that she was a friend of yours."

"Like I said, I'm sorry."

"How did you meet?"

"We met at Newton College. I was an elementary ed major, and Helen was studying art history. There were a lot of kids from wealthy families at that school, but we were among the few who were there on full scholarships. We bonded over that. Goodness, that seems like so long ago, now," she said, checking the time on her cell phone. "We never really fit in there, especially after we fought to get the chancellor fired."

"What was your beef with the chancellor?" I asked.

"He was diverting donations from alumni for his personal use. He lived very extravagantly off money that had been donated to support scholarships for students. Well, Helen and I, as scholarship students, just wouldn't have been able to live with ourselves if we didn't do something about that."

"Did you get him fired?"

"No, not exactly. We staged a few protests and got some other students interested—even got a couple of newspaper articles written about him—but when finals approached, we all lost steam. Funny thing is, at the end of the summer, he announced that he was going to retire. I think those alums woke up to what he was doing—Helen and I woke them up—so they threatened to cut off their donations unless he left." Stella checked the time again. "Is there anything else, Frank? I should be leaving soon."

"Just one more thing. I went to Jake Horgan's funeral this morning. Such a tragedy! I feel so bad for the family. I noticed you stopped by to pay your respects, too, at the gravesite."

"I would have liked to attend the whole service," she said, "but I was afraid my presence would be too much of a distraction. I didn't want his funeral to become about me."

"I suppose Ashley had a stronger claim to be at the funeral. He did work for her, after all."

"Fuck her!" Stella blurted, slamming her chair back. "Jake worked for me, too, remember? I had just as much right to be there as she did." She stood up, closed her eyes, and turned away from me.

I gave her a moment to recompose, then dived right back in. "Then why didn't you go to the funeral and make *her* stay away? What's so special about Ashley?"

Stella turned back to face me but didn't look directly at me. "Like I said, I didn't want to make a scene. Sometimes you have to be the adult when faced with unreasonable people, and that was one time I felt like I had to be the adult. That's why I let Ashley go to the funeral, while I stayed away. Frank, I hate to be rude," she said, taking a couple of steps away from me and toward her office, "but I should go now. I've got that meeting coming right up, as I told you earlier."

"Yeah, I suppose I should go, too," I said, getting up from the chair. "Oh, before I forget, did Stan tell you we met?"

"Yes. He mentioned that he found you and your friend in the river," she said, walking back toward the table and sliding the chairs back into place.

"An inglorious way to meet," I said.

"I can only imagine. Then again," she said, looking right at me again, "it does make you seem a whole lot less threatening, doesn't it? Comical, almost."

"Maybe that's just me: nonthreatening and comical." I waved my left hand, palm up. "Anyway, I'm glad I got to meet him. His name kept coming up in conversations around town. It helps to put a face to the name. Looks like he's in some trouble now, though, because of the fire."

"Stan will be fine," Stella said. "He's rarely in trouble, but when trouble finds him, he's remarkably good at escaping unscathed."

"So you aren't worried about him? That maybe he's losing his job—or worse?" I asked.

"Not at all," she said. "He has friends looking out for him." She reached into a pocket and pulled out her phone, then looked at the time. "And now, Frank, please excuse me. I have to go."

I figured I'd be pushing my luck if I asked for another quart of ice cream, so I just said goodbye and walked out. She'd handled the surprise visit well, but at least she confirmed some of what I'd heard, such as Jake's affair with Ashley. At least, it seemed like she did, with the way she turned away from me at first, then how she wouldn't look at me directly after she had turned back around.

She was awfully cool about Stan, though—too cool. There was something about their relationship that felt off to me. Stan had showed more passion about his friendship with the mayor than his marriage to Stella, while Stella got more emotional about Jake than about Stan. They were both ambitious and worked hard. From what I'd seen, they spent more time on the job than with each other. I couldn't tell if Stella and Stan still loved each other, or if they were just reluctant to let go and move on. To move forward.

CHAPTER 27

After I left Stella's ice cream factory, I realized that I hadn't eaten lunch yet. I was in the mood for some home-style cooking and conversation, so I drove to a diner not far from the John Deere plant in northern Dubuque, a place called Fred's, the "Friendliest Diner in Dubuque"—or so the sign said. I was looking for a good burger and fries, to get some idea of what folks thought of the congressional race—if they thought of it at all.

I'd just missed the lunch rush, but the place was still half full. John Deere memorabilia hung on the walls: old advertising signs, product manuals—even a few spare tractor parts, like spark plugs and a piece of green sheet metal with the Deere logo. I sat at the counter, near a couple of guys looking at menus and a table of four who were digging into their food as if their hands were forklifts and their mouths empty warehouses. I swear I saw one guy pick up an entire burger and slide it into his mouth in one smooth motion. Guess he was in a hurry.

It was hot inside the diner. The windows were open, which offered about as much relief as the corner fans that just moved the hot air around. I tried to strike up a conversation with the other guys at the lunch counter, but all I got was a word or two back. Maybe they didn't like my hat, either. After I ordered food, I caught the server in between delivering trays of saturated fat and asked him if folks were talking much about the campaign. He looked at me as if I'd asked him what was in a hamburger. He just shook his head and said folks around there had more important things to worry about, like paying their bills.

I was about to give up when one of the guys at the table behind me spoke up and asked if I was a reporter. I let him think so. It turned out that folks around there weren't terribly fond of reporters, especially the ones from out of town, so when I told him I was from St. Louis, I didn't score any points with that, either.

He humored me, though, after a few thinly veiled insults about the journalism profession. "I don't care who wins that damn primary, because they're both socialists, anyway." That was enough to get others in the diner riled up. Before I knew it, half the customers were arguing about the two candidates. So much for having better things to worry about.

The arguments pro and con for each candidate were pretty straightforward and, not surprisingly, mirrored the themes from the campaign ads I'd heard. Mayor Andelfinger had experience and knew how to get things done. I didn't see much passion from his supporters, though. It seemed to me that they just figured he'd bring money to the district and maybe get a few things fixed.

Adler's supporters called the mayor a crook and too full of himself—a contention that one guy tried to dispute by pointing out that the mayor had never actually been *convicted* of anything. About half the crowd thought that was really funny, just not the guy who'd said it. Adler's supporters said she was tenacious and that she'd proven her mettle by going toe to toe with the big shots at John Deere. During her tenure as union chief, she'd won a couple of big victories, not the least of which was her role in keeping the plant open a few years back, when it had seemed a hopeless cause.

The diners were doing a fine job of keeping the arguments going without my help, so I listened and watched. At one point, as folks began to settle down, I asked, "Is Adler enough of a local to win people's trust, given how

Dubuquers feel about outsiders?" That set off another round of arguing and insults, most of which were aimed at me. Every time an out-of-town reporter comes to Dubuque, locals get asked that same question, or so I learned when someone chucked a spoonful of mashed potatoes just over my head.

The guy sitting next to me told me that he was sick and tired of visitors calling the city a backwater and its residents isolated hicks, and he gave me some helpful suggestions for where I could put the next issue of my newspaper or whatever I wrote for. I tried to point out that I'd never used the words *backwater* or *hicks*, but all I got was a less-than-forgiving "Fuck you!" as he got up and left. Another guy yelled out that, of course, they'd vote for an out-of-towner like Adler. It didn't matter that she wasn't from Dubuque; it only mattered what she would do for the city if she won. Someone then called me an elitist hack, which I figured was one of the nicest—and most confusing—insults I'd heard in a while.

Most of the customers had to rush back to the plant, so the restaurant emptied quickly. I lingered a little longer, to give them all time to get out of the place, in case one of them resented me a little more than the others did. I was looking toward the front door, watching the last straggler exit, when the server dropped off my check; he tapped on the counter to get my attention.

"Hey, mister. I have a quick story for ya. There was this woman—let's call her Mrs. Johnson—who was born in Waterloo. But her family moved to Dubuque when she was just a baby. She lived here all the rest of her life, ninety-three years' worth. When she died, the obituary headline read 'Waterloo Native Dies in Dubuque.'" He paused for effect; then he said, "Those guys—they're a bunch of fuckin' hypocrites, and they tip lousy, too. That union chief, Ms. Adler, she's in her mid-forties and has lived in Dubuque over forty years. You heard 'em. They called her 'an out-of-towner.'"

I thanked him for the story and left a twenty-dollar bill to cover my twelve-dollar tab. I'd heard that story before and hadn't paid it much attention. Maybe I should have. When I got outside to the parking lot, my rental car had two flat tires.

<h1 style="text-align:center">CHAPTER 28</h1>

The rental company sent a guy to change out the deflated tires for new ones, and I was back in business about an hour later. With the deadline approaching for submitting my article to *Wandering Gourmet,* I used the time to look over some of my notes. I had gotten a lot of research done at the convention before the fire started, but I still needed a few quotes to liven it up.

Once I was mobile again, I went back downtown to visit a couple of stores and talk to the owners. I stopped first at a brewpub and ordered a flight; I didn't want to offend them by not giving their beer a proper chance.

It was midafternoon, so the place wasn't too busy, yet. I asked the owner and the brewmaster about the craft-food fad, and they agreed that there were a lot people who'd grown up with gardens, but they reminded me that many more, including they themselves, had grown up thinking that dining out meant getting a burger at McDonald's—a treat to look forward to. They'd been well into their twenties before they realized how much good food and beer they'd been missing.

They'd opened their brewery about three years before, and it had been growing every year. I remembered when I'd visited, back when they were still new at it all. I was pretty sure then that I'd never go back. Though they had learned quite a bit since then—and the beer they brewed was definitely better now—I didn't have the heart to tell them that they still had a ways to go.

I left the brewpub and walked a couple of blocks down Main Street. The sun was burning hot, and sweat was rolling down my face and the back of my neck. After sampling five beers, though, I didn't much mind.

Farther down Main Street, I passed a small bakery that I hadn't noticed before, Tilly's Cupcakes, so I went in to check it out. Someone was fond of frilly decorations. The windows were partially covered by lace curtains. Ceramic angels sat in windowsills, while unnaturally blue paintings of country farmhouses hung on the walls. A plush white area rug was placed in front of the glass case that was filled with a few dozen cupcakes. The decor was enough to stifle my appetite, but looking at those cupcakes, I figured I could eat something.

The owner, a woman who I assumed was named Tilly, placed one carrot cake and one red velvet cupcake that I ordered in a tidy cream-colored box and sealed it with a red ribbon. She looked familiar, so I asked if she'd been at the convention center. She stuttered a yes, then apologized for being cagey about it, confessing that the fire had started at her booth. She felt terrible about it but was dumbfounded about how it had happened.

She'd had the oven and power cords inspected before the convention started. No one from the city suggested there could be a problem. The city report I read indicated that the fire had ignited a stack of papers and boxes near the electrical outlet and that's how it had spread, but Tilly didn't remember stacking any papers back there. When she realized a fire had started, she tried to snuff it out by slapping at it with a towel, but that seemed only to make things worse. She was pretty sure those boxes weren't hers, though, because she saw the word *cream* on one of them, and she knew that she hadn't packed any cream for her cupcakes that day. Cream? Ice cream, maybe? I thanked her for the chat, paid for the cupcakes, and left, forgetting to get a quote from her about the value of small-batch cupcakes.

I sat on a bench on Main Street and ate the red velvet cupcake, watching the tourists and office workers scurry down the sidewalk. At one point, a group of seven men walked in front of me, all wearing blue dress shirts (one with pinstripes—a rebel!), all in black slacks and black oxfords, six of them pulling suitcases behind them that bounced up when they hit the same cracks, their hair uniformly short, and their waistlines uniformly wide.

They felt a long way away from me, as though they were actors on a movie screen playing their parts but just for my amusement. I nibbled on the cupcake, watching the scene progress, wondering who were the heroes and who the villains. The guy wearing a bright red tie, pulling a suitcase with one hand and looking at an iPhone 6 in the other—he was definitely a jerk, self-centered and cold, probably the boss. The guy at the back of the pack—the one whose oxfords were popping out at the seams and whose belt was too big for his waist—he was recently divorced and had just been passed over for a promotion. They were living the kind of lives that I'd wanted once but that I couldn't imagine going back to now. I had walked away from everything, and nearly everyone, and started over. Did that make me brave or just selfish? I'd felt like both. Anyway, Tilly's red velvet cupcake tasted really damn good, and that's all that mattered at that moment.

I walked another block down the street to The Wired Bean, the place Stella had mentioned when I interviewed her the first time, for a cup of coffee and to start the outline for my article. After I got an espresso, I found a seat at a small patio table, between two men wearing three-piece suits playing with their tablets and a woman in a sundress doing a crossword puzzle. None of them budged or looked up when I wiggled past them to get to the empty chair.

I was ready to slow down after a day that had begun with a funeral and had peaked with the slashing of my tires. I sent a text to Jefferson but didn't hear back, so I picked up a copy of the *Dubuque Register* and scanned a few pages. One of the casinos was planning an expansion, and the campground at Miller Riverview Park had had a busy but profitable Fourth of July holiday. A new poll showed the mayor had a comfortable lead on Laura Adler in the Democratic primary. The obituary for Jake Horgan noted that Richard and Lynn Johns had set up a scholarship in his name at Loras College. And near the back, in the business section, was a brief note that Ashley Johns had signed a deal with a small supermarket chain in Chicago to sell her ice cream and chocolates.

<h1 style="text-align:center">CHAPTER 29</h1>

I finished throwing together an outline at the coffee shop and then went back to the motel for a nap. After a quick shower, I dug through my suitcase and found a clean shirt and drove back into the city to meet Jefferson for a happy hour drink at the Commodore Lounge, the bar at the Ice Harbor Inn. He had a seat at one end of the bar, but there were no other empties, so I stood next to him at the corner.

The place was so packed I could barely see the faux fishing nets and pilot wheels, which I assumed had been hung to shift attention from the cracked mirrors and the ripped vinyl floor tiles. I could also barely see the bartender—or, rather, she could barely see us. We finally got our drinks, elbowed our way through the masses of office workers and vacationers, and headed to a back corner, next to a fiberglass statue of Neptune, where there was a gap in the crowd. Jefferson had been busy, checking with the police about the investigation into the convention center fire.

"Here's the good news," he started. "We're free to poke around all we want, as long as we keep it quiet and don't go ambushing the mayor or any other politicians publicly. There's no love lost between the mayor and the cops I talked with, but they have to watch their backs, too. They'll share what they know; we just can't let on that they've helped."

"That sounds promising," I said.

"I suppose. The bad news is that they're about to close the investigation and move on. So they might be sharing what they know now, but they won't be out there looking into anything else about the fire."

"So we're on our own with that."

"Yes. We have to do our own digging…" he said, looking at me like a first-grade teacher telling his students to work quietly. "Discreetly."

"I got it," I said, looking back at him like one of those students who had no intention of being quiet. "So what have you learned from them so far?"

"That's the other bad news. I didn't find out much beyond what was in the report they just released. They're confident about where the fire started, that it was probably an overloaded circuit that set it all off."

"That reminds me. Earlier today I met the person who owns the booth where the fire started. Her cupcake business is in a storefront just down the street. She seemed really rattled by the fire, even apologized to me for her role." I took a quick sip of my drink, then tilted my head toward Jefferson. "The odd part—what stood out to me—is that she swore her whole setup had been inspected and approved: the oven, the wiring, everything. She didn't understand how a fire could have started after that."

"Did she say who inspected it?"

"I didn't ask, but she said it was someone from the city."

"Maybe I should talk to her about it, too," Jefferson said.

I gave him the store's name and told him where to find it, feeling a little shamed, like I should have known to ask for a name. "There's one other detail she mentioned," I said. "She told me that the fire started around a stack of boxes, and at least one of them had the word *cream* on it. She didn't think it was hers, because she hadn't made any cupcakes with cream filling for the food fair."

"Cream? Like ice cream?" Jefferson asked.

"That's what I was thinking," I said. "Stella's booth was just across the aisle from where the fire started. But before you go and turn Stella into an arsonist, let me just say that it seems a little too... too convenient for that box to show up there. Stella seems bright to me. If she was going to start a fire at that convention, she wouldn't do it with a box from her own business."

"Unless she believed it would be burned up in the fire," Jefferson said. "I don't remember the police notes including anything about labels on boxes or papers at the site where the fire broke out. I would assume they were too charred to be useful."

"Seriously, I can't believe she would take a chance like that."

"Fair enough. You've talked with her; I haven't." Jefferson rubbed his forehead. "But we shouldn't rule anything out at this point. If she's not involved, how did the boxes get there?"

"Good question. What other news do you have?"

"They know about the locked exit doors; they just don't have an explanation for them. They didn't note the problem with the doors in the report, because the mayor's office didn't want it in there."

"They got political pressure to leave it out?" I asked.

"Yes. I think it's just temporary. Since they couldn't explain it, they didn't want the public to know about it right now. I held my tongue on that. I was afraid I'd step on some toes if I challenged them about that. It seemed like it was out of their hands, anyway." He shrugged his shoulders. "I've got a friend back home in St. Louis who works at the convention center there. I got him asking around about doors like that, to see if he can help us come up with a theory about what happened." He looked over at me. "What about you? What else did you do?"

I told him about the funeral, the diner and the slashed tires, my chat with Stella. I'd had just as busy a day as he had, yet somehow I felt like I'd been a lot less productive. I turned up a couple of interesting tidbits, but I didn't feel like I'd discovered much that moved us along.

"Oh, one other thing," Jefferson said. "I had the marriage record pulled for Richard Johns. Stella was right. His birth name was Richard Johnson. He changed it when he got married."

"OK," I said. "So Stella's right: he's a pretentious ass. So what?"

"Maybe that's all it means." Jefferson scratched his head. "Then again, maybe it says he's the kind of person willing to do just about anything to get ahead."

"And how does that make him different from every other rich bastard?"

"Now, now, Frank. Not everyone out there with money is a crook or got their money by cheating."

Truth was, my views about the wealthy were probably closer to Stella's than to Jefferson's. I refused to believe that people who went from nothing to being rich did so legitimately. I was sure that they'd screwed over plenty of people along the way. The difference between me and Stella, though, was that I didn't harbor the same hatred for them. Sure, I wouldn't trust most rich people with my wallet, but I didn't wish them ill. I just wished they'd spend more of their money on the things *I* was selling. Before I could explain the subtleties in my position to Jefferson, my phone rang. It was Courtney Baker, the mayor's chief of staff.

"Frank, this is Courtney. I don't know why I'm even bothering to share this with you, given the shit you've pulled around here, but something's happened that just doesn't sit right with me."

"I'm glad to hear from you," I said, "to find out we're still on speaking terms."

"Don't get excited about it. Look, I don't have a lot of time. You probably saw the news that the mayor suspended Stan Mueller for four weeks for his role in the convention fire."

"Yeah, I heard about that."

"Well, the part that didn't make the news is that the mayor pulled some cash out of his campaign funds and gave it to Mueller, to make up for the lost pay."

"We should all have friends like that," I said. "I don't suppose there's a paper trail for that transaction?"

"Hardly. No. But I wanted to give you a heads up about it. It's something you should keep in the back of your mind as you talk to people around here."

"What makes you think I'm still investigating anything?"

"Oh, Frank, don't be coy. I know you went to Fred's Diner today and got people all worked up. I know what you're up to. That you won't let this go."

"So why rat out your boss? That can't be good for your job security."

"Neither is working for a crook. Look. I've said too much already. Don't mention this conversation to anyone or try to use me a source. I'll deny it and crucify you in the process."

I said a quick "Thank you" before she hung up; then I slid the phone back into my shirt pocket.

"What was all that about?" Jefferson asked.

"It looks like the mayor's chief of staff has turned on him."

Chapter 30

Happy hour was winding down and we were hungry, so we decided to split a pizza for dinner. We walked down the street to a cozy pizza joint with an imposing stone oven. Most of their business was takeout, but they had a half dozen small tables squeezed between the front window and the counter. All were empty when we got there. We ordered the *enorme con tutto* and sat at a table by the window.

"What's going on with Lonna?" I asked.

"I don't know, Frank. I don't know. I haven't had to do the dating thing for so long, I feel out of whack. I don't feel like myself. I don't like being confused."

"What's confusing you?"

"I feel like she's sending mixed signals. She plays it cool most of the time, like she's indifferent to me. When I show up, I can't tell if she wants me around or not. Then, out of the blue, she'll start flirting with me—just a little wink or a flash of skin, enough to make me believe again that it's worth my time to stick around. By the end of the night, she kicks it up big time and wants me to stay with her, to sleep with her. I can't figure it out. Does she want to be with me or not?"

"Have you asked her that directly?"

"Why would I do that?"

I laughed. "*You* may not do it, but normal people do it to get answers to the questions you're asking. It beats guessing. Maybe you should try it."

"But what if she says that she doesn't want to get serious with me? Then I've wasted time and energy courting someone who doesn't want me back." Jefferson threw up his hands and sat back.

"You really have been out of it for a while, haven't you?" I said. "Maybe she does like you, but it's the dating-seriously part she's not ready for. Have you thought about that?"

"No," Jefferson said. "Why wouldn't she want to date seriously? Why bother with any of this if it's not meant to be real and lasting?"

"Not every relationship has to end in marriage. Maybe she doesn't want to go there again. Maybe she's just looking for something fun, with no demands."

"She can look all she wants, but that's not what *I'm* looking for. That's not what I'm about."

"If she doesn't want to date you seriously, wouldn't you rather find that out now, and not put more time and energy into chasing her?"

"I wish I'd known that before we started into this. I wish she would have told me up front. That's what I wish."

Our pizza showed up, and Jefferson shut down. To take the focus off his troubles with Lonna, I told him about Adam, about how it was a nice distraction to spend time with someone like that while I was in Dubuque. After we finished eating, Jefferson begged off for the night. He said he needed some time alone, to think things through. I believed him, and I didn't mind. I had other plans. I wanted to go back to Aquoqua and poke around a little more, and I didn't want Jefferson looking over my shoulder this time.

<h1 style="text-align:center">CHAPTER 31</h1>

I drove from downtown Dubuque to Aquoqua, windows wide open to let the air blow around me. It was still hot, but I'll take the breeze over AC any day. The sun was getting low on the horizon. In another hour or so, the light would soften, blanketing the landscape for a few precious moments with a golden hue before yielding to darkness.

Down in the bottoms, however, that golden light had already gone, and the air was cooling. I pulled into the parking lot at the marina and walked up the stairs to the Hungry Point Bar and Grill.

The place was busier this time, and loud. There was only one open seat at the bar, on a corner opposite the door, and most of the tables were full, too. I went to the bar and sat down next to a woman who was wearing a black Harley T-shirt over a bathing suit. She turned to say hello, then went back to talking to her friends. The bartender, Rick, came down my way.

"You're back. That hat of yours looks better now. I like the weathered look." He looked up and down the bar. "What are you looking for this time?" he asked.

"A beer," I told him. "How about a Potosi IPA?"

"Coming right up."

I looked around the bar, scanning the crowd. I didn't see anyone I'd met the last time I was there, but everyone looked happy. I felt like I was crashing a frat party that had broken out on the river and moved into the bar when

the beer ran out. Rick came back with my drink. "Here ya go. Three bucks."
I gave him five. I commented on how busy the place was. Rick told me they
just finished Tuesday trivia, a big hit with the regulars.

"This area reminds me a lot of where I grew up," I said.

"Where's that?"

"Brice Prairie, Wisconsin. Just north of La Crosse."

"You grew up near the river?"

"I grew up *on* the river," I said. "Until I was twelve. Then my dad got a new
job, and we moved to a big city. To St. Louis."

"Must have been one helluva change in your life, but at least you were
still near the river." Rick walked around the end of the bar to tend to the
customers at the tables.

"So you're not from around here, huh?" The woman sitting next to me
turned away from her friends and back to me.

"No," I said. "I suppose the hat gave me away."

"No. I just heard what you told Rick. I'm Debbie. I come here just about
every day."

"Frank," I said, reaching out to shake her hand. "You must live around
here, then, if you come here so often."

"Sure do. Born and raised in Aquoqua."

"I bet you know the mayor and Stan Mueller, then."

"Sure. Known them a long time. Why? You know them, too?"

I told her I was a reporter, that I'd come there to write a profile of the
mayor for a national magazine and got caught in the fire at the convention
center. She didn't seem too bothered to talk to a reporter.

"I don't care if you quote me," she said. "I've got nothing to hide."

"I hear Stan is taking the blame for the fire," I said.

"That Stan, he's a good guy. Real solid. I doubt he did anything wrong up
there that caused that fire. I wanted to marry him at one time, you know."

"No, I didn't know. He'd be a good catch, I suppose." I took a sip of beer, then looked over at her. "How long ago was that?"

"Quite a few years back. Before he got married."

"I suppose you must have been disappointed when he chose Stella over you."

"No, not Stella. Before he got married the first time."

A previous marriage? That was news to me. "Stella is Stan's second wife?"

"Sure. He got married right out of high school, to Mike's—the mayor's—sister, Gretchen. They'd been sweethearts off and on since seventh grade. Moved into the family house just down the road right after that."

"I guess their marriage didn't work out, since Stan later married Stella?"

"Now that's a real sad story. She died young—carbon monoxide poisoning. Power went out for a couple of days when Stan was on a hunting trip. She brought a generator into the house to keep the fridge going, but I guess she didn't know that was a bad idea. She kept it running all night. Stan found her in bed, dead."

"That's terrible. They must have been devastated, both Stan and the mayor."

"Stan wasn't the same guy after that. Kept to himself a lot more. Not long after she died, he got a place to live in Dubuque. He couldn't bring himself to sell the old house, though. Still goes there sometimes, but I don't think he'll ever live there again."

"What about you? After he lost his first wife, did you think about dating him?"

"Oh no. I was already married by then. I called him a couple of times, offered my support, but I never heard back from him."

"How did he meet Stella?"

"Let me think." She scratched her head and looked down. "It was a while after Gretchen died. I think they were set up—like a blind date thing maybe?

I don't exactly remember that part. I know she'd been out of town awhile, like for a year or something. She went somewhere to learn how to make ice cream. Or at least the kind of fancy ice cream she wanted to make." She leaned toward me. "Looks like it worked out good for her, huh?"

"Yeah, I'd say so. So where do you suppose someone would go to learn how to make ice cream like that? Where do you suppose Stella went?"

She leaned back. "That's a good question. I don't remember exactly, but maybe somewhere in Wisconsin? They have a lot of dairy up there, so maybe she found an ice cream school in Wisconsin?"

"Maybe so," I said. "They don't have any children—Stan and Stella—do they?"

"They sure don't. I don't think either of them ever wanted kids. Maybe that's why they got along so well. They both work real hard, you know. Stella with her ice cream and Stan with all he does for the mayor. Seems like that makes them a pretty good match."

Debbie got distracted by her friends again, and bartender Rick, who'd been watching us chat but trying not to be obvious about it, walked down to check on me. "You need another beer?" he asked.

"Not yet. Still working on this one."

He turned to Debbie and told her the time, like it was part of their nightly ritual. She quickly paid her tab, said it was nice to meet me, and left. Within a couple of minutes, her friends paid up and left, too. Rick came back and slid another beer in front of me.

"On the house," he said. I had been in my share of bars and knew that most bartenders weren't so quick to comp a drink. I wondered what Rick was up to.

"That Debbie—she's quite a talker, isn't she?" Rick asked.

"She's not any chattier than other folks I've met, I guess."

"Did she help you out with your story?"

"I suppose. Honestly, at this point I'm not sure where I'm going with the story, anyway. I hate writing these fluff pieces," I said, then drank the rest of the first beer. "Debbie, though—at least she told me a few things about Stan that I didn't know. He's had a tougher life than I expected, with his first wife dying and all."

"Yeah. That was awful. He deserved better."

"So that's when he moved away?"

"He never exactly moved away. Still owns that house. He just never stayed down here as much as he used to after that. When he does, he keeps to himself. We don't see much of him."

"Still, meeting Stella must have been a blessing. They seem like a good pair."

Rick didn't respond right away, instead taking a couple of steps toward the sink and turning on the water. "I'm trying to decide how much I should actually say to you. Whether it would be better for all concerned if I just kept my mouth shut. Then again, if I wasn't planning on talking more, I shouldn't have just said that, should I?"

"You don't have any obligation to tell me anything, you know," I said.

"I know. But if you keep asking questions, you're gonna find out a few more things, anyway. May as well hear it from me instead of from someone who might object more strongly to your poking around."

"I appreciate it. What is it you think I should know?"

"I don't much care for Stella. I think you'll find that to be true of most folks around here. Sure, we were glad that Stan found someone new, but we were hoping he'd do better."

"What's wrong with Stella?"

"I don't have a lot to go on, truthfully. It's just more of a feeling than anything. Something about her I don't trust. She left town for a year when she was... what... maybe twenty-two? That got a lot of folks wondering."

"Debbie mentioned that. She said Stella went somewhere to learn how to make ice cream."

Rick smiled. "That's possible, I suppose. I just don't know why it would take a whole year of study to learn how to do something that most folks can learn in an hour or two. Making ice cream ain't that hard."

"True, but maybe there was more to it, like learning how to make it on a bigger scale. And managing a business." Rick didn't look convinced. "So if she wasn't learning how to make ice cream," I said, "then why do you suppose she left town for a year?"

"I heard she got knocked up, that she went somewhere where she could hide out until she had the baby, then come back as if nothing had happened."

"How long ago was this? And why would she have to leave town to give birth?"

"It would have been a couple of years before she met Stan. Why'd she go away? I can't speak to that for sure, but there are still folks who don't look favorably on the idea of a woman having a baby when she's not married. Maybe that's who she comes from."

"Maybe." I looked down at my beer and tried to figure out if Rick's analysis had any merit. It seemed possible, but I wasn't sure. "Anything else you think I should know, Rick?"

"Just watch your back. You're not very subtle in the way you go about asking questions. Some folks might not take too well to that."

"I've noticed," I said. "Since we seem to be getting along so well, can I ask you one more not-so-subtle question?"

"Go ahead."

"If I wanted to find Stan's house, where would I go from here?"

"It would be real foolish on your part to go down there. But it's your life. He's been spending more time down there since he got suspended. Hiding out, I guess. He's always been protective of that place. Doesn't get a lot of visitors."

"Naturally, I wouldn't go where I wasn't welcome, especially now, after dark. But say I wanted to swing by during the day tomorrow, where would I go?"

"That wouldn't be much better. But if you wanted to give it a try, I'd suggest driving up very slowly and making plenty of noise, to give him notice that someone is there. Or you can stop in here, and we'll give him a call for you. The house isn't hard to find, though. Just take the road south of the marina, then the first left. Follow it around until it nearly ends. Stan's house is the second-to-last one."

I thanked Rick and left him another nice tip, then walked out and down the stairs. I was curious to find out if Stan was around tonight, but I didn't want to get noticed, so I left my car parked at the bar, threw my hat inside it, and walked down the road toward his house.

Chapter 32

The moon was waning; just a sliver was visible above the horizon in the darkening sky, but it gave me enough light to see the road as I walked from the bar. A light breeze had stirred up, replacing the heat with the cooler air it picked up off the water. For the first time all day, I wasn't looking for a rag to wipe my forehead.

There were a couple of trucks parked at the boat ramp, their die-hard owners still out on the river trying to catch a fish or a break from their families. Just south of the parking lot, houses lined the road on both sides, each one elevated some twenty feet above the ground, a sentry standing watch over Old Man River. Some residents used the space underneath the house as a garage, a convenient place to park a Ford F-Series truck and a boat trailer. For others, that space was ideal for storing an old washing machine, chicken wire, or plywood. A few dogs barked as I walked along the road, but none gave chase. The windows were open on most of the houses. As I walked down the road, I could hear a TV show from one house and dishes clanking from another, but otherwise Aquoqua was quiet.

I didn't really have a plan for what I was going to do when I reached Stan's house, didn't know what I expected to find once I got there. I figured that since I was in the area, why not snoop around a little and check out his house? What could go wrong?

I walked about ten minutes until I reached the crossroad, took a left, then followed it around as it curved back to the right. The road narrowed, and the gravel gave way to hard-packed dirt, just wide enough for a single car. On my right, a few houses rose above the flood plain, set further apart from each other than the ones I'd passed earlier; to my left, a backwater channel of the Mississippi lazed by.

It was another ten minutes before I got close to what I figured was Stan's house. I drifted to the other side of the road so I could get a good angle to look inside. It was like most of the others, elevated some twenty feet above the ground on sturdy concrete pillars. It looked like a simple ranch house, longer than it was deep, with cream-colored vinyl siding. A cedar staircase rose up the side, doubling back on itself and ending at a small porch that extended out by the front door; that staircase just might have been the fanciest part of the whole house.

Two silver pickups were parked next to the stairs. Stan must be home, but why two identical pickups? Maybe one was a spare. I stopped and leaned against a tree, a swamp white oak. There were two rooms lit up in the front of the house. All the windows were open, and I could hear someone talking. Stan wasn't alone. I decided to stay put for a few minutes and watch, to see if I could figure out who might be keeping him company and what they might be talking about. Shadows flashed in front of the windows as the voices got louder, but I couldn't make out a word. Whatever it was, they said it with emphasis. At one point, when they were screaming at each other, they stopped in front of a window and stood toe to toe.

I jumped when I heard glass shatter. The yelling continued; then I saw an arm swing, followed by a loud smack and a shriek. They separated and disappeared from the window; all I heard were footsteps racing across the floor until a door opened and slammed shut. I saw someone race down the stairs and get in one of the pickups. I stumbled back a couple of steps and laid down flat on the ground as the truck's diesel engine roared to life. The driver slammed the truck into reverse and swung around. I tried to make out who was driving, but the cab was too dark. As the truck flew past me, though, moonlight flashed over her face. It was Stella. She gave the pickup some gas and sped down the dirt road and around the corner, out of sight.

I looked back up and saw a figure standing on the front deck, head turned in the direction the truck had just left. Stan, I assumed. I dropped my head back down and didn't move. After a couple of minutes, I didn't hear anything except what I thought might be the sound of a door closing. I cautiously peeked up and looked around under the house and didn't see anyone. When I looked back up at the top of the stairs, Stan was gone. I scanned the windows on the front of the house, but I didn't see him there, either.

I lifted my head up a little higher and saw Stan standing ten feet from me at the foot of his driveway. He ran over to me, grabbed me by the back of my hair, and yanked me up, throwing me against a tree.

"What are *you* doing here?" he yelled as he wrapped his right hand around my neck, pushing my head back against the tree.

"Lost my keys?" I spit out.

"Don't try to get funny with me now," he said, his eyes focused and furious.

"Sorry to hear about your suspension," I said as he gripped my throat more tightly. "I guess the mayor's giving you up."

"I'm getting really tired of you poking around in my business."

I was having a harder time breathing, so maybe the lack of oxygen impeded my judgment. "Looks like Stella's dumping you, too." That didn't go over well with Stan.

"My life is none of your goddamn business," he said, smacking my head against the tree for emphasis. "What I do for the mayor is none of your business. Whatever is or isn't going on with me and Stella is none of your business." He gripped my throat tight enough to panic me. "Do you understand me?"

I couldn't move and was beginning to feel light-headed when I heard the sound of shotgun fire. Was it from the river? Stan loosened his grip on my throat just enough so I could sneak in a quick breath.

"Let go of 'im, Stan," I heard someone say.

"He won't let up on me. He needs to learn some respect."

"He's just doing his job, Stan, just like you do. Now let him go before I come up there and kick your butt."

Stan released me and stepped back. I heard the *put-put-put* of an outboard motor get louder as Big Dan pulled up to shore. "Mr. Dodge, this would be a good time for you to leave."

"I was just thinking the same thing," I said. "Thanks for the assist."

"I didn't do it for you."

I brushed off my clothes and made my way back to the parking lot, walking at a much faster clip than on the way down. When I got to the car, I fumbled the keys twice trying to push the button on the remote to unlock the door. Once in the car, I took a deep breath, pushed the ignition button, and sped out of there.

I felt lucky. Either Big Dan had a great sense of timing, or he knew something was up. Regardless, if he hadn't shown up, I'd be in a lot worse shape than I was. I'd pushed the limits with Stan, gone too far, or maybe I'd just been too careless about how I did it. At least it wasn't a complete waste of time. Stan was on edge. He'd been in the spotlight, the public face of blame for the fire and two deaths. I could've been wrong, but I got a feeling from Stan, a sense of growing righteous indignation, as if he felt like he was being blamed unfairly. All the poking around I was doing was just compounding that resentment. I figured I could take advantage of his fragile state, but I needed to regroup first, to catch my breath. I drove back to Dubuque and right to Adam's place, where I could quickly forget about the day's events.

CHAPTER 33

The opening chords of Johnny Cash's "Big River" woke me up, so I picked up the phone to see who was calling. It was Helen Kraft.

"I hope I didn't wake you, Frank," she started.

"Of course not," I stammered, rubbing my eyes.

"Oh, good. This won't take long anyway. I have some news that I thought was best heard from me directly."

"Did you die?" I asked.

"Funny. No, dear. No one died. I got a call this morning from the editor of *Wandering Gourmet* magazine, Gordon Harper. He was in such a state of distress over that article you were supposed to write for him."

I sat up, my throat suddenly dry and tight. I forced myself to swallow.

"Gordon was so committed to giving you a chance to show what you could do, Frank," she continued. "To giving you a well-deserved opportunity to showcase your skills for a national audience."

"What are you trying to say, Helen?" I swallowed again.

"It's that darn deadline," she said. "The one you missed. Gordon is under pressure to fill pages, of course. He has his own deadline and just can't wait any longer for your piece. He was so torn about what to do, so he called me for advice."

"Why you?... And what did you tell him?"

"We're old friends, Frank. I think I mentioned that before. I didn't *tell* him to do anything, I just listened. I listened as he described the torture he was putting himself through. He came to realize that he was very nearly out of options, so he asked me to write the article instead." She got quiet for a moment. "I was reluctant to do it, of course."

"'Reluctant,' my ass!" I blurted, my voice trembling. "You probably invited it."

"Oh, Frank, there's no need to be paranoid. Gordon's an old friend of mine who needed help. I had assured him earlier that you'd be able to deliver this piece on deadline, so I felt responsible to step in and help out."

"What do you mean, you 'assured him'? Are you saying that I got that assignment because you recommended me?"

"Not exactly, Frank, but he did ask my opinion about you. Of course, I gave an enthusiastic recommendation. I figured it was the least I could do, given our prior misunderstandings." She paused again. "But it doesn't matter now. I'm sure you had a very good reason for missing the deadline—and I'm sure you'll get other opportunities like this—but I'm sorry to say that this assignment is no longer yours."

I sat up in bed, unable to believe what I was hearing from her.

"I know this must be a terrible shock, Frank," she said. "I wish it had worked out better for you. And as much as I'd like to help you process your feelings, I promised to send Gordon a draft this afternoon, so I must get to working on it. I'm sure I'll see you soon, Frank."

Helen hung up, and I sank back into bed, despondent. The phone rang again; this time it was Gordon Harper at *Wandering Gourmet.* I let it go to voice mail. There went another paycheck. For Christ's sake, I'd been in a goddamn fire that killed two people. Couldn't Gordon have given me a couple of extra days? And he gave it to Helen, of all people! I bet she'd been talking to him behind my back all along, looking for a chance to swoop in and steal the story at the first sign of weakness.

If only people around here were more cooperative, had been a little more forthcoming, I might have finished that piece on time. I'd wasted too much time chasing after people who didn't want to talk to me, because I wasn't one of them, wasn't part of their tribe.

Adam rolled over and grabbed his phone. "Shit. I need to go. It's later than I thought." He rolled back over and wrapped his arms around me. "But I don't want to. What was all that about, with the phone call?"

"I don't really want to get into it." The feel of his body against mine, his hands rubbing the back of my neck, was soothing. I felt my anger let up.

"Whatever. Your call."

"Thanks for letting me come over last night," I said. "I needed the company."

"Are you going to tell me what happened yesterday?"

"Not right now," I said, before changing my mind. "Part of it is just this fucking city. I can't figure it out. I feel like everywhere I go, I get in trouble. No one is approachable, because I'm not from here."

"I'd say you got awfully close to me," Adam said, kissing my neck.

"Yeah… but that's different, I think."

"How?" he asked, pulling back just a little. "I'm a born-and-bred Dubu-quer, just like those other people you're complaining about. I've heard peo-ple talk shit about us—about us Dubuquers—that we're all reserved and standoffish." He sat straight up. "Maybe it's not us. Maybe it's that the people who are complaining are condescending assholes."

I sat up and looked at him. "Are you saying that I'm the problem? That I'm a condescending asshole?"

"No. Well, maybe a little. Look, Frank, you can come on strong sometimes, from what I've seen. Maybe you just need a lighter touch around here."

Maybe Adam had a point, but my style seemed to go over just fine most everywhere else. Why should I have to change who I am just to please people here?

"I'll think about it," I said. I checked the time again and sat up. "But right now we both need to get to work."

"You're right." He rolled onto his back and stretched, then moved over to the side of the bed and sat up, picking up his boxers and sliding them on. "You know, we've spent almost every night together since we met. It's been cool. And I don't know if this is the best time to ask, but where are we going with this? What do you want from me? After all, you don't live in Dubuque, and I won't be moving any time soon. If it's just a casual thing, that's OK, I guess, but I'd like to know."

I sat up and looked at him. His back was still turned to me, so I reached over and touched his shoulder. He quit looking for his pants and turned to face me. "When I first met you," I told him, "I figured this would be a casual thing, for the reason you just said: we live in different cities." I sank back into the bed. "I don't know what I think now. I feel lucky to have met you, to have had your companionship during this whole mess. But I don't know what to tell you about what comes next. I'm here, in Dubuque, until I figure out what happened with the fire, but I have no idea what I'm doing after that." I rolled on my side and touched his shoulder again. "How about I take you out for dinner tonight? We can talk more then."

He said "OK," shrugged his shoulders, and went back to getting dressed.

"Do you have any special dietary requirements?" I asked.

"What do you mean?"

"You know. Are you vegan, vegetarian, pescatarian, gluten-intolerant, lactose-intolerant, allergic to nuts or shellfish? That kind of thing."

"No," he said, letting himself laugh.

"Good. That'll make it easier to agree on a place to eat."

Adam finished dressing, and we made plans to meet at Maria's Italian Kitchen at seven for dinner. After a quick kiss, I was out the door and on my way back to my motel room. I didn't know what else he could want from me at that moment. I'd come to Dubuque on a writing assignment, not on a love quest, and I had plenty of unfinished business to deal with back home. I didn't know if I was ready to take on anything new.

I took a quick shower, put on fresh clothes, and drove back into town. I gave Jefferson a call to let him know I'd be working on the article; I couldn't bring myself to tell him that I'd lost it. He had plans for the morning anyway and suggested I call him in the afternoon. I went back to The Wired Bean, for coffee and to sort through my options. They weren't as busy as the time before, so I found a small table inside, in a quiet corner, where I set up shop.

I looked over the outline I'd put together the previous time I'd been there: a brief history of the origins of the boutique food movement, with no reference to Midwestern gardens; a quick sketch of the variety of vendors at the convention, with no mention of the fire that had disrupted it; some data on the growing size of the Midwestern boutique food economy, again with no accounting for home gardens; and a wrap-up with a couple of quotes about the prospects for future growth. I could have knocked out fifteen hundred words today, no problem. It wouldn't have been the least bit novel, but it would have delivered what they wanted, and I would have gotten paid three grand.

I was just starting to get pissed off again when my phone rang. It was Jake Horgan's father. The family had time to meet with me, but, he said apologetically, it had to be right away. The rest of the day was looking pretty busy, he said, and tomorrow wouldn't be any better. He gave me directions, and I told him I'd be there in twenty minutes.

I packed up my computer and notes and left the coffee shop. The Horgans lived in southwest Wisconsin, just a few miles south of the Dominican monastery at Sinsinawa. I knew the area well.

During the previous year, I'd spent a week at the monastery for a personal retreat. I'd written about the founder of the Dominican monastery, Father Samuel Mazzuchelli, a man who'd given up a comfortable, privileged life in Milan, Italy, to live a spare life on the sparsely populated frontier of what was then the western United States. I admired that.

I crossed the Julien Dubuque Bridge and followed Highway 20 to Menomonie Road toward Sinsinawa, then snaked through the countryside to reach the Horgans' home. They lived in an old farmhouse, a two-story building covered in white clapboard that'd been built at the end of the nineteenth century. A small apple orchard grew on one side of the gravel driveway, while a row of boxwood hedges lined the other. It was just midmorning, but the sun was already high and hot. I pulled up to the house and was no sooner out of the car when Jake's father came out the front door to greet me.

"Thanks for coming on such short notice," he said, offering his hand to shake. "I'm Darrel, Jake's father. My wife, Carol, had to run into town to pick up a couple of things, so she won't be able to join us." He had a strong grip and a confident but unassuming air. Darrel was tall—taller than I was anyway—dressed in black slacks and a light blue dress shirt. His fingers were as thick as the hair on his knuckles, his head covered with fine gray mat trimmed short.

The Horgans lived on the two hundred acres that Darrel's great-grandparents had bought after the Civil War. His family ran an impressive operation. It was a dairy farm, mostly, but they planted about a hundred acres of vegetables, too. In the past decade, they'd changed their farming practices so they could get their produce and dairy products certified organic. It wasn't an easy transition, but it was paying off. It had been Jake's idea.

We walked inside, into the comfort of the air-conditioned front parlor. The room was decorated with antiques—family heirlooms, Darrel told me. He pointed me to an armchair next to the doorway, then sat in a matching chair next to it. On the walnut table between us, there was a framed five-by-seven portrait of Father Mazzuchelli. The wall opposite us was covered with portraits, most of them photographs, but a few oil paintings were mixed in.

"That's our family tree," Darrel told me. "Those two paintings on the top right—those are my great-grandparents. If you follow the male lines down and toward the center, you'll get to me and my family."

I spotted the photo of Darrel and his wife, just above two younger people, Jake and his sister.

"That's the most amazing family tree I've ever seen," I said. Darrel smiled. "It shows a lot of pride in where you come from." I lowered my head, took a deep breath, and looked back up at Darrel. "I can't imagine how you must feel right now."

"It's been rough," Darrel said. "Jake was a fine young man. We were very proud of him."

"So tell me about him. Describe him for me."

"It's hard to know where to start. Well, he loved people, was outgoing and friendly. Sharp as a tack and honest. The kind of person you wanted as a friend and were proud to call son."

"I know he was working for Post-Modern Chocolates, but he went to college before that, right?"

"Yes. He got a degree in business from Loras."

"Business, huh? Was he interested in farming, too, given the family occupation?"

"Yes, he was. I'm not sure if he was ever going to take over our farm, though. He liked it around here, but the idea of living out on the farm full time didn't appeal to him too much.

He figured that if he got a degree in business, he could help us keep the farm going—maybe come up with some new ideas for us—but I don't think he was ever going to be the one running the show."

"A business degree... I bet he had a lot of options about where to work."

"Absolutely. I think he could have gotten a job anywhere he wanted. At least, that's what we told him. He loved Galena, though, and wanted to stay there."

"He'd worked at Post-Modern Chocolates for a while, right?"

"Yes. Oh, he loved that business, and Ms. Johns gave him a lot of input. He helped come up with new flavors. And he ran the shop, too. He even started thinking about becoming a chocolatier himself. He had a good palate."

"I guess that's why Ms. Johns was at the funeral, because Jake was so important to her business."

Darrel blushed, cleared his throat, and mumbled, "Yes."

"If I remember right, he also worked for an ice cream parlor before he worked at the chocolate shop, right?"

"That's right." Darrel fidgeted, and I was afraid the questions were getting too uncomfortable for him.

"It must have been tough for Jake at times, being stuck in the middle of a feud between two strong personalities."

"Like I said, Jake was a people person, so he was real good at charming his way out of a bad situation. He'd worked for Stella—for Mrs. Mueller—for a long time, since high school. We were all surprised when he went to work for Ms. Johns, but he told us that the ice cream store was in trouble anyway. He thought it was going to close soon."

"I guess he was right. Mrs. Mueller closed that store not long after Jake left, right?"

"That's right. She had that accident with the freezer, and that seemed to tip her over the edge. She just couldn't get it back on its feet after that."

"About the farm... Is your daughter going to take it over when you retire?"

"Yes, I think so. Amy and Jake talked a lot about the future of the farm. They were like best friends in a lot of ways. When we adopted Jake, she was old enough to watch out for him, so they spent a lot of time together."

"Jake was adopted?" I asked, leaning forward. "I didn't know that."

"Yes. We adopted him at birth. We never treated him any differently, of course, but we never felt like it had to be a secret, either. He was our son, period. That's how we thought about it."

Darrel checked his watch. "Hmm. I didn't realize we'd talked that long already. I'm glad you could stop by when I called, but I've got to rush you out now. We've got friends stopping in a few minutes. I need to get some lunch together."

"There's no need to apologize," I said. "Thank you for taking the time to chat with me, especially given the circumstances."

"I hope that helped," he said. "Did you get what you needed?"

"Yes, I think I did. If I have any other questions, is it OK if I contact you again?"

"Of course. We'll be around, but we'll have a lot of friends and family stopping by the next couple of days."

So Jake had been adopted. I didn't know if that mattered in any way, but it might. Darrel also called Stella by her first name, before he corrected himself. Maybe it was just because Jake had worked for her for so long, but they were obviously familiar with each other. Very familiar, I'd guess. That seemed like something I wanted to know more about.

CHAPTER 34

Since I was close to Galena, I figured I'd find a coffee shop there and get back to sorting through my options. I might have lost the assignment from *Wandering Gourmet*, but that didn't mean that I couldn't find another magazine that might be interested in the same topic. As I was pulling into a parking spot on Main Street, my phone rang. It was Ruby.

"Hi, Frank," she said. "How are you?"

"OK, I guess," I said. "I got a scolding this morning for missing the deadline for my article on boutique food, but I'm fine otherwise."

"Oh, no, Frank. Did you get more time to work on it?"

"No," I told her. "They gave it to Helen Kraft."

"Oh, no! What are you going to do?"

"I'm not really sure, but I'm going to start by seeing if I can repurpose this article for another magazine."

"That sounds like a good idea, Frank. Like we talked about before: sometimes you just have to keep pushing ahead. I know you have a lot on your mind, so I won't take much of your time. I found out a little more about the Dubuque mayor and those art dealers from Chicago."

"That didn't take long," I said. "What did you find out?"

"That Internet is something else. A few weeks ago, I had a librarian show me how to look things up using that Google, and I'm just so fascinated by it. It's so much quicker than searching through card catalogues and microfilm!"

"That it is. The main trick is understanding what you're looking at, knowing the source, so you can figure out how reliable it is."

"Of course. But that's true for anything you read. Anyway, I did some searches on Mayor Andelfinger and the Johnses, looking for a connection—any connection—and it sure didn't take long. First, I found a photograph of the mayor posing with six people. It was taken at a party on the night he was sworn in as mayor, I think. I recognized the Johns family right away—Richard, Lynn, and Ashley."

"They were at his inaugural party?"

"Yes, they were."

"Who were the other people in the picture?"

"It was Joseph and Anita Baker and their daughter, Courtney."

"Courtney Baker?"

"Yes, that's right. Do you know her?"

"Yeah. She's the mayor's chief of staff. Interesting. What do you know about her parents?"

"If I remember it right, the caption in the photo said Mr. Baker is a real estate developer and Mrs. Baker is an attorney."

"So they have money. At least I know how Courtney got the job now."

"Don't jump to conclusions, Frank. I'm sure it helped her to have those connections, but the mayor wouldn't do himself any favors by hiring someone for that position who wasn't going to be good. She must have had some experience at it, too."

"You're probably right. Then again, how hard can the job be? He's the mayor of Dubuque, not Chicago."

"Well, I don't know about that. But I did find out one more thing: an article about the Bakers buying a piece of art. A painting, I think. It was just a couple of years ago. I bet they bought it through the Johnses."

"OK," I said, with little interest.

"Don't you see, Frank?" Ruby asked. "That's their connection to Dubuque. That's probably how the Johnses know the mayor: through the Bakers, Courtney's parents. I don't find it so surprising now that they would donate to his congressional campaign. They've known him for a while."

"I understand what you're saying, Ruby, but I'm still not really convinced. I get why they might throw some money to his campaign, but I still don't understand why they would donate so much. Keep digging, Ruby. See if you can find any other links between the mayor and those two couples. I'd also like to know how much the Bakers have contributed to the mayor's campaign."

"OK, Frank. I'll let you get back to whatever you were working on."

"Thanks, Ruby. Oh, one more thing. I have something else I'd like you to check on."

"Yes? What is it?"

"When I talked to Stella the other day, she mentioned that she and Helen were involved in some kind of protest on campus that might have gotten attention. Can you use your magical searching skills and see if you can find out anything about protests at Newton College in Illinois in the early or mid-1980s?"

"Sure. I'll start on that today."

I thanked her and hung up. I wasn't quite ready to get back to my notes after all. I realized that I had another stop to make in Galena before I settled into a coffee shop.

Chapter 35

I walked along Main Street, past the stately DeSoto Hotel, down to Post-Modern Chocolates, then a little farther, just two doors down, until I found the storefront for Ashley's newest venture. It was easy to find, thanks to the neon sign in the picture window with the words "Frozen Expressions: An Ice Cream Emporium" spelled out in Gothic script. Ashley had somehow managed to snag Stella's old storefront, and now she was using it to sell her own brand of ice cream. Standing in front of the shop, I realized that, even though I'd sampled the chocolates and been to Ashley's house, I hadn't yet been inside the Post-Modern Chocolates store, so I went back to check it out first.

The inside was dark, with antique chandeliers casting a dim light around the inside of the store. One wall was lined with small, cast iron café tables, just big enough for two chairs that were just uncomfortable enough to discourage lingering. Atop each table, perfectly centered, sat a vase with fresh flowers carefully arranged, a single yellow rose poking out above a circle of hosta leaves and lady's mantle. Above each table hung an elegantly framed print of an old advertising poster for Belgian chocolates. A mahogany counter ran the length of the store, with glass cases underneath, each individually lit, to show off the variety of chocolates on sale that day. Each case had a theme: milk chocolate truffles in one, dark chocolate truffles next to it, nut clusters in a single case, which was next to the flavored barks.

The case at the far end was filled with chocolate-flavored pastries: éclairs, flourless tortes, and small cakes. Three clerks—"Chocolate Ambassadors," as Ashley called them—stood watch over the cases, ready to guide each customer on a journey to discover their "secret chocolate passions"—their words, not mine.

One of those clerks, Brittney, ensnared me soon after I walked in; they weren't very busy yet. She gave me the standard overview: regular chocolates, seasonal offerings, and specials of the day. I asked if I could sample a couple of chocolates, and she pointed me to a white plate in the center of the counter that was covered with pieces of bark broken into small chunks. I put a small piece in my mouth and let it melt: dark chocolate with raspberry. Delicious, but far from their best.

I took my time looking over the chocolates in each case, making small talk with Brittney. She was tall with lightly tanned skin and silky blond hair that hung halfway down her back. She wanted to be a veterinarian, so she was majoring in biology at the University of Dubuque. This was her third summer working at Post-Modern Chocolates. Her experience showed. With no one else waiting to buy, she took me through the chocolate offerings with confidence and ease and in tempting detail. She assured me that they'd get a lot busier in the afternoon but that during the week the mornings were always slow. By afternoon, customers would have to take numbers; on weekends, some would wait as long as an hour for a chance to buy chocolates.

I tired of the small talk, so I told her I was sorry to hear about the death of her co-worker, Jake. She looked down, and I thought she might cry. He'd been very popular and had practically run the business, she told me. He knew everything there was to know about the shop, and people trusted him. He treated everyone fairly, with no drama. Now that he was gone, Ashley—"She," as Brittney referred to her—was trying to run the shop on her own, but she just wasn't too good at it, especially now that she had an ice cream store to manage as well. The staff was worried that she had spread herself too thin. "But she wasn't a very good manager even when she just had the chocolate shop," Brittney whispered to me.

I picked out a half dozen truffles and a three-inch-round flourless chocolate torte that I planned on sharing with Adam later that night. Brittney pulled each truffle from the case using a pair of silver tongs and placed them on a small silver tray. She handed the tray to a different "Ambassador," who put the chocolates into a white cardboard box, sealing it with a single strand of red ribbon tied at the top into a heart-shaped knot. I thanked Brittney for chatting with me and walked down to the ice cream store.

If you walked directly from Post-Modern Chocolates to Expressions Ice Cream like I did, you wouldn't have much trouble figuring out that there was a connection. The storefront had a similar layout, with the same cast-iron café tables and the same vases—just minus the flowers. Instead of old posters advertising Belgian chocolates, the walls were decorated with prints of famous paintings, such as Van Gogh's *The Starry Night*, Picasso's *Girl Before a Mirror*, and Kandinsky's *Composition VIII*. Persian rugs in colors that complemented the framed prints were laid out atop the oak flooring from one end of the store to the other.

The ice cream cases lined the other wall, but instead of a mahogany countertop, the cases had a mahogany base topped with pieces of glass that curved up toward the servers, with wide, brushed steel doors on the servers' side that, when opened, made for easy scooping. At the far end, an antique brass cash register sat atop a pink marble countertop—next to a five-by-seven framed portrait of Jake. I found out later that the cash register was just for show; the store used an iPad to handle payments.

Like the chocolate shop, the flavors were grouped in each case according to a logical scheme. Fruit flavors were in one case, chocolates in another, which were next to the vanilla-and-nut varieties; the specials were in a case at the end—green tea and basil pine nut on that day.

That's where the similarities between the shops ended, though. At Frozen Expressions, the atmosphere felt chaotic and hesitant. The three clerks behind the counter—"Ice Cream Ambassadors"—were frantic with tasks that had nothing to do with connecting customers with their secret ice cream passions. I walked in and looked around for a few minutes before anyone behind the counter even acknowledged I was there. I was the only customer, but I was more than they were ready to deal with.

I stood at the counter a little longer before someone came over to help, a young woman named Tori. When I asked for a sample of the Aztec chocolate, she looked confused and asked her co-workers if it was OK to give away a free taste. They both thought it was probably OK; then one of them noticed a bowl of small plastic spoons atop the counter and yelled out, "I remember now. That's what these are for," as she pulled out a single spoon.

Tori opened the steel doors, reached in, and broke the little spoon as she tried to scoop out a little bit. "Sorry," she said, giggling. The second try went better, but I was afraid to ask for any other samples after that. Instead, I just got a small scoop of the Aztec chocolate in a cup, which Tori seemed OK with.

As she was taking my cash, someone pushed through the front door, slamming it against a wall, and immediately began barking out orders. "Why haven't you put the flowers out yet?" "Would one of you please write today's specials on the chalkboard and put it outside? Now!"

It was Ashley. Her face had a deeper scowl than usual. She'd tied her hair into a bun, probably in a rush as she'd left her house; a clump of it fell apart and rolled down as she raced into the store. Instead of the elegant black blouse I was used to seeing her in, she wore jeans and a purple T-shirt. She nearly reached the back of the store before she saw me.

"What are you doing here," she growled.

"Just a little more research for my article in *Wandering Gourmet*," I lied. "I wanted to visit your two stores before I called the article done."

"Why do I find that hard to believe?" She looked around at her scurrying staff, let out a heavy sigh, then turned back to me. "Just stay out of the way."

"I'm about done here anyway. Looks like you're off to a rocky start with the ice cream store."

"That's an understatement," she said. "It's impossible to find good help these days." She turned back toward her staff and barked out a few more orders.

I finished my ice cream and left Ashley to attend to her mess. I was ready to settle into a coffee shop for a light lunch and to brainstorm ideas for an article to salvage out of this trip. The Coffee Depot was nearby, so I walked back up Main Street, past the Old Stockade and across Franklin Street to a single-story brick building. It was an intimate place, with just eight small tables and four armchairs. I ordered a salad and an espresso and staked out a table where I could spread out and look over my notes. Not long after I had everything out and ready to read, my phone rang again. It was Jefferson.

"Frank? It's Brian. Where are you right now?"

"In Galena, sorting through some notes."

"You still working on that article?"

"Not exactly."

"Well, you might want to come back to Dubuque, as soon as you can. I've got some news: a couple of things about the fire that I want to tell you about, but I don't want to get into it on the phone. When can you be back here?"

Jefferson wasn't one to dick around, so I told him I'd meet him in an hour at The Wired Bean.

CHAPTER 36

When I got back to Dubuque, Jefferson was sitting at a table on the patio of The Wired Bean. I ordered an espresso and went back out to join him.

"So what's this big news that you've discovered?"

"I made some progress looking into that fire," he began, keeping his voice low. "The official report concluded that the fire was an accident, but I'm pretty damn sure it was intentional."

"What makes you so sure now?" I asked, matching his low volume.

"A couple of details stand out to me. First, the sensors on the sprinklers had been tampered with; they had to have been. I found out what kind of sprinklers they had at the convention center. They have these little glass tubes that are filled with alcohol; they're sensitive to heat. When the alcohol heats up, it expands. If it gets too hot and expands too much, the glass pops. That turns on the sprinklers. Each sprinkler has its own tube, so if one goes off, they don't all have to go off." His eyes narrowed. "That's how it's supposed to work anyway." He leaned toward me and spoke, his voice barely audible. "Someone painted over the glass in that hall, which made those tubes a lot less sensitive."

"Couldn't that have been unintentional" I asked. "I mean, someone could have done that accidentally when they were repainting, right?"

"Sure, but once you get about thirty feet away from where the fire started, there's no paint at all on any sensor. I checked—all of them."

"The only sensors that were painted were the ones near where the fire started?"

"That's right. I think someone knew exactly where the fire was going to start, then went to work to make sure the sprinklers didn't kick on until the fire had spread out some."

"What about the exit doors?"

"Well, they're never supposed to be locked, but a lot of times they are, because someone gets worried about a thief sneaking out through a side exit. My buddy in St. Louis told me that doors like those were supposed to have a delay on them. If you push the bar, an alarm sounds, then in about twenty seconds, the door opens. That's enough time for security to get there and find out who's trying to leave. That delay can be overridden, though, when a fire alarm goes off. That's the way they're supposed to work. But we know the doors at the hall didn't open at all." He tapped on the table. "That can happen, but someone has to lock the bars in place, so that they can't be pushed open. It has to be done manually... on every door. And there's only one key that works on those locks."

"That doesn't sound very accidental to me."

"That's what I'm saying, Frank!"

"So it looks like someone wanted to start a fire and wanted to create panic, but they maybe didn't want it to get out of control?"

"Yeah, very good, Frank. That's exactly what I think. They didn't plan on the panic getting out of hand and a bunch of people running around in chaos trying to save themselves. That mess lasted long enough for the crowd to do some serious pushing and shoving, which is why so many people got hurt and two of them died."

"Do you think they—whoever sabotaged the room—just got the timing wrong? That maybe they assumed the fire would get put out sooner, so the crowd would have less time to freak out?"

"That could be. I'm not convinced that they were out to kill anyone. It seems like they just wanted to cause a good fright."

"Who do you suppose they were trying to scare?"

"That's a good question. The fire started real close to the booths for the chocolate lady and the ice cream lady, two people who don't exactly get on well. Maybe they got booths assigned so close to each other, so when the fire broke out, it would look like either could be a victim or a suspect."

"Except that the person taking the blame at the moment is married to the owner of the ice cream shop."

"That's right. Stan Mueller's fingerprints are all over this—at least figuratively. He had access to the room, and he had all the tools to pull this off. If someone had spotted him poking around in the conference hall, they wouldn't have questioned it. They would've just assumed he was there doing his job."

"How much of this do the local police know?"

"All of it," Jefferson said.

"So they're covering up some of the details, hoping the public buys the accident theory?"

"Yes and no. The report that came out—they called it preliminary. If the story changes later, they can always say that their investigation turned up something new. Of course, the investigation is really on hold now. Probably for good, but not many people know that."

"Why are they sitting on this? What's in it for them?"

"It's not so much what's in it for them as what they could lose if they keep going at it. Stan Mueller is the mayor's man, a good friend. If they go after him, they risk alienating the mayor, and they aren't willing to risk that for this case."

"Even though two people died?"

"Yes, even though two people died. They were accidents. No one pulled a trigger and shot someone."

"But they'd be alive today if that fire hadn't been started, or if the safety systems hadn't been tampered with."

"I know what you're saying, Frank, and I agree, but those two folks are dead, and nothing's going to change that. The cops here—the leadership anyway—believe that finding out the whole truth might add more tragedy to what's already tragedy enough. They aren't willing to go there."

"They didn't count on us being here, though, did they?"

"Damn right," Jefferson said, smiling. "Oh, there's one more thing. I don't know if this really matters, but there's a detail in all this that bugs me."

"Go on."

"The kid who died..."

"Jake Horgan?" I asked.

"Yes, Horgan. The older guy who died, he probably got pushed around and fell. I can picture that happening. It was really crowded, and there was a lot of confusion, a lot of people pushing other people. His head hit that hard floor and cracked. Horgan also died from a concussion. Hit his head on something, probably a table in the booth." Jefferson paused. "He was inside the booth, though, with what—two or three other people? That's what bothers me. I can't picture what happened to cause him to hit his head. Was he pushed? If not, how did he fall?"

"Are you implying that his death wasn't an accident?"

"I'm saying that I just don't know. And that bugs me."

"A few people can panic just as easily as a big group can."

"You might be right, Frank. But it's something I can't stop thinking about. I want to get a look again at how things were set up and see if I can figure out how he might have fallen."

"Do what you've gotta do," I said. Then I told him what Ruby had uncovered about the apparently tight connections between the Johns family, Courtney Baker's parents, and the mayor. I couldn't bring myself to tell him about my unannounced visit to Stan's place. "What should we be doing next?"

"I'd like to talk to Stella Mueller, to hear directly from her what happened before the fire started. Let's go pay her a visit."

CHAPTER 37

We left the coffee shop, got in Jefferson's truck, and drove toward Cathedral Ice Cream. Before we got far, though, we detoured to Tilly's Cupcakes for a quick stop. Jefferson wanted to check with her on some details about what had happened Friday morning.

We parked in front of the store on Main Street, and, after waiting a few minutes while Tilly dealt with a customer, Jefferson introduced himself and asked if she had time for a couple of questions about the fire at the convention center.

"Of course," Tilly said.

"Tell me what you remember going on around you, just before the fire began."

"I can try, but we were busy. I remember a lot of people standing in line to buy our cupcakes, but I can't remember much else."

"I'm sure whatever you can remember will help us. What were you doing before the fire started?"

"I was rushing around. I remember that. We were running low on the red velvet cakes—they were very popular that day—so I had to make another batch," Tilly said. "I took out some batter from the refrigerator and filled about six baking trays."

"I assume those trays went in the oven after you filled them?" Jefferson asked.

"That's right."

"Was the oven on all day, or did you turn it on just when you needed it?"

"We ran it only when we baked. That's what we were told to do."

"Who told you that?"

"I don't remember his name, but it was the inspector from the city."

"Would you recognize him if I showed you a picture?" Jefferson asked.

"Yes, but you don't need to do that. I saw his picture in the newspaper. He's the one I guess they're blaming for the fire, the one the mayor suspended."

"Stan Mueller?" I asked.

"I guess so, but like I said, I don't remember his name."

I pulled out my phone and found the picture of Stan Mueller that ran in the *Dubuque Register*. "Is that him?" I asked, holding the phone up for her to see.

"Yes, that's him. He's the one who inspected my booth right after we set up."

Jefferson nodded. He was feeling satisfied with himself. "One other thing," Jefferson said. "Think back to just before the fire started, as best you can. I know you were busy, but what was happening around you?"

"Like I said, we were really busy, so I didn't notice much outside of our booth." Tilly stopped to put a few more cupcakes out on display. "Now that I think about it, I remember hearing a couple of people arguing. Their voices were loud. Angry loud. I'm very sensitive to negative energy, so that's probably why I remember that."

"Where was it coming from?"

"Right next to me, from the chocolate booth."

Jefferson was completely focused on Tilly. "Uh huhh. Now, what do you recall about the argument itself. What were they arguing about?"

"I'm sorry, but I really don't know. I just tuned them out. I remember that the louder of the two was a woman, but I think a man yelled back. I'm sorry, but I just don't remember anything else."

We thanked Tilly and left the store, getting back in Jefferson's truck for the short drive to Cathedral Ice Cream. "I thought that went well," I said.

"Yeah. It's hard to imagine that Stan Mueller is blameless, isn't it?" Jefferson asked. "He had access to everything to start the fire and could have easily tampered with the equipment. He personally inspected the booth where the fire started. I just haven't figured out the why, what motivated him. Even if the fire was just supposed to scare someone, who the hell was he trying to scare and why?"

"You don't think he was looking out for his wife—for Stella?" Even though I'd heard Stan and Stella fighting the night before, it still seemed likely to me that Stan would start the fire to help Stella. "That fight between Stella and Ashley is pretty damn bitter," I said. "Maybe Stan thought it was time to convince Ashley to get out of the way for good."

"That's a possibility," Jefferson said. "That's why we need to talk to her, to Stella, to find out just how possible it might actually be."

After we parked near the front door and got out of the truck, Jefferson turned to me. "Frank, I know you've already talked to her a couple of times and you have some kind of rapport with her, but I'd like to ask the questions this time. You gonna be cool with that?"

"Go for it," I told Jefferson. After my last visit with her, I'd probably burned through some of that rapport anyway. I didn't have a problem with Jefferson taking the lead this time, even if I also had a couple more things I really wanted to ask Stella about. Sure, Jefferson could take the lead, but I had no intention of staying completely quiet while Jefferson had all the fun.

Chapter 38

We walked into the ice cream factory and waited in the front lobby. Stella was standing in her office watching over the production process, but she spotted us quickly. This time she was in no rush to greet us, though, making us wait a few minutes before she finally came over to say hi.

"What a surprise! I get two visitors this time. Is everything OK, Frank? I thought we covered all you needed to know the last time you were here."

"Don't worry. Everything's fine. We've just learned a little more about the fire and realized that we hadn't had a chance to hear your experience during it."

"I see. And who's this?" she asked, looking at Jefferson. "You look familiar."

"Brian Jefferson, ma'am. I think we met before, on the cruise."

"Speaking of horrible events," Stella said, trying to force a smile. "Please, call me Stella. None of that 'ma'am' shit."

Jefferson asked her to talk about the day's events, what she'd been doing before and up to the time the fire broke out. I just stood by and watched, paying attention to how she presented herself and how Jefferson reacted. I didn't have any reason to think Stella was involved in the fire, but Jefferson didn't assume anything. He was a skilled and patient interviewer. Asking nonthreatening questions to put her at ease, even asking about which ice cream had been the most popular that day (salted caramel with candied pecans). He could have been a good therapist. By the time we got to talking about the fire itself, Stella was relaxed and downright chatty.

"Let's talk a little about what was happening just before the fire started. About the time Frank got an unsolicited sample of your ice cream. What was that about?"

Stella blushed and looked down, fighting back a barely perceptible grin. "I'm still embarrassed about that. Sorry again, Frank," she said, turning to me and allowing that smile to break loose. "You know the story between me and Ashley by now. Sometimes I just can't restrain myself when I get around her."

"Did you do something at the convention center to set her off?" Jefferson asked.

"I'm afraid I did," she confessed. "I gloated. You see, the day before the conference began, I read a review of her chocolates in a Chicago publication—her hometown, you know—and it was brutal. I was, understandably, overjoyed to read that someone finally saw her for what she really was."

"You must have felt—I don't know—vindicated by the review."

"I sure did," Stella said. "Vindicated. Exactly. Maybe I was feeling cocky, too—just a little, you know? I made copies of the article and brought them to the convention center. I put a copy on the table at Ashley's booth, right in front of her, and repeated my favorite quote from the article: 'the chocolate equivalent of a starving artist's sale, but less satisfying.' Ashley didn't take it too well. She threw the paper at me and swore I was behind it, threatening to get even with me."

"Were you behind it?" Jefferson asked.

"How could I be?" she asked. "I don't have the connections she does. Someone from Chicago must have come through Galena and visited her store."

"How would that have worked?"

"Oh, it happens all the time. Galena draws a lot of vacationers from Chicago, and they probably had a list of places they'd heard were popular and wanted to review." She twirled her hair, then seemed to catch herself and quickly stopped. "It happened to me all the time when I had the storefront in Galena. A few times a year, a Chicago paper would publish a review of my ice cream. Always favorable, of course."

"So what exactly was going on between you and Ms. Johns when we stepped in the middle?" Jefferson asked.

"After I gave her a copy of the review, I went back across the aisle to my booth. A few minutes later, I saw Ashley whispering something to a few people and pointing at me. Well, one of them was an old friend of mine who came over and told me that Ashley was telling people that my ice cream had made people sick the day before, that I'd given them *E. coli*! *E. coli*! You'd think someone in the food business would know that you don't get *E. coli* from ice cream—*Listeria*, maybe, but not *E. coli*. What an idiot! Well, anyway, I was so pissed off that I just reacted. She was staring at me from across the aisle, looking so smug. Well, I looked down at my table and saw an ice cream scoop, so I turned around and dug into the rocky road behind me with as much force as I could muster. I gathered up a big ball of it, then turned back around and flung it across the aisle as hard as I could, without looking around first or aiming properly. That's how it ended up on your face, Frank." She touched me on the shoulder as she said my name.

"At least it makes for a funny story now," I said. "And I got a quart of ice cream out of it, too."

"It was one of his better looks," Jefferson said. "How much damage did the fire cause to your operation?"

"We lost almost everything we had in that booth. All of our product, absolutely. All the ice cream either melted or was contaminated by the smoke, so we threw it all out. What the smoke didn't ruin, though, the water coming out of the sprinkler system pretty much finished off. We didn't have a lot of expensive equipment, but we lost a freezer and all of our marketing materials."

"You were lucky that no one from your booth got hurt."

"Absolutely."

"How many people did you have working for you that day?"

"Three, not counting myself, of course. Four is about all we can fit into a space that size."

"You may not have noticed this," Jefferson said, "but how many people did Ms. Johns have working at her booth?"

Stella paused for a minute, looking away as though trying to picture the Post-Modern Chocolates booth in her head. "I think they had four, counting Ashley and Jake."

"That's what I remembered, too," Jefferson said. "Tell me what happened when the fire started, or when you noticed that something was wrong."

"I smelled the smoke but didn't think much of it at first. I assumed that someone had just overcooked something. When the smoke got thicker, though, and people starting to hurry around, then I knew it was time to get out. I grabbed the cash drawer and told my employees to run for the exit. We'd made the trip from our booth to the exit so many times that we got out quickly. I just assumed everyone else got out like we did. I was shocked when I heard later about some people getting trapped."

"And about Jake's death," I interrupted. Jefferson shot me a look.

"Yes, of course," she said, looking back and forth between me and Jefferson.

"I know this is difficult, Stella," Jefferson said, "but I have to ask. Your husband, Stan... It looks like he's getting the blame for the fire. What do you think about that?"

"I don't think it's fair at all. I can't imagine that Stan would do anything on purpose that would put people at risk. He's very good at his job."

"So you believe he's innocent, that he didn't do anything wrong."

Stella twirled a curl of hair again. "The truth is, between you and me—and don't you dare write about this, Frank—I've been worried about Stan. He's been very distracted lately. Personally, I think the mayor has him doing too many things. I think he's spread too thin. So while I'm sure that Stan didn't do anything intentional, I can't help but wonder if he inspected the hall too quickly, because he had so many other things that needed to get done, too."

"So you think he could be responsible... but maybe because of neglect?" Jefferson asked.

"That's right. But I don't *know* that to be the case, of course," Stella emphasized. "It's just something I thought about since the investigation began."

"I'd like to ask a little bit more about Jake," I said, looking out of the corner of my eye at Jefferson, who frowned. "Is that OK?" Stella nodded.

"Everyone I've talked to has had nice things to say about Jake," I said. "He seemed like a stellar young man."

"Yes, he was. People really liked him."

"He'd worked for you for quite a while, before Ashley hired him?"

"Yes. I hired him when he was a senior in high school."

"Did he work for you while he was in college, too?"

"Yes, the whole time. He'd work weekends during the school year, then full time in the summers."

"So it must have felt terrible when Ashley hired him. Like an insult."

"I wasn't happy about it," she said. "Not at all."

"I hesitate to bring this up," I said, watching Jefferson fidget a little. "There was a rumor I heard in Galena. Apparently some folks thought that

Jake might be… was probably having an affair with Ashley. Had you heard those rumors, too?"

Stella almost looked relieved, relaxing her shoulders and eyebrows. "I'm sorry to say it, but yes. It wasn't just a rumor. It was true."

"Why are you so sure?" I asked.

"Because Jake told me."

"Is that why he left your shop for Ashley's? Because they were already lovers?"

"I don't know if the affair started before or after he left me," she said with a shrug, "but I think he'd had his eyes on her early on and jumped on the chance to get closer to her, so to speak." Stella's face turned a subtle shade of red.

"What did he tell you about the affair?" I asked.

"He didn't say much. He told me he was in love with her, and that she loved him back. Typical twenty-four-year-old nonsense."

"Do you think Ashley was in love with him?"

"I doubt it. I don't think she can love anybody but herself." Stella paused. "I'll give her some credit, though. She recognized his skills for running things. It didn't take her long to put him in charge of the store. That's the only time she showed good judgment." She put her hands on her hips. "I was ready to do the same thing, of course, but he left me before I could promote him."

"When was the last time you and Jake talked?"

"Oh, we stayed on friendly terms. Sure, I was disappointed—hurt, even—but I had too much respect for him to shut him out. I took the high road and acted like I was OK, even though I wasn't. We kept in touch, chatted from time to time. On the day he died, we snuck in a quick conversation at the Post-Modern booth, when Ashley wasn't around."

"Jake was a lucky guy, lucky to have found someone like you to stick with him, even when he screwed up," I said. "And lucky to have had folks like the Horgans to adopt and raise him."

Stella moved uneasily, avoiding any eye contact with me or with Jefferson. "Yes. He got some good breaks early on. Too bad it didn't last."

"Thanks for putting up with us," I said. "Did you have anything else you wanted to know, Brian?"

"No. Thank you, Stella. This was very helpful."

When we got outside Cathedral Ice Cream, I said to Jefferson, "Damn! I wish that we'd gotten a look at one of the boxes she uses, to make sure it had the word *cream* on it."

"I did, and it does," he said.

Chapter 39

After visiting Stella, Jefferson was on a roll and wanted to go back to Aquoqua, to talk to Stan directly. He thought he knew enough to turn up the pressure, to find out if Stan would come clean about anything. I told him that sounded like a great idea, except that there might be a problem.

I came clean and told him I'd gone back to Aquoqua without him, that I'd spied on Stan and heard him fighting with Stella, that Stan caught me spying on him, and that Stan might have choked me to death if Big Dan hadn't shown up.

To my surprise, Jefferson didn't lose his cool. "Frank, I've learned to expect you to do stupid things. I'm almost disappointed when you don't. I'm glad you didn't get hurt, but, honestly, no matter how mad Stan was, I don't see him as the kind of person who would have really hurt you. I think he would have caught himself if Big Dan hadn't stopped him first."

"It sure didn't feel like it at the time," I said.

"Did you at least find out anything interesting?"

I gave him the highlights of what I'd learned at the bar before I snuck out to Stan's, that Stan had been married once before Stella, to the mayor's sister, that she'd died from carbon monoxide poisoning when Stan was out of town.

"Man, that's awful," Jefferson said. "It must have nearly killed him."

I told him the other piece of news that I'd picked up, that Stella had fled town for a year when she was in her twenties, that she floated a cover story about learning how to make ice cream, which seemed plausible when she came home and did just that: made ice cream. "Some people didn't buy it, though," I told him. "Some thought she was pregnant and too embarrassed to stay in town and face people."

"I'm surprised you didn't ask her about that just now," Jefferson said.

"I did, but indirectly."

"When?" Jefferson paused. I let him think about it for a minute, to see if he'd make the leap I was making. "Wait. You said that the Horgan kid was adopted, right? Are you telling me that Stella was his mother?"

"I'm not sure, but I have a hunch. There are things about it that just make sense, like the timing for one. He was twenty-four years old, which would make him about the right age."

"Who would the father be? Stan?"

"I doubt it. From what I learned last night, they didn't meet until Stella was back in town, after she would have given birth."

"I guess we have another thing to ask him about, don't we?"

Jefferson didn't like the idea of dropping in at Stan's place unannounced, a reluctance that seemed entirely reasonable to me. He had a better idea anyway. He wanted to offer to meet Stan somewhere with Big Dan as chaperone, maybe at the Hungry Point Bar and Grill.

We parked at the marina and went up and into the bar. A few people turned to look at us, and even though I was afraid I'd pissed off folks in Aquoqua by asking too many questions about Stan Mueller, nobody gave either one of us a second look. When we sat at the bar, even Rick the bartender didn't seem all that bothered.

"Wasn't sure if I'd see you, again," Rick said. "I was glad to hear that Big Dan found you before Stan did something he woulda regretted."

"Me, too," I said.

"Good. That's why I tipped him off—Big Dan, that is. I sent one of the regulars down to his place to let him know what was up. I figured you were about to check out Stan's place in spite of what I advised you not to do, and I knew that Stan wouldn't be none too happy about it."

"Thanks for looking out for me."

"Didn't do it for you," Rick said. "So what are you looking for today?"

We asked Rick about getting in touch with Stan Mueller and Big Dan and meeting them at the bar. Rick thought that sounded like a good idea, but he couldn't promise that either would show up.

He tried Stan's number first but didn't get an answer. Big Dan didn't have a phone, so Rick asked one of the customers to watch the bar; he told us he would run down to Big Dan's place in a jon boat and talk to him directly. He put a couple of beers in front of us and left. About a half hour later, he came back and said he'd convinced Big Dan to host a meeting of the minds at his house. Big Dan promised that he could get Stan to show up, but he needed about an hour.

Jefferson wasn't crazy about going down there, partly because that meant we needed to go by canoe again, but he was mostly bothered by the isolation. He felt vulnerable down there, and he didn't like feeling vulnerable. We milked our beers for another hour while sticking to small talk with Rick. After enough time had passed, Rick set us up with the canoe again, and we shoved off. "Shit! Here we go again," was all Jefferson had to say. Like last time, I did all the paddling; Jefferson sat in front, and unlike last time, he didn't even bother to hold a paddle.

Since we knew exactly where we were going this time, the trip felt a lot quicker. The surface of the water was smooth, our canoe cutting graceful V-shaped ripples in the water as we moved downriver. It was hot as hell again and so dense with humidity that it was hard to tell where the air ended and the river began. My clothes were saturated with sweat just a few minutes after we set out.

We were quiet on the paddle down, Jefferson breaking the silence to remind me to let him do most of the talking and threatening to shoot me himself if I blindsided anyone with one of my hunches. I felt nervous but excited. I had no idea what to expect and wondered if Stan would try to choke me again.

When we pulled ashore, the dogs came running at us, jumping up on the driftwood fence at the front. Big Dan was sitting in a rocker by the front door, in no hurry to get up just because we had made it there. "Tie up where you did before," he said, then turned and spat some tobacco juice on the ground. "Stan's here, too. Come on inside, and let's talk this thing out."

I could smell wood burning when I got in the cabin, which surprised me since it had been so warm. Big Dan wasn't trying to heat up the place, though; he'd stoked up his stove so he could boil a kettle of water. "I thought I'd make some tea for us," he said. It'll help us all keep calm."

I watched as Jefferson carefully scanned the cabin. I imagined that he was looking for anything that could be a potential threat and noting how to get out quickly if he needed to.

"First thing I want to do is apologize to you, Stan," I said. "I had no right to be at your house last night. I won't offer any excuses. It was a dumb move on my part."

Stan stood near a window, dressed in worn blue jeans and a camo shirt. He was staring out the window but not looking at anything in particular. He didn't turn around when I spoke, but he nodded his head just enough for me to notice.

Big Dan took a cast iron kettle off the stove and poured water into four cups, all hand-thrown pottery, each one brown and a slightly different interpretation of round. "This is a calming tea," he said. "It's based on a recipe

I got from a Sauk medicine man, but I threw in a couple of extra leaves to soften the taste. All of it comes from herbs I collected from the forest or grew myself. I'd tell ya exactly what's in it"—he paused and looked up at me and Jefferson—"but then I'd have to kill ya." A big smile covered his face, but I wasn't entirely confident that he was joking. He handed us each a cup, then ordered us to drink it and sit down.

That was enough to break Stan's trance. He followed Big Dan's orders, taking a sip from the cup and settling into a chair next to the window. Jefferson and I sat at the table that served as Big Dan's dining room, with Jefferson taking the seat that was closer to the door.

Jefferson didn't waste any time getting the ball rolling. "Thank you Stan, for talking with us. And thank you, Big Dan, for having us here at your house again." He looked at each of us directly as he spoke. "There's not a delicate way to approach this anymore, given everything that's happened. You know we're not here in any official capacity. Frank may or may not write about any of this. That part is still negotiable," Jefferson said, looking at me. I nodded my agreement.

"I may or may not share what I learn with the police," Jefferson continued. "That's a decision for later. But we are here to get to the bottom about what happened at the convention center on Friday. I ordinarily wouldn't give a flying fuck about it, but two people are dead, and I could have been one of them. So I plan on dogging this case until I know exactly what happened. Everything. Do you understand what I'm saying?"

Stan nodded but didn't look at us, his left hand rapidly tapping the side of the chair he sat in.

"I'm gonna start with the things I already know," Jefferson said. "I know that someone tampered with the fire sensors, that the glass cylinders were painted to make them less sensitive. I also know that the only sensors that were painted were the ones within about thirty feet of where the fire started.

"I know that you are one of just a few people who could have gotten in and painted them, who would have known what painting them would do."

Stan took a sip of his tea, then turned to look at Jefferson, his gaze intense but masking whatever he was feeling. Big Dan looked down at his mug and stirred his tea with a cinnamon stick. I wondered if he was afraid to look up and face the reality of what Stan had done.

Jefferson continued to lay out the details to Stan. "I know you inspected the electrical systems at the booth where the fire started. The woman who ran the booth, the cupcake baker, saw your picture and recognized you, verified that you were the one who told her that her setup was OK.

"In spite of your inspections, a fire started there anyway, at that very spot, and probably from an overloaded circuit. You approved a setup that was inadequate for the power that her oven and other equipment would use."

Still no response from Stan, even with Jefferson staring him down. He turned up the heat a little more.

"I know you had the access and the opportunity to mess with the sensors and to tamper with the electrical systems," Jefferson continued. "The official report more or less said the same, blaming you for the start of the fire. It's just that they called it negligence instead of arson." I saw Stan raise an eyebrow at that, but otherwise he held steady.

"I also know that you placed boxes from Stella's ice cream company near the cupcake booth," Jefferson said, "near the power outlet that overloaded. I suspect that you moved a bunch of other papers, too—kindling, I suppose. You put everything in place to make sure that a fire would start and that it would burn hot for a short time."

Stan took another sip.

"The only part I'm having trouble with is the why," Jefferson said. "What did you think would happen by starting that fire? The whole thing looks like an attempt to go after Ashley Johns, because of the ongoing fight between her and your wife. It feels like that's what I'm supposed to think, but I'm having a hard time with it. I found out that the mayor had suspended you for a month, but that he was secretly paying your salary from some campaign funds, and that made me very curious."

Big Dan looked up and at Jefferson, then over at Stan. Stan looked down at his cup, avoiding Big Dan's gaze.

"The other part that puzzles me is why you locked those exit doors," Jefferson said.

"I never touched those doors," Stan said, breaking his silence.

"If you didn't lock them, then who did?" Jefferson asked. "And why?"

"I can't speak to that. I don't know who did. I just know it wasn't me."

"Stan," Big Dan jumped in. "I practically raised you and Mike, treated you two like you was my own. I showed you what it takes to survive out here on the river, and how to live a life with honor, with respect for yourself and for the life all around us. I showed you how to take care of yourself but also to know your limits, to let friends help you out, 'cause you're gonna need it. We all need it sometimes." Big Dan stood from his chair, his checks glowing red.

"But most of all, Stan, I taught you to be responsible," Big Dan said, his voice cracking. "To own up to the things we done, with no self-pity and no excuses. Now, I don't know everything that's happened to you since you moved away from this place, but those values shouldn't matter any less now. If you did something wrong, it's time to say so. No more hiding." His hands trembled slightly. "I've got you covered, just like I always done. But I can't help if I don't know what happened, what you did. So this time right now, this would be the time to talk. It's not gonna get any easier later."

Stan nodded.

Chapter 40

It was getting late in the day and dark inside the cabin. Big Dan walked around and lit four kerosene lamps, then settled back in his chair. With each wick lit, the smell of smoldering oil grew a little stronger, eventually crowding out the scent of the herbal tea that had been boiling since we'd arrived.

"There's a certain key that locks the push bars on those doors, right?" Jefferson asked.

"Yes," Stan said.

"Who would've had access to that key, besides you?"

"We kept it on a ring in the maintenance room at the convention center. Anyone who could get in that room could get to the key."

"And who would've known that those doors could be locked and what key to use?"

Stan didn't answer right away, swishing the remaining tea in the cup and taking another sip first. "Not many people, I suppose. Besides me there was Jim Davis, who oversaw the day-to-day operations at the convention center. There might be one or two others who would know, too."

"Where was this Davis when the food fair was being set up?"

"Florida," Stan said. "He'd been on vacation for about two weeks and didn't come back until after the fire."

"So basically we're just supposed to take you at your word that you didn't lock the doors."

"I suppose so."

Jefferson sighed, unconvinced. "Fine. So tell me, why start that fire at all?"

Stan pursed his lips and sat up straight in the chair.

"Stan," Big Dan said, glaring at him.

"You're asking me to... to turn on—to betray—the only person who's stuck by me," Stan said.

"I'm asking you to be true to your roots. To take responsibility for what you done."

Stan got up and looked out the window again, his fists clenched. "I was asked to do something to make Stella look bad." Stan looked down, then turned back to face Big Dan. "I was asked to make Stella look bad. That fight with Ashley Johns was getting too big. It was out of control and starting to hurt Mike's campaign. That's what I was told." He grimaced. "The fire was supposed to make it look like Stella had lost it. That she had finally gone too far in her war with Ashley. Stella was supposed to get blamed for the fire, so it would drive her out of business and end the war with Ashley Johns for good. No one was supposed to get hurt, though, much less die."

"Who would ask you to do something like that?" Big Dan asked. "To turn on your own wife."

"Mike, of course," Stan replied. "But a mayor can't say things like that directly, so Courtney Baker, Mike's chief of staff, asked me to do it." He turned back to the window.

"What did the mayor have against Stella?" Jefferson asked.

"It's not my place to ask those questions," Stan said. "I just do what I'm asked to do."

"If you were going to guess about it, what would you guess?" Jefferson asked.

Stan stood silently for a minute. "If I had to guess, I'd say it was because the Johnses had given the mayor a lot of money for his congressional campaign," he said. "I suppose you could assume it had something to do with that."

"That put you in a really tough spot, Stan," I said. "To have to choose between hurting your wife or refusing to help your boss and best friend."

Stan looked over at Big Dan, who looked like he was about to say something but thought better of it.

"Stella's a strong woman," Stan said, using a phrase that's normally a compliment, but it didn't sound that way when Stan said it. "She always finds a way to survive, to win. I figured this wouldn't be any different. That she'd come up with a new plan to do something and would probably come out better off than before. That's the story of her life: She always finds a way to come out ahead."

"Still, you must owe the mayor big time," Jefferson said. "To take his side over your own wife's."

"I do," Stan said. "I do."

Big Dan faked a cough and got up from his chair. He walked across the room to a table and picked up a photo that was in a small frame, one that looked like he might have made himself from wood he'd found in the forest.

"Look here at this picture," he said, putting it on the table between me and Jefferson. There were four people in it: Big Dan was easy to identify, but I could also pick out a younger Stan Mueller. I assumed the other guy was the mayor, Mike Andelfinger.

"Who's the woman in the photo?" I asked.

"That's Gretchen, Mike's sister," Big Dan said.

"Stan's first wife?" I asked.

"That's right," Big Dan said.

"I'm sorry about what happened to her, Stan," I said. "It must have been hard."

Stan didn't speak; he just kept staring out that window.

"It was a terrible accident," Big Dan said, his voice strong and reassuring. "A terrible accident. We was all real close when they was kids."

Big Dan walked back to where he'd been sitting before and sat down. "We went on a hunting trip," he said. "Opening weekend of deer season. Me and Stan—we took Mike along with us. Twisted his arm real good to get him to go. He hated hunting and fishing and could barely pitch a tent on his own, but we was always hoping that maybe we could turn him into a river rat. I've got a small cabin a few miles from here, downriver where the flood plain opens up wide. There's always a lot of deer there. So we figured we'd go down for a couple of days and see what we could get." He cleared his throat. "The weather was pretty good when we left, but a cold front blew through. Nature's way of telling us that fall was over. We was ready, but the big change in the temperature was still a slap in the face. Back up here around Aquoqua, the wind blew so hard that it knocked out power for most of the area, at least for a few hours. That happened pretty regular back in those days, so most folks weren't too bothered by it. Most everyone owned a generator, so they could get by just fine."

Big Dan looked over at Stan, like he was looking for a signal about whether or not to go on. Stan didn't do anything to discourage him.

"Gretchen," he continued, "she was kinda like Mike in that she wasn't built for life down in the bottoms. Don't get me wrong: she loved the river and got out on the water a lot. She was plenty smart, too. But she just didn't really have the makeup and the know-how for living a simpler life." Big Dan looked over at me and Jefferson. "When the power went out, she got a generator out of the garage. She knew enough to get it started and hooked up an electric heater in the bedroom, but she didn't know that she needed to vent it. When we got back from hunting, we was feeling good about our haul, so we stopped at Stan's house for a beer. Stan heard the generator running and found Gretchen in bed, dead."

Stan walked over to the table and picked up the picture. "I was crazy about her, since junior high school. I never pictured myself married to anyone else." He looked at the picture for a couple of minutes, not saying a word, and we didn't interrupt.

"The thing is," Stan said, "she never really loved me back." Stan put the picture back on the table and went back to his chair and sat down. "She didn't want to get married... to me, anyway. She wanted out of Aquoqua. Wanted to live in a big city like Minneapolis or Chicago. But Mike talked her into marrying me. He sold her on me. Told her that the three of us had to stick together, that we were going to do great things, the three of us. We knew that Mike had big ambitions, so I promised her that I'd stick close to him as he climbed the political ladder—like we all knew he would—and that we'd follow him out of here to bigger and better things. She was young enough to buy all that, I guess, so we got married right after we graduated from high school." He picked up a piece of loose wood on the chair. "When Mike went off to college, we stuck around Aquoqua, where I did construction and whatever other work I could find. I was killing time until Mike finished school, and I was more comfortable doing that down here than up in Dubuque. Gretchen put up with it, most of the time. She'd sometimes get restless and run off to Dubuque for a weekend with her brother. Mike—he almost never came back, but we did manage to coax him down to go hunting with us.

"The day we found Gretchen dead," Stan continued, "we were all in such a good mood when we got back. Even Mike had bagged a deer. When I heard the generator running, though, I got a sinking feeling in my gut. I'm the one that found her, that saw her first. I'll never forget it—when I opened the door and saw her there in bed. She looked so peaceful that it didn't hit me at first that she was dead. She always looked so beautiful when she was sleeping." Stan looked down at his hand and spun his wedding ring around a few times.

"Her death," he went on, "well, it nearly killed us—all of us. She and Mike weren't just brother and sister, they were best friends. Being the same age, they'd shared damn near everything their whole lives. Mike wanted her on the inside when he entered politics. She probably would have managed all his campaigns eventually." Stan looked at Big Dan, then back toward the window.

"After she was gone," he continued, "I thought about killing myself for a while. I was sure I'd never find anyone like her again. Didn't even want to. Mike wasn't the same after that, either."

"What happened to Mike?" I asked.

"He pulled away. Sure, we spent a lot of time together, but it wasn't as much fun anymore. Everything became about his future. About doing whatever he had to do to get into politics, to win elections." He dug harder into the chair and pried loose a sliver of wood. "Before Gretchen died, he'd talked a lot about what he wanted to do once he was in office, the ideas he had for helping people. After she died, all he talked about was winning."

Big Dan got up and poured us each a refill, then walked to a cabinet, pulled out a bottle of schnapps, and added a splash to each mug. "It changed all of us," Big Dan said. "One day the people who mean the most to you are right there. Then—just like that—someone's gone. It makes you rethink everything you thought you knew. You know your life will never be the same."

"Will never be quite as good," Stan added.

I felt a couple of tears welling up, but I held them back. "You sound like a man who's known his share of grief," I choked out to Big Dan.

"I lost my own wife about fifteen years ago. Heart attack, no warning. One day we're hunting for morels and kidding around, and the next she's gone. It's hard enough when you know it's coming, finding a way to say goodbye and all, but what are you supposed to do when it's all sudden like that? Got no chance to make your peace with each other."

"Like you said," Jefferson jumped in. "You find a way to get yourself up every day and keep yourself busy until it doesn't hurt as much anymore. Sounds like you did that, Stan. You stuck with the mayor. And you even got married again."

"I couldn't stay in Aquoqua after that," Stan said. "Couldn't bring myself to live at the old house in Aquoqua, where Gretchen had died. I moved up to the city and got a job at the University of Dubuque—where Mike was going to school—in the maintenance department, fixing things around campus. It was a good job, perfect for me at that time. I've always been good with my hands, so I didn't have to think much. I worked a lot of overtime, so I earned enough to rent an apartment."

"How'd you meet Stella?" Jefferson asked.

"Not long after Mike was elected to the city council—right after he finished college—I started going to this new ice cream shop near my apartment in the North End. That was Stella's first place. I liked the ice cream a lot, so I went three or four times a week. Every time I went, we'd talk a little more, until one day we realized that we liked each other, so I asked her out. She reminded me of Mike in some ways—her ambition, especially. She wanted to be the ice cream queen, and nothing was going to get in her way. We got along well and figured we'd be better off together than if we both stayed single, so we thought we'd give marriage a try. I suppose that doesn't sound all that romantic, but we'd each had our share of disappointments and didn't have any fantasies about what we were doing."

"Are you still?" I asked.

"Still what?"

"Are you still better off being together than separate?"

Stan took a small sip of his tea, looked out the window, then drained the rest of his cup in one long swallow. "I don't know," he said. "Probably not. Seems I can't do much right these days."

"The other night, when I was outside your house, it sounded like you and Stella were arguing," I said.

"Probably," Stan said. "Been doing a lot of that lately."

Big Dan put the schnapps back in the cabinet, then turned back to face me and Jefferson. "OK. So you have your confession," he said. "So what do we do now?"

"That's a good question," Jefferson said. "I think we should start by getting back to town. It's almost dark, and we still have to paddle that damn boat—canoe—back to my truck."

CHAPTER 41

Big Dan offered us a ride back to the Aquoqua marina, and Jefferson was quick to accept. Before we left, Stan admitted that he was the one who had run me off the road after I visited Ashley.

"I wasn't trying to run you off the road," he insisted. "Just wanted to give you a little scare. You surprised me when you swerved out of control." It was somehow reassuring to know that Stan was responsible for the accident, but I'd have felt better if he'd showed at least a hint of remorse about it.

"I suppose you're the one who put the fish in my truck, too?" Jefferson asked.

"Yeah," Stan said, with a sly smile. "I saw you get out of it in Galena and wanted you to know that you were being watched."

"But fish parts? Really? I can still smell them."

"I'd been out on the river earlier in the day. I thought it was a good way to clean out my truck."

We left; Stan stayed at the cabin to wait for Big Dan to get back. I tied the canoe to the back of Big Dan's jon boat, and we got in. Big Dan fired up the motor and turned on a spotlight, and we were quickly moving away from shore and back to Aquoqua. The air was as still as when we'd paddled down to Big Dan's cabin, and the heat still hadn't let up.

"Stan's a good man," Big Dan said over the putter of his motor, "even if he's quicker to anger these days and maybe's done some things I wished he hadn't. He and Mike—that friendship is strong. Maybe too strong. Stan looked after him so much when they was growing up, defended him from the other kids. Even rescued him a couple of times, like I told you about. Then when Gretchen passed, it was like they'd been welded together." Big Dan swerved to avoid a log, then throttled back.

"Do you think that's a good thing?" I asked.

"It was for a while, but I'm not sure anymore. I've told Stan that it was time to get his own life back. To think for himself and be more independent."

"Why?" I asked "What are you worried about?"

"Mike's not the same person I remember. Sure, he always had ambition, but I believed he'd put it into something good. When he got on the city council, he fought for better schools and to bring back the riverfront. Even after he became mayor, I had a feeling that he was going to be a good one. That he'd fight for the little guy and win more than he'd lose. He even got us some money down here in Aquoqua, for some overdue fixes, even though we're not part of the city."

"But something changed?" Jefferson asked.

"Yeah, something changed. I can't tell you exactly when it happened. Maybe it was Gretchen's passing, like Stan said. Maybe you never get over losing a twin sister. Maybe it wasn't even all at once." Big Dan scanned the water ahead of us. "I noticed a difference when he got in with the bigwigs, after he became mayor. You could see that he loved it, the attention and feeling the power. Hell, when he was a kid down here, he used to complain about those same people, the ones who lived in the big houses up on the bluffs. He resented them, felt like they'd never take him serious." Big Dan steered around more driftwood.

"All that attention and being part of the inner circle," he went on, "it made Mike even more ambitious, made him covet more power. I could be wrong about him, of course, but I've known that boy since he was born. He ain't the same. He ain't the little sprout that I used to know." He scowled. "Stan is starting to see it more clearly, but I wish I could get him to do something about it. I'm just not sure Stan has it in him to cut ties with Mike."

As we got near Aquoqua, Big Dan killed the engine, and we drifted into the boat ramp. He jumped out of the jon boat, helped us to shore, and we pulled the canoe up the ramp.

"I'll keep working on Stan," Big Dan said. "Maybe I can get him to tell the police what he did. Even if he does, though, you're gonna have a hard time pinning anything on Mike."

"Leave that part to us," Jefferson said. "Every crook makes a mistake somewhere, and the mayor's no different. I'll find what we need to nail him."

When Big Dan pulled away, Jefferson and I carried the canoe back to its home under the marina bar. Rick came down and complimented us for staying inside the canoe this time.

Once we were back in the truck and driving toward Dubuque, I checked my phone and saw that I had several texts. "Shit!" I said. "I was supposed to meet Adam for dinner. To talk about our future."

"You two have a future?" Jefferson asked. "You told me he was just a nice distraction while you were in Dubuque."

"I don't know. I'm not sure what I want right now, but I didn't help anything by standing him up tonight."

"Take it easy on yourself, Frank," Jefferson said. "It's not like there's much you could have done different. We got caught up in talking to Stan, and you couldn't call Adam, because your cell phone didn't work down there."

"That may be true, but I don't think it's going to make Adam feel much better."

I scrolled through the texts, all from Adam, beginning with "@ Maria's; got a table near the back." Each subsequent message expressed increasing dismay, ending with "This is fucked up. Thought you were better than this."

I'd come to Dubuque to write a quick article for a national magazine, for the exposure and the good payday, and in the process, I'd met a guy I really liked. This could have been a great trip, could have gotten me back on track. But I'd screwed up the writing assignment, and now I'd probably screwed things up with Adam, too. All the time we'd been spending trying to figure out who or what caused that damn fire—it had better be worth the trouble.

Chapter 42

Back in Dubuque, Jefferson dropped me at my car. I sent a quick text to Adam: "Sorry! Give me a chance to explain?" I waited a few minutes for a response, and when it didn't come, I drove down to Lonna's Livery for a nightcap, hoping I might bump into Adam there.

The bar was busy, but I didn't see Adam anywhere. Lonna walked down, said hi, and asked where Jefferson had been hiding out. She hadn't seen him in a while and missed him. I told her I'd say hi from her. She got busy refilling drinks and chatting with regulars, so I finished my beer and went back to the Clear Lake Inn.

I needed to do something to take my mind off Adam, so I pulled out the articles that Ruby had copied for me, starting with the one panning Post-Modern Chocolates, which it had called "the chocolate equivalent of a starving artist's sale, but less satisfying." It had run in *Chicago Magazine*; I didn't recognize the name of the reviewer, Steven Gold.

The piece noted the popularity of Post-Modern Chocolates in Galena, which the writer called a "tourist town," a subtle dig at the credentials of the people who made Ashley's chocolates popular. After all, the article implied, those chocolates were obviously made to please the unsophisticated palates of the rubes in flip-flops and halter tops who visited the town. The piece also mentioned that Ashley had had a store in Chicago that failed, a not-so-subtle reminder that she was at least a one-time loser.

The reviewer's main complaint about the chocolate itself was that Ashley was trying to pull one over on her customers by mixing in a type of chocolate called CCN-51. I had to look that up. CCN-51 stands for Colección Castro Naranjal-51, a cacao plant that had been developed by Homero Castro to save Ecuador's cacao industry from years of declining production. Ecuador had once grown one of the world's most desirable varieties of cacao, but a disease called witch's brew had nearly destroyed it. Castro went on a mission to develop a cacao plant that would resist the disease; he finally got it right on his fifty-first try, hence the name.

The earliest plants went into production in the 1960s and were not only resistant to witch's brew but also highly productive; they grew a lot more pods than the traditional plants. Everything looked rosy—until people tasted it. Early reviews were brutal. Experts described its flavor with words like "acidic" or "sour," comparing it to dirt and rusty nails. Castro's focus on breeding a plant with a higher yield and disease resistance had come at the expense of flavor, as it often does. Unlike consumers of most other industrial ag products, though, chocolate lovers cared. Castro's efforts looked like a failure when he died in a car accident in June 1988.

Demand for chocolate kept growing, though, and the big companies struggled to keep up. A new way of processing CCN-51 was developed, which made it taste less like sludge, and that was good enough for the mass producers, who started mixing CCN-51 into their factory-made chocolate bars; hardly anyone noticed.

Serious chocolate nerds continued to hate CCN-51, however. One of them was a man named Ed Seguine, who is one of the world's foremost experts on chocolate and just might have the best-developed palate on the planet. He said that CCN-51 tasted like "acidic dirt" and would love nothing more than for it to disappear forever. That's not going to happen, though. Nobody cares now if a manufacturer includes a little CCN-51 as one of their ingredients, as long as they're making chocolate bars for the masses. If you call yourself a chocolatier, however, slipping a little CCN-51 into a truffle is viewed as favorably as a bartender lacing a cocktail with arsenic.

So this reviewer for *Chicago Magazine* accused Ashley of slipping a little CCN-51 into her gourmet mix, polluting her fine cacaos with an inferior and cheaper ingredient. Those sounded like fighting words to me, so I figured I'd head back to Galena the next day and find out for myself if Ashley was the cheater the reviewer had made her out to be.

CHAPTER 43

After a restless night, I woke up early—too early—so I took a long shower, hoping that the water and a strong cup of coffee would get me going. I went back to The Wired Bean, a place I had been often enough on this trip that the barista knew to start a double espresso as soon as he saw me. While I was waiting for Jefferson to show up, I sat at a table outside and called Ruby.

"How goes your research, Ruby?" I asked.

"I don't have a lot of news right now," she said, "but I did find out that the Bakers, Courtney's parents, donated almost as much money to the mayor's campaign as the Johns did. Boy, that's hard to say: 'the Johns.' Is that right? Or should it be 'the Johnses'? I'm never sure."

"I suppose the sticklers would prefer 'the Johnses,' but I think you're OK either way. I know what you mean. Anyway, so you found out that they're both top donors. Well, we pretty much expected that to be the case. I'm not sure it makes much difference at this point." I took a small sip of espresso, but it was still too hot. "Did you have any luck with that search on Stella and Helen in college?"

"Oh, how could I forget that one?" Ruby said. "Yes, I did. Let me find those articles I copied. Just a minute." I heard some papers shuffling before Ruby got back on the phone. "Here it is. There were protests on campus in 1984 against a professor who some students said was making demeaning comments about women."

"How do Helen and Stella figure into it?" I asked.

"It says that the protests were led by Helen Kraft, who was president of the student council, and a campus activist named Stella Wulff. That must be her maiden name, Wulff. They were angry with a sociology professor who told students in his classes that wives were supposed to be submissive to their husbands and that sometimes a man was justified in using force to keep his wife submissive. Oh, my—what nonsense! I can see why those students would be upset."

"What happened to the professor?" I asked.

"I found several articles about those protests, Frank, and I'd say that the students won, but it wasn't exactly an easy win."

"What do you mean?"

"When the protests started, the college president condemned the professor's statements but insisted that the professor could say whatever he wanted, because he had tenure.

That didn't quiet things down, so the students kept protesting and eventually got on national TV. That's when the president announced that the professor had agreed to stop teaching, although he didn't resign his position."

"So the protestors won, right?"

"Yes, I'd say so, but I found another article from a few months after that announcement that said the president of the college was resigning. He was accused of paying the professor under the table to get him to quit teaching. When that was discovered, the university ordered a complete audit and found a lot of unnecessary expenses. They said he—the president—had spent too much money furnishing his office and on travel."

"Huh. That's not quite the way Stella told the story, but she didn't exactly lie to me, either." I stirred the espresso to help it cool, then took another sip.

"Thanks for looking that up, Ruby. If I ask you to research something new, will you hate me?"

"No, Frank, of course not. This is so much fun, I don't mind at all. What else should I look up?"

"Last night I reread that bad review of Post-Modern Chocolates. The writer accused Ashley Johns of slipping inferior chocolate into the mix, something called CCN-51. Using it to stretch the good stuff, I guess. That substitute is supposed to have a bitter taste, so if you're an expert, you should be able to tell that it's there. That made me wonder if anyone else ever noticed. Could you search around a little more and see if you can find any other reviews of Post-Modern Chocolates?"

"Of course. I'll go to the library this morning."

"Keep an eye out for any mention of CCN-51 in other reviews."

"OK. I'll do that." She paused. "How was your day yesterday?"

"Brian and I got busy tracking down some leads about the fire. We had a revealing chat with Stan Mueller. He admitted that he was responsible for starting it."

"That's great, Frank! What will you do now?"

"Getting the truth from Stan was a big deal, but we still have a lot of questions that need answers. We're going to be busy today trying to nail down a couple more pieces."

"Well, good luck with that, Frank. It sounds like it might be coming together. I'll let you know if I find anything out at the library."

Jefferson showed up just as I finished talking to Ruby. He got his usual—a large dark roast, black—and sat down with me. I told him about the article I'd reread and the research I'd asked Ruby to do, but he seemed distracted.

"What's up with you this morning?" I asked.

"What do you mean?"

"Your mind is somewhere else."

"Of course, it is. Look, I don't really care if that woman put rat shit in her chocolate. I'm more focused on how we're going to get to the mayor. He should be your priority, too, Frank."

"He is, Brian. But I have a feeling that this is important, too."

"Great. Another one of your fucking hunches," he said before catching himself. "I'm sorry, Frank. You're right. I haven't slept well the last couple of nights. I'm tired of being away from home. Counting Hawaii, it's been two weeks since I slept in my own bed. Two weeks since I saw my girls. I'm ready for this to be over. I'm ready to go home."

"So what do you want to do now? What's our next step?"

"I think it's time for a frontal assault. No more dicking around. Let's go pay a visit to that chief of staff... what's her name again?"

"Courtney Baker?"

"Right, Courtney Baker. Now that Stan's named her as part of the plot, I think it's time we find out what she has to say for herself and the mayor."

Chapter 44

City Hall was just a few blocks from The Wired Bean, so we left our cars behind and walked. The four-story brick monument to local government had opened for business in 1857; it has more than a passing resemblance to Boston's Faneuil Hall. We walked up the front steps and straight to Courtney's office, a small two-room suite at the end of the hallway.

Her secretary sat at a desk just inside, guarding the passage to twin ten-foot oak doors that were wide open when we walked in. Before the secretary could ask, "Who the hell are you?" Courtney spotted us and came out to intercept us, her thin heels clicking like crickets as she crossed the pine floor. She looked equal parts intrigued and annoyed, but when we asked for a few minutes of her time, in private, she agreed. We followed her into the office, and she slid those big doors shut behind us.

The inside of her office was Spartan chic, spare in quantity but with eye-catching quality: a nineteenth-century oil painting of Dubuque in muted reds and blues, a twelve-foot-round Persian rug with complementary colors in the middle of the room. On her desk, next to a laptop computer, was a table lamp with a stained-glass shade, probably Tiffany. Given how beautiful the rest of the office was—the walnut wainscoting and crown molding, the oak floors—she didn't need to add much to impress visitors.

"I don't think we've been introduced," Courtney said, extending a hand out to Jefferson. "I'm Courtney Baker."

"Brian Jefferson."

She walked past me without shaking my hand and sat down in a leather desk chair that was jacked up about as high as it could go. "Please, have a seat," she said, pointing to two oak chairs in front of her desk. We followed orders. "What can I do for you two?" she asked, leaning back.

Jefferson didn't waste any time. "We had a long chat with Stan Mueller last night and thought you might like to comment on what he said." Courtney's eyes flitted from Jefferson to me and back, but she didn't say a word. "He told us that he started the fire at the convention center." Courtney sat up. "That he tampered with the sprinklers—told us exactly how—that he rigged the cupcake baker's electrical outlet to overload, and that he piled combustible material around the outlet to catch fire."

"I told you there was something suspicious about him, about Stan, didn't I, Frank?" she asked, excited about the news. "Didn't I ask you to keep an eye on him? So what do we do now? Now that we know that Stan Mueller was responsible?"

"We call it a good start," Jefferson said. "A curious thing came up in that conversation, though." Jefferson paused, looking Courtney directly in the eyes.

"What's that?" she asked, holding his gaze.

"He said you ordered him to do it."

"And I guess you believed him," she said, without looking away from Jefferson. "Oh, please! Why on earth would I do such a thing? He's just trying to shift the responsibility to someone else." She leaned back in her chair.

"Stan said you told him to do it," Jefferson responded, "on the mayor's behalf."

"So the mayor's involved, too? Did he also blame Obama and Putin? Maybe the pope had a hand in it, too! You can't seriously believe him, can you? He's just trying to save himself."

"Didn't seem like it. He and the mayor are closer than conjoined twins." Jefferson kept steady eye contact with Courtney. "No, I believe him. I think the mayor wanted it done but couldn't tell Stan directly, so he told *you* to tell Stan to do it."

"What an intriguing conspiracy, Mr. Jefferson! Why exactly would the mayor want someone to start a fire at a major convention? Especially when he was campaigning for higher office?"

"When it comes to politicians and why, I just follow the money. The top two donors to his campaign are Richard and Lynn Johns and Joseph and Anita Baker. The Bakers, of course, are your parents."

"And what does that prove?"

"Let's start with the Johnses. Their daughter, Ashley, runs a fancy chocolate shop."

"And an ice cream business, too," I added.

"Right, now ice cream, too," Jefferson said. "She has a rivalry with Stella Mueller, who also runs an ice cream operation. In fact, Stella Mueller and the Johnses have a long-standing feud of their own. They make the fight between the Hatfields and McCoys look like a couple of bitch slaps. Sometime before the convention, Ashley decides she's going to open that ice cream business."

"This is sounding like a soap opera," Courtney said, "not a plot to commit arson."

"There's more," Jefferson said. "When the booths are set up for the convention, Ashley and Stella just happen to be right across an aisle from each other. The woman who ran the booth where the fire started told us that she saw some of Stella's boxes near the faulty outlet. Everything was set up to make it look like Stella was responsible for the fire."

"So where did that plan go wrong, I wonder?" Courtney asked. "After all, the fire and police investigators concluded that it was just an accident. No one said anything about arson."

"That's true. No one mentioned a few other key details, either. Like the fact that several emergency exit doors were locked when they shouldn't have been." Jefferson paused, his right index finger lightly tapping on the chair's armrest. "No, I think that's when the plan changed—had to change—after two people died in the fire. The mayor and the Johnses might have wanted to see Stella look desperate enough to start a small fire, but they weren't willing to ride it all the way to a manslaughter conviction. No. When those two people died, someone panicked, so they had to come up with a different plan. They decided to push the story that it was a terrible accident and move on to fight another day."

"Impressive, Mr. Jefferson. You've obviously given this a lot of thought. But even if there was any truth to that story—and I'm certainly not saying there is—what makes you think that I'd be willing to stick my neck out and help you? All you have right now is the word of an admitted arsonist and some flimsy circumstantial evidence. You expect *me* to be the one who reveals the details of whatever plot supposedly exists and, in the process, take the fall for it. But you haven't given me any reason why I should turn in my boss and throw away a political career that's on a fast track." She leaned forward and looked Jefferson directly in the eyes. "You must have something more concrete, something more damning, don't you, Mr. Jefferson? Or else why would you come to me now?"

"We also have the part about the mayor paying Stan a month's salary from campaign funds," I said, "to make up for the suspension."

"Frank, any decent lawyer will rip that testimony to shreds." She got up, walked around the front of the desk, and sat on the edge. "No, gentlemen," she nearly whispered. "I'd like to help you here, but I've already held your hands more than enough. If you expect me to give you more than I already have, to say anything that could conceivably implicate me, then you need to have my back, too. You need to have some solid evidence on your side, something tangible and convincing that would hold up in court. If you can get that, come back to me. Until then, there's nothing more I can do."

Courtney got up from the desk and gestured toward the door. "I have a meeting in a few minutes with the mayor. You know how to reach me if anything changes."

We left her office and walked back down to Iowa Street. "What do you think?" I asked.

"Went better than I expected, really," Jefferson said. "I think she wants to talk. And I think she's ready to rat out the mayor. So that's good."

"But she also wants us to come up with some concrete evidence that would back up our theory about what happened, and we don't have much there. I don't think anything is going to magically turn up, either."

"I agree," Jefferson said. "At this point, we're probably not going to find a smoking gun. Maybe that doesn't matter, though." He looked at me as his eyes opened wide, and a slight smile worked its way up to a full-on grin.

"What do you have in mind?"

"Look. It's possible to get to the truth without having all the best evidence. Sometimes you just have to give folks a little extra motivation to talk."

"So how do we motivate Courtney Baker to tell what she knows?"

"I have an idea," Jefferson said. "Follow me."

CHAPTER 45

We walked back to Jefferson's truck and got in. Jefferson wanted to know more about the painting that had been mentioned in Helen Kraft's article, the one she'd written about stolen Nazi art that had caused the split between Stella and the Johnses.

I'd left a copy of the article back in my motel room, so we called Ruby and asked her to read the highlights to us, as well as the article about the art that the Bakers had purchased. It took her about five minutes to find the articles and call back. I put her on speaker phone.

"In Helen Kraft's article, there are three paintings that are mentioned: *The Lion Tamer* by Max Beckmann, *Portrait of a Woman* by Picasso, and *Seated Woman* by Matisse."

"Thanks, Ruby," Jefferson said. "Now take a look at the article about the Bakers' purchase. What does it say? What did they buy?"

"Let's see. It says they bought a Picasso, a painting called *Portrait of a Woman*. Isn't that interesting?" she said. "That must be the same one that Helen Kraft wrote about, right?"

"That's a hell of a coincidence," I said.

"Does the article say anything else?" Jefferson asked.

"Not much. Just that they plan on loaning it out for a while to the Dubuque Museum of Art. Maybe it's still there."

"No mention of who they bought it from?"

"No, there sure isn't."

Before we hung up, she said she was still searching for any other reviews about Post-Modern Chocolates and hoped to let me know something soon. We thanked her and walked the half-mile to the Dubuque Museum of Art. As we were en route, I sent another text to Adam, apologizing again and asking to see him in person. After making me wait a few minutes, he sent me a quick "call me tonite."

It wasn't too hard to find the painting at the art museum. It was displayed on a second-floor wall, behind a door in a room with modular walls protected by a couple of cameras but not much else. The painting hung on the wall in a simple walnut frame, with cylindrical wall lights casting a gentle light evenly over its surface. Every detail on the deformed woman's face was visible: the wide open eyes, one of them oversize; a split nose, with a nostril that appeared to come out of an ear; the hourglass-shaped breasts, the left one larger than the right, maybe to balance the oversize right eye.

We hadn't been standing there very long when a woman came up to us and started describing the painting. She introduced herself as Marie Gebbs, the director of the museum. "Picasso painted several images of women that he called *Portrait of a Woman*. This one was probably painted in the 1920s. We don't know a lot about its history or the woman who might have inspired it."

"It's pretty damn twisted," Jefferson said. "He didn't think much of women, I guess."

"He had difficult relationships with women, that's true," the director told us. "His first wife had several breakdowns and was institutionalized. He also had a wife and a mistress who each committed suicide. I've wondered how much that influenced his paintings."

After making sure it was OK, Jefferson took a picture of the painting with his cell phone.

"How did you acquire this piece?" I asked. "It must have really stretched your acquisitions budget."

"We don't own the painting," she said. "It's on loan from a private collector."

"I see. So that's the Joseph and Anita Baker referred to on the panel, I guess."

"Yes, that's right. They wanted to share this painting with the community."

"How generous. I imagine that would have been an expensive piece for your museum to purchase."

"Absolutely," she said. "Only a small portion of our annual budget is set aside for purchases, and this one would have been well beyond our means. Our permanent collection typically grows only by donation. We put together shows using pieces on loan from collectors, plus we host exhibits that travel from museum to museum."

"Just out of curiosity," Jefferson said, "if I wanted to buy a painting like that one, how would I go about it?"

"The most likely way to buy a painting like this would be at auction. Sometimes, though, private collectors sell pieces directly. I think that was the case for this one."

"The Bakers had some kind of connection, I suppose, who let them know this was for sale?" Jefferson asked.

"Something like that. The Bakers knew an art dealer in the Chicago area who helped them with this purchase. I imagine that they discussed the type of painting they were looking for." She clasped her hands in front of her. "They might even have asked the dealer to look out for pieces by Picasso. I'm not sure of all the details."

"Would you have any idea who the art dealer was?" Jefferson asked.

"I believe it was Richard Johns. He's quite well known in the art world."

We thanked Ms. Gebbs and left the museum. "Let's go back and visit with Ms. Baker one more time," Jefferson said. "I have an idea."

CHAPTER 46

I thought we were going back to Courtney too quickly, wondered if we had enough to motivate her to talk, but Jefferson was smiling and confident and insisted we were good. I admired his confidence, but I didn't get it. We got back to City Hall barely two hours after we'd last seen her. She was in her office again and not overjoyed to see us back so soon. She came out to greet us—or maybe to shoo us away.

"Back already?" Courtney asked. "You weren't gone very long. Maybe you left something behind—like your judgment?"

"Funny, but you're right. Partly right anyway," Jefferson said. "We left without your side of the story. We came back to get it."

Courtney looked at Jefferson, then at me, and back to Jefferson before gesturing us into her office, reluctantly. Jefferson and I sat in the same chairs as before. Courtney followed us in, closing the doors behind us.

"I told you not to come back unless you had some kind of real evidence," she said. "Exactly what do you think you've discovered in a couple of hours?"

"Are you familiar with the term *Raubkunst*?" Jefferson asked.

"Why would I be? It sounds German, not a language I speak."

"*Raubkunst* is the term used to describe art that the Nazis stole during World War II. Those Nazis—they loved art, especially the famous pieces they stole to put in their own homes. Hermann Göring had one of the biggest collections: hundreds of pieces worth a couple hundred million bucks at the end of the war. No one knows exactly how much art the Nazis actually took, but we know that a lot of what they stole never turned up after the war."

Courtney sat down behind the desk. "I don't have all day, Mr. Jefferson. Maybe you should just get to the point and skip the Nazi history lesson."

Jefferson looked unfazed. "Every now and then, a few pieces resurface, like the ones that ended up in the hands of a hoarder named Cornelius Gurlitt, whose lifestyle was what we now would call off the grid. When he was low on cash, he'd sort through the thousand-plus rolled-up canvases in his apartment, pick one, and go to a friendly art dealer who would sell it on the down low for a share of the profit."

Courtney picked up her cell phone to check the time, then leaned back in her chair.

"Even when these pieces show up," Jefferson continued, "it's sometimes impossible to figure out who owned it before the Nazis stole it. Some families were wiped out by the Holocaust, of course; others just didn't have any records of what they owned before the war; some families sold their art at a discount so that they would have money to get away from the Nazis. There's a decent list out there of the paintings that were probably looted by the Nazis, but it's got a lot of holes in it. Art dealers and museums that worry about their reputations stay away from art where the ownership chain is murky, especially if the trail get lost around World War II."

"And what exactly does this have to do with me and the fire at the convention center?" Courtney asked. "Or anything in Dubuque, for that matter?" Courtney tossed her cell phone onto the desk.

"A few years back," Jefferson continued, "Richard Johns had a deal to sell a painting of... disputed origin. He had a buyer who wanted it but was publicity shy. When the name of that painting showed up in an article about art looted by the Nazis, that buyer backed out and the Johnses lost a big commission.

"In fact, they lost a lot of business for a while. Their buddies in the art world apparently thought they should've been a little pickier about what they sold." He leaned forward slightly. "By the way, that article about Nazi art, the one that named the painting the Johnses wanted to sell, was written by Helen Kraft. I believe you know her."

"I'm familiar with her work." Courtney looked unmoved.

"I've been over that article a dozen times since I got a copy of it. It's a great read. Sorry, Frank," Jefferson said, glancing at me quickly before turning back to Courtney. "Curiously, Stella Mueller took some heat for leaking the name of the painting to Kraft. Seems the Johnses had confided the details of the impending sale to Stella not long before Kraft named it in her article.

Stella denied telling Kraft about the painting, of course. I didn't give it all much thought, until recently." He pulled out his cell phone, brought up the photo of the Picasso at the Dubuque Museum of Art, and passed the phone to Courtney. "Do you recognize this painting?" he asked.

"Sure. That's the Picasso my parents bought, the one they lent to the art museum." Courtney sat up straight and looked right at Jefferson. "You aren't suggesting that *my* parents bought looted art, are you?"

"In her article, Kraft named three paintings that were known to have been stolen by the Nazis and that didn't resurface after the war." Jefferson picked up his phone and showed it to her again. "This painting, the one at the art museum here, was one of them." He put the phone back in his pocket and pointed at Courtney. "We know that your parents and the Johnses are friends. We've found photos of them together at public events. We know that Richard Johns was the dealer who helped your parents purchase this painting." He sat up straight, his eyes narrowed. "What we don't know is if your parents were willing participants in the deception or just dupes."

Courtney leaned forward and rested both elbows on the table.

"We also know that both your parents and the Johnses are major donors to the mayor's campaign," Jefferson continued. "Your parents have donated a load of cash to the mayor over the years." He sat back and folded his arms. "Maybe that's how you got your job."

"That game won't work with me, Mr. Jefferson," Courtney jumped in.

"Then let's cut the games, Ms. Baker." Jefferson dropped his arms to the side and leaned in again. "We know you told Stan to start the fire at the convention center and that you were doing it because the mayor asked you to. Stan's willing to testify to that. If you want to save your own butt, you need to talk to us. Now." He locked eyes with Courtney. "And if you won't save your own butt, just think of how embarrassing it will be for your parents—and for your mayor and the City of Dubuque—when we call the *New York Times* and tell them that a painting stolen from Jews slaughtered during the Holocaust has turned up in a Midwestern city settled by a lot of Germans. As you folks in politics like to say, 'Those are terrible optics.'"

Courtney sat back and turned away from us, lost in thought. We sat quietly for a couple of minutes before she finally spoke.

"It didn't have to be a fire," she said. "The mayor wanted a disturbance of some kind, something that would look like Stella was trying to sabotage Ashley's chocolate business. The Johnses wanted her out of business, and the mayor felt like he had to go along. They were—are—his biggest contributors and promised more support—more money—if he helped with this one thing: taking out Stella. The mayor couldn't ask Stan directly, so he told me to talk to him, to see what Stan would come up with. It was Stan's idea to start the fire. He didn't tell me about that plan, and he certainly didn't tell the mayor."

"The mayor wasn't a little concerned about asking Stan to ruin his wife's business?" I asked.

"Honestly? No. He knew that Stan was more loyal to him than to Stella," Courtney said. "Sad, but it's true."

"How could he be so sure that Stan would go along with that?" I asked.

"Like I said, Stan's loyalty to the mayor runs deep. They've been through a lot together, suffered together. That counts for a lot more than a marriage certificate to a second wife. Besides, Stan and Stella hadn't exactly been getting along great lately anyway."

"Well, it looked like he was right about that much," Jefferson said. "I'm ready to put a wrap on this, and with your testimony, I think we can do that. Will you go to the police with us? Tell them that it was the mayor who ordered Stan to create the mess?"

"If I agree, then you won't tell anyone about the painting?"

"I haven't decided yet," Jefferson said. "It depends on how cooperative you are with the police and whether you help us nail the mayor and the Johnses."

"I'll help," she said. "I'll help."

Chapter 47

Courtney Baker, chief of staff to the mayor, confessed directly to the chief of police. It didn't take long for the media circus to stake out police headquarters. The mayor came in for questioning, voluntarily, and tried unsuccessfully to slip out past the reporters who were lined up with cameras rolling, eager to capture his fall off the cliff. Images of the impeccably dressed mayor wearing a perplexed expression were plastered all over the regional news outlets.

Courtney Baker was given immunity from prosecution in exchange for testifying, which was enough to get Mayor Michael Andelfinger arrested for conspiracy, although he was promptly released on bail. Prosecutors hoped to collect enough additional evidence to bring manslaughter charges as well, for the two people who had died in the fire.

The mayor's donors, Richard and Lynn Johns, weren't charged with anything, at least not right away; Courtney's testimony about their role wasn't damning enough, and the mayor wasn't giving them up. He was, in fact, steadfastly denying the whole conspiracy. Stan Mueller was facing arson and manslaughter, though he was expected to catch a break if he cooperated. At least, he might have caught a break had he lived.

When police went down to his house in Aquoqua Thursday afternoon to bring him in for processing, they found him dead. He'd brought a generator into his bedroom, closed all the doors and windows, and let the thing run all Wednesday night while he fell asleep. Like his first wife, Gretchen, Stan died a peaceful death from carbon monoxide poisoning.

I was shocked but not surprised. In a short time, he'd lost both Stella, his wife, and the mayor, his best friend. It was losing the mayor that hurt the most, I suspected. After Stan lost Gretchen, he'd put everything he had into the mayor, built his whole life around being the mayor's most essential aide. After he turned on Andelfinger—ratted out his most loyal friend—Stan must have realized that he didn't have anything left for himself. His purpose was gone, and I guess he wasn't inclined to stick around and start over. From everything I'd heard about him, all the praise from people who'd known him a long time, I suppose he was also broken up over the two deaths at the convention center. If that was true, he did what Big Dan had been telling him to do: he took responsibility for his actions. I'm sure Big Dan could have come up with a dozen better options. We would never really know what was going on in Stan's head, though. Stan, like most people who kill themselves, didn't bother to leave a note with a tidy explanation for his suicide.

I called Adam in the evening, and he agreed to meet me for dinner, to talk things out. When the news of the conspiracy hit the press, he softened up a bit; maybe it made me seem like less of an asshole for standing him up the previous night. "I assumed that was just your chickenshit way of telling me to leave you alone, for having the nerve to ask where this thing was going," he said. "Maybe I overreacted... a little."

I told him about the whole series of events, from the details of how we escaped the fire to Stan's suicide. He thought it was one hell of a story—which it was, of course—just not one that *Wandering Gourmet* was going to publish. I couldn't avoid the Big Talk for long, though.

Adam confessed that he was surprised at how much he'd come to like me, how quickly he'd gotten attached. "I'd given up on finding a guy to settle down with as long as I lived in Dubuque," he said. He was willing to give it a shot, a relationship, if I was, even if it meant doing it long-distance. "What do you want?" he asked. "Do you think we could have a future?"

I felt the same way about him, felt the same surprise at how it had all happened and how easily. When we'd met at Lonna's Livery, I figured this was just going to be a pleasant diversion with a nice guy while I was on the road. That first night, neither one of us said anything about the future, about relationships or commitments. But I liked him. Really liked him. He was smart and curious, passionate and tender. I could picture myself with him for a long time. Just not at *that* time. My life was already too cluttered. I doubted that I had much left in me to give. No, I needed to attend to unfinished business, and he deserved better than to get dragged down into it.

That's not exactly what I told him, though. "I really like you, Adam, but I don't think I'm cut out for a long-distance relationship. If the circumstances were different," I said, "maybe if we'd met at another time when I had less going on, then I might have been willing to give it a shot." It sounded like bullshit, and I knew it, but if he was going to be mad or disappointed, I wanted him to be mad at me instead of feeling like something was wrong with him.

Adam stood up to say goodbye, then reached into his backpack and pulled out a rolled-up sheet of paper. "This is for you," he said. "I drew it a couple of days ago. I want you to have it." I stood up and gave him a long hug before finally letting him go.

When I got back to my car, I unrolled the paper Adam had given me. It was a charcoal sketch of me, a profile sitting on a barstool, with a fedora on my head and a beer in a hand.

After dinner, I met Jefferson at Lonna's Livery to toast the end of the case. He was ready to get home, and, honestly, I needed to get back to St. Louis and take care of business, too. He and Lonna were chatting casually when I showed up. She got me a beer, then wandered to the other end of the bar.

"Looks like you and Lonna worked things out," I said to Jefferson.

"We reached an understanding," he said.

"What's that?"

"I understand that she doesn't want what I have to offer." He took a sip of beer. "How about you and Adam? You gonna keep up with him?"

"No," I said. "He wants more than I have to give." Jefferson nodded. "But look at you," I said. "In two weeks, you've met two women who were hot for you. You still got it!"

"Yeah, I suppose," he said. "Look, about Cassie, the woman I met in Hawaii. I didn't want to admit this, but truth is, she dumped me, too. Said I was moving too fast for her. She was just in Hawaii for fun. So those two women I met—neither of them was looking for anything serious." He winced and shook his head. "I don't really feel ready for this dating thing, Frank. I don't want to fuck around. I want to find someone who's serious about commitment, about making a life with me. I just don't know how I'm going to find that."

"You're trying too hard, too soon," I said. "You need to take some time off from relationships. Spend time with your daughters. Buy some damn art to bring a little life to that barren new apartment of yours. There's no rush."

"I'm not twenty anymore..." he said.

"And you're not ninety, either. You'll be fine."

"Guess I'll have to be."

We had more drinks and less personal conversation the rest of the night before Jefferson went back to his room to pack. He was leaving first thing in the morning, anxious to get going early and settle back in at home. I told him I'd be a little behind him and would call when I got to St. Louis. I had one more drink after he left. I sat at the far end of the bar, by myself, avoiding eye contact and conversation as the bar filled up, already regretting my decision to leave Adam behind.

CHAPTER 48

I had another restless night, tossing and turning; I couldn't stop images of the fire and Adam from flooding my mind. When sunlight began breaking through the tattered shades in my room, I felt relieved. I showered, packed, and checked out of the Clear Lake Inn by nine. I was heading back to The Wired Bean for coffee and a snack when I got a call.

"Frank, it's Ruby." She still had an old phone, a landline with no add-ons, so I didn't think she understood that her name would come up on my phone when she called. "I bet you're glad to be going home. Too bad you didn't get to finish the story for that New York magazine, though."

"Yeah," I said. "There'll be other opportunities, I guess."

"Look, Frank, I know this is late, since it looks like you've got everything figured out, but I wanted to tell you about something I just found."

"What is it?"

"You asked me to look for any other reviews of Post-Modern Chocolates—bad reviews especially—remember?"

"Right. I almost forgot. Did you find anything?"

"Well, not really. She got a lot of good reviews. That one from Chicago was really the exception. But I did discover something else."

"What's that?"

"I was really struck by the line in the bad review that compared Post-Modern Chocolates to a starving artist's sale."

"Yeah," I said, smiling. "'The chocolate equivalent of a starving artist's sale, but less satisfying,'" I quoted. "I thought that was pretty clever."

"Exactly. Well, I got the idea to look around for that phrase—I don't know why, it just stood out to me. Well, I found another article that used a similar phrase. It was about a Caribbean cruise; it said, 'the cruising equivalent of a starving artist's sale, but less satisfying.'"

"Huh. That's exactly the same. Was it by the same person who wrote the review of Post-Modern Chocolates?"

"No. It was written by Helen Kraft."

"Someone stole a line from Helen Kraft? Helen Kraft wrote a line worthy of being stolen?" I said.

"Actually,' she said, "I'm not sure if it was stolen at all."

"What do you mean?"

"Well, the bad review of the chocolate shop was written by someone named Steven Gold. The thing is, I can't find any other articles by a Steven Gold. Nothing. I thought maybe I was doing something wrong, so I asked for help, but the reference librarian couldn't find any other articles, either. She even tried to find a Steven Gold who was a chocolate expert, but that didn't turn up anyone, either."

"What do you make of that, Ruby?"

"Well, this is just a guess, of course, but what if Steven Gold was just a pen name for Helen Kraft? It would make sense, after all, since she is friends with Stella Mueller. She might have agreed to write a bad review to help Stella, but she didn't want it to look too obvious."

"I wouldn't put it past them," I said. "But the thing is, the article had a very specific critique, that Ashley was using an inferior type of chocolate, mixing it in with the good stuff. I know Helen. Her palate's no better than mine. I'm sure she wouldn't have noticed that on her own. So how did she know it was in there, and what it was called, I wonder?"

"That's a good question, Frank. What about that young man who worked for her? Didn't he used to work for Stella, too?"

"Jake Horgan?" I asked.

"He's the one who died in the fire, right?"

"Yes," I said. "He worked for Stella for years before he switched sides, but they didn't part on very good terms. Stella blamed him for sabotaging the freezer, for causing the accident that shut her down at a critical time."

"Yes, that was the story," Ruby said. "Maybe there's more to it than we know."

"Maybe so."

I thanked Ruby and promised to stop in Friesburg for lunch the next time I was in the area.

Could Jake have been spying on Ashley for Stella? Maybe I didn't have all the answers, after all. When I got into Dubuque, I drove through downtown and turned east on Highway 20, onto the Julien Dubuque Bridge and back to Galena.

CHAPTER 49

I grabbed a parking spot on the south end of Main Street and walked the couple of blocks to Frozen Expressions, assuming that Ashley would most likely be there, terrorizing her new employees. I was right. When I walked in, I heard her screaming at two of them: "That's too much! A level scoop! A level scoop!"

When she heard the tinkle of the bell over the door, she turned to look, then refocused her anger on me. "Get out! You've done enough damage already!"

She picked up a scoop and looked like she was ready to pull a Stella, but she thought better of it and set it back down.

"Last time I checked, I wasn't the one who started the fire or sold Nazi art," I said.

That was enough for her to change her mind again, but instead of flinging ice cream at me, she threw the scoop, which flew about six inches to the right of my head, bounced off the front door, and landed at my feet. I picked it up and walked it over to her.

"I'll be out of your hair soon enough," I said. "I just wanted to clarify one thing. Then I'll be gone for good."

"Why should I talk to you about anything?" she asked, throwing the scoop into the sink.

"You don't have to, but this is one thing that you might not mind. It's about that bad review that was published in *Chicago Magazine* just before the convention started."

"What about it?" she snapped, stepping toward the counter, her eyes narrowing.

"I've done some background work on it. I'm pretty sure that the person who wrote it used a pseudonym. I think the article was written by Helen Kraft."

"Oh, I knew that right away."

"Why were you so sure?" I asked, confused. Ruby had stumbled into that conclusion after a few days of research, but Ashley knew right away? She stammered something unintelligible, then turned her back to me, grabbing a towel and wiping down the counter.

"It's because of Jake, isn't it?" I asked after a pause. "He was spying on you." Ashley covered her mouth with the towel. "Jake saw you making chocolate, saw you mixing in CCN-51 with the rest of your chocolates. And he told Stella, didn't he?"

"Yes," she said, softly.

"I'm sorry, Ashley," I said.

"I don't need your fucking pity," she said, turning to face me, tears in her eyes. "Look, I knew it was a mistake, using CCN-51, but the business was barely viable. I had to find a way to cut expenses. CCN-51 isn't as bad as some people say. The processing has improved the flavor so much that very few people can tell the difference." She sneered. "I bet you couldn't tell the difference right now."

"You're probably right," I agreed.

"On the other hand, it helped me turn the corner. It made the chocolate shop profitable enough that I could convince my parents to invest in Frozen Expressions, so I could pair ice cream with my chocolates."

"So when the article came out and said you were using CCN-51, you were afraid that it would turn customers against you, that both of your businesses could be in jeopardy?"

"Of course I was. Wouldn't you be?"

"Hell, yes. And I'd also feel pretty damn pissed. Being betrayed is bad enough, but when the traitor is also your lover…"

Ashley's face turned bright red and tightened up. I couldn't tell if she was about to cry uncontrollably or if she was going to strangle me, or both. As I stood there trying to decide if I should hand her a napkin or run away, I remembered what Jefferson had said earlier about Jake's death, how it had puzzled him. Sure, he could understand how an old guy got pushed down and smacked his head; that guy was in the middle of a big crowd that was panicking. Jake, though, was in a small vendor's booth with just a couple of other people whom he knew. Tilly, the cupcake baker, thought she heard an argument next door in the Post-Modern booth. *They* were arguing, Ashley and Jake.

"You pushed him," I said without thinking.

"What?" Ashley said, shaking her head and stepping back from the counter.

"You were arguing with Jake when the fire started, yelling at him for giving up your secret. You got angry and pushed him hard. As he fell down, he hit his head on the table." I walked up to the counter, to get closer to her. "You killed him," I whispered. "It may have been unintentional, but you killed him just the same."

"Get out!" she screamed. "Get out of my store, and don't ever come back!" She picked up the ice cream scoop and threw it at me, missing again but breaking a shade on a table lamp. She reached over and picked up another scoop and threw that one, too, with better aim. If I hadn't ducked, it would have hit me square in the forehead. The Ice Cream Ambassadors turned to see what was going on.

"I'm going!" I said, taking a couple of steps back. "But throwing shit at me and kicking me out isn't going to change anything. I hear that confession is good for the soul. Maybe it would even help someone like you to come clean."

"To whom?" she asked. She looked back at her employees, stepped toward me, and then in a hoarse whisper said, "Who the hell am I supposed to tell this to? Jake's parents? Would they feel better if they knew their precious son had been double-dealing? Would they be comforted knowing that his boss and lover pushed him in a fit of rage, killing him? Or maybe you think I should tell the police?" Her jaw clenched. "They already ruled his death accidental, which it was," she said, intensely but barely louder than breathing. "Confessing to them wouldn't change anything for anybody."

"I don't know how you can keep something like that to yourself without it ripping you apart," I said, raising my voice slightly.

"I don't buy this sudden empathy for me, Mr. Dodge. Now get out of here, before I have another blight on my conscience," she breathed, grabbing a knife and holding it up.

I didn't see any reason to keep arguing the point with her, so I left. Besides, she did confess... to me.

Chapter 50

I drove back to Dubuque to get one last coffee from The Wired Bean before heading out of town. I filled my travel mug with dark roast this time and bought a croissant filled with milk chocolate from Post-Modern; I was curious to find out if I could taste any bitterness. I couldn't—not in the chocolate, anyway. On the way out, I saw Stella sitting at a café table on the patio. I stopped to say good-bye.

"I'm so sorry for your loss," I said, wishing that I had a better way to offer condolences.

"Thank you, Frank. This has been a terrible week. I'm glad it's almost over."

"What are you going to do now?"

"First, I'm going to give Stan a good send-off. He'll be cremated, like he wanted to be. We're going to take his ashes and scatter them in the Mississippi near Aquoqua. Let him rest for good back home." She picked up a napkin and wiped a few tears from her eyes.

That's how I'd like to go out, too, I thought. Scatter my ashes in the backwaters around Brice Prairie, Wisconsin, where I grew up.

"After that, I'm going to take a vacation somewhere. Anywhere," she continued. "And how about you, Frank? What will you be doing next?"

"Heading home. I need to spend some time in St. Louis. Get a few things in order. Try to get a few things written."

"Helen told me that you lost the assignment to write about the food convention. That's a shame. I'm sure it would have been very well written."

"Thank you," I said. "I lost track of time trying to figure out what happened with the fire, and I missed the deadline."

"You'll have other opportunities, I'm sure."

I had one last thing I really wanted to ask her, but I hesitated. She'd been through a lot, lost a lot, and I didn't want to keep poking at her wounds. Still, I couldn't contain my curiosity. "Stella, I don't mean to pry... Actually, I do. I was wondering... Jake Horgan... He was your son, wasn't he?"

Stella nearly spit out her coffee. "My son? What have you been drinking, Frank?"

Her reaction confused me. "He was twenty-four years old, right?"

"Yes. When he died, he was twenty-four. So?"

"And about twenty-five years ago, you left town... for a year."

"At least you're good at math, Frank," she said. She looked at me, puzzled, like she was trying to decide whether it as worth her effort to explain to me that two plus two equals four. "I went to Madison, to get an MBA," she finally said. "I wasn't running away from Dubuque, and I certainly wasn't pregnant." She placed a hand on her cheek. "Why on earth would you think so?"

I looked her over carefully, trying to figure out if she might be lying. "It was just a guess, based on the timing. And a couple of other things, like the fact that you visited Jake regularly at his parents' house and that it didn't seem like it should take a year to learn how to run an ice cream shop. That's all."

Her expression changed from being puzzled to looking annoyed. "I went to Madison for school, to get an MBA, to learn how to run a business. I visited some ice cream shops while I was there, to see how they did things. But I went for the degree. As far as Jake goes," she said, "I've known his parents forever. His father is my first cousin."

A black Chevy Suburban pulled up in front of The Wired Bean, and a window rolled down. Stella stood up, acknowledged the vehicle, looked back at me, and said, "I have to go. My ride is here. It was nice to meet you, Frank," she said, shaking my hand and her head. "Good luck with your writing, but try not to let your imagination get the best of you."

Stella got in the back seat, and, as the Suburban pulled away, I couldn't see who was driving, but I caught a glimpse of Helen Kraft in the passenger seat, turning around to say something to Stella after she got in.

CHAPTER 51

I had one more stop to make before starting the five-hour drive home. I dropped off the rental and picked up my car from the repair shop. On the way out of town, I detoured to Aquoqua, to the Hungry Point Bar and Grill and asked Rick if I could borrow his canoe one more time. He didn't object.

The July heat wave hadn't let up, but I didn't care. The trees shielded most of the midday sun, and I was getting used to the humidity. I slipped off my shirt and paddled slowly down to Big Dan's place.

I could hear a light breeze rustling through the tops of the oaks and cottonwoods, but none of its cooling power reached down to river level. As I made my way through the backwaters, I wondered how many times Stan had passed through, how many fish he had taken out of this river.

I got to Big Dan's cabin and pulled ashore; I tied up just as the dogs came running toward me, with Big Dan not far behind. The dogs recognized me, or my smell, and quickly shifted from looking out for Big Dan to begging for my affection. I obliged, rubbing the tops of their heads until Big Dan made it to the fence and ordered them back to the cabin.

"Didn't think I'd see you again, Frank," he said.

"I wasn't sure if I should come by. If I'd be welcome."

"Ah, hell, none of this was your fault. I don't blame you for what happened."

"That makes me feel good, to hear it from you, even if I feel a little responsible anyway. It never crossed my mind that Stan might take his own life."

"It crossed mine," he said. "I just didn't expect it so soon, else I would have kept him close to me. I feel like I let him down."

"You did everything you could for him, Big Dan. If having someone like you around isn't enough to give a guy the strength to forge ahead, well, then I don't know what would do it."

"That's awful nice of you to say, Frank. I'm still gonna miss him something terrible," he said. "Anyway, you showed up at just the right time. I was about to pay honor to Stan in my own way, with a little ceremony I thought up that steals from different traditions." He put both hands on a fence post and raised his chin. "Care to join me?"

"How can I say no? What do you have in mind?"

Big Dan went back inside his house and came back out with a small birch-bark canoe, just a foot and a half long. "I made this myself a while back," he said. He also had two beeswax candles, both small enough to fit inside the little canoe. "I was thinking that these candles could stand for the spirits of Stan and Gretchen. That by floating them down the river, maybe we're helping to reunite them in the next world." He held the candles up for me to see. "Fuckin' corny, I know," he said.

"Damn right it is," I said. "But I like it. I like it."

Big Dan put the candles in the canoe and pulled out a box of matches. "Go ahead and light 'em," he said. "Oh, wait here just a minute. I forgot one thing." He went inside his house and came back with a bowl of dried leaves.

"Sage," he said, "as long as we're mixing and matching spiritual traditions." He lit the leaves, and when the smoke was plentiful, he used a feather to direct some smoke around me, a little more over himself, and a final wave over the little canoe. When the sage was done burning, Big Dan set the small canoe in the water and gave it a gentle push. As it drifted slowly away from shore, he wished them, Stan and Gretchen, peace in the next world and scattered the rest of the sage on the water. We watched as the canoe floated away and the sage slowly spread out.

When the canoe was just out of sight, I turned to Big Dan and gave him a bear hug. "Would it be OK if I stopped in again?" I asked. "The next time I'm in the area?"

"That'd be all right," he said.

I paddled back to Aquoqua, got back in my car, and drove south on Highway 52, back toward St. Louis.

CHAPTER 52

Once I got within range of the Quad Cities, I called my brother, Mark, and told him that I was going to be in St. Louis for a few days.

"That's great, Frank," he said. "I'm looking forward to it. We don't get to spend a lot of time together, just you and me. I've been a little worried about you lately, after the trouble you've run into. I'd be real upset if something bad happened."

After that uncharacteristic emotional outburst, we made plans to meet for a beer and catch up. I promised I'd tell him about the whole fire investigation, and he promised to share a few really good fish tales.

It wasn't long before I was on Interstate 74 and my mind was wandering. Adam was right. Whatever problems I thought I had in Dubuque were on me. Plenty of people reached out and helped me, had helped me over the years, but I hadn't let it register. I'd never admit that to Adam, of course, or anyone else.

My thoughts drifted back to the fire and who did what. I was impressed at how easily we pulled everything together, how all the pieces had fallen into place with so few surprises. It had seemed so easy. Had it been too easy?

So much revolved around Stella. She'd been the target of the fire, a fire that was supposed to have discredited her and ruined her business. Sure, she hadn't been injured, but it had ultimately cost her a friend, Jake, and a husband. Those damn emergency exit doors. We never figured out why they'd been locked or who'd locked them. Stan had insisted—had sworn—that he'd had nothing to do with it, yet he was one of only a handful of people who had access to the keys that locked them, and his assistant had been on vacation for a couple of weeks before the fire. Somebody had locked those doors, but if not Stan or his assistant, then who? Who else could have had access?

Stella. Of course. It had to have been Stella. She'd almost certainly had access to Stan's keys, would have known where Stan kept them. She and Stan had obviously been fighting; their marriage was in deep trouble. But to lock those doors—well, she would have had to know that something was going to happen at the food fair. But how? Stan wouldn't have told her; I'd bet anything on that. He really believed he was about to ruin her business. But if he hadn't told her, that left only the mayor... or Courtney Baker. Courtney Baker. Courtney would have known what was going on; she was the one who'd ordered Stan to do it in the first place. Had Courtney and Stella worked together? What if it was Courtney driving that Suburban at The Wired Bean in the morning, the one that picked up Stella... the one with Helen Kraft in it.

Stella... Courtney... Helen. Could it be? Was it possible that the three of them had somehow orchestrated this whole thing? Courtney setting up Stan and the mayor; Helen writing incendiary pieces to stoke the rivalry with Ashley and cast suspicion on her; Stella sabotaging the saboteur to turn a fleeting embarrassment into a disaster that couldn't be brushed aside so easily?

I doubted that there was much I could do at that point to prove any of this, but I had an idea. I thought I might be able to chip away at one part of the story. I pulled off at an exit and called Darrel Horgan.

"Mr. Horgan? This is Frank Dodge, the reporter." I was getting used to using that title for cover.

"Oh, yes. Hello, Mr. Dodge. What can I do for you?"

"I hate to bother you at this time of the evening. I talked with Stella Mueller just before I left town. She mentioned that you two are cousins."

"That's right," he said. "Her mother and my father were siblings."

"So that means that Jake was… what… your first cousin once removed?"

Silence. I didn't hear a click, so I assumed he didn't hang up.

"No," Darrel said, breaking the silence. "Jake was my son."

"It's OK, Mr. Horgan. Stella told me that she was Jake's mother, that she hid out for a year when she was pregnant."

"Mr. Dodge, I'm not comfortable with these questions. I don't see what it has to do with anything we've discussed."

"I know. I'm sorry. It's just that Stella was still pissed off that Ashley, Jake's lover, had been allowed to attend Jake's funeral while she, Jake's biological mother, had been banned."

"Nobody told her she couldn't go to the funeral. That was her decision."

"When did Jake learn that Stella was his birth mother?"

There was another short silence. I'd learned a long time before that you can get away with saying just about anything if you say it with confidence.

"When he was in college," Darrel responded. "We're not comfortable keeping secrets, my wife and I. When we adopted him, we agreed to let Stella have some contact with him, so she visited regularly while he was growing up. We were going to tell him when he was in high school, but we put it off when he started working for Stella. It seemed a little complicated at that time."

"So Stella didn't mind when you told him?"

"She did. She was afraid he was going to hate her for giving him up."

"Did he?"

"No. He was shocked about it—a little angry for a while, too—but they got through it."

"When you told Jake—was that around the time he left Stella's ice cream business to go work for Ashley?"

"Yes," Darrel replied. "Look, Mr. Dodge, I don't mind answering your questions, but I'd like to know what you plan on doing with Jake's story. How much of this are you going to write about?"

"I don't know" I said. "but at this point, I probably won't include these details about Jake. It's not my intention to be disrespectful to him at all. But you have to admit, he was in a very awkward position. Not only did he leave Stella to go work for her most bitter rival, but he became that rival's lover. Stella must have been hurt, and Jake must have felt very conflicted."

"That's a fair summary."

"Did you know Jake was spying on Ashley for Stella?"

I heard a heavy sigh. "I don't know what you need me for, Mr. Dodge. You seem to have all the answers already."

"Did Jake talk to you about it? About the spying?"

"Yes."

"What did he say?"

"Jake was a fine young man, good-hearted and well-meaning, Mr. Dodge. But he didn't always have good judgment. He had divided loyalties. I tried to help him sort through all that, but ultimately he had to decide for himself what to do. He was looking for a way to keep them both happy. I warned him that he was unlikely to succeed at that. That someone was going to get hurt. We just didn't know that it would be Jake."

I expressed my sorrow, again, for his loss and thanked him for talking to me.

Knowing that Stella was, in reality, Jake's mother didn't prove anything other than that she could keep a secret and lie to my face convincingly. I still had nothing concrete to prove that she, Helen, and Courtney had been responsible for the fire, no evidence to convict them, but the more I tossed it around in my head, the more certain I was. I had a harder time understanding what it was all for, though. I imagined that Courtney must have seen some political advantage to getting rid of the mayor. Stella seemed intent on bringing Stan down, too, but I didn't understand why she needed all the drama to do it. Helen? Well, she was obviously along for the ride.

If I was right about the three of them, then Jefferson and I had also been part of their play—had been played. For the first time, I felt sympathy for the mayor, and I felt even worse for Stan. I had underestimated the three women, each of them and collectively, and I was pissed off at them, and at myself, even if I admired the planning and discipline that had gone into pulling it off. I was pretty sure that Jefferson wouldn't feel the same way, though.

At the next rest area, I pulled over and sent a text to Helen Kraft: "Got a story to pitch: ice cream maker, writer, & political aide plot a fire to take out a boss & a husband; three dead, but get away with it." A few minutes later, she texted back: "It'll never sell. Not believable."

Chapter 53

I got into St. Louis late and worked quickly to empty my car and get into bed. What I wouldn't have given for one good night's sleep! Too bad that wasn't in the cards.

When I woke up, I felt almost as tired as when I'd gone to bed. Even a shower didn't make me feel any better. I pulled out the French press and made a strong cup of coffee, then gave Jefferson a call to tell him my theory.

He wasn't buying it, probably because he didn't want to admit that we'd been manipulated. He kept insisting that I didn't have a shred of evidence to back up my theory, and he was right. I didn't. All I had was a few seemingly disconnected facts and intuition, and that was never going to convince Jefferson of anything.

After I put on a fresh set of clothes, I drove to a long-term-care facility in south St. Louis.

"We didn't expect to see you again, Mr. Dodge," the clinic director said to me after I entered.

"I didn't expect to be back," I said. "How's he doing?"

"Not well. He doesn't seem to know where he is now, and he no longer recognizes friends and family. He's not talking, either. We get him out of bed less than we used to, because he doesn't have much strength any-more."

"How much longer does he have?"

"It's hard to say, but he could go on for months like this. We make him as comfortable as we can. If it's any consolation, I'm pretty sure he doesn't have any idea who he is or what's happening anymore."

"It's no consolation," I mumbled. "What room is he in?"

"One-twelve."

I walked down the hall, stopping to pluck a few flowers from a vase in the TV room. When I got to room 112, I stopped in front of the door and peered into the room. I could see the foot of the bed and the outline of feet under a bed sheet but nothing more. I took a deep breath and walked in. His head was slightly elevated, but he was otherwise lying flat. His eyes were open, but he didn't seem to be looking at anything in particular, definitely not the episode of The Price Is Right playing on the TV on the wall in front of him. His breathing was slow but deep, and he smelled like he'd been left to rot in the sun. The younger Greg Williams would be appalled if he could see what he'd come to. Alzheimer's had robbed him of the essential things that made him human, had turned him into a machine that took in liquid food through a tube and shit it out into a bag.

I'd brought along a small bottle of his favorite cologne, Chanel for Men, and splashed a little on his neck. I leaned in and gave him a quick kiss on the cheek. "Happy anniversary, babe. It was twenty years ago today that we had our first date."

Epilogue

I settled back into St. Louis, ready to stay put for a few weeks while I sorted things out. Back in Dubuque, the sorting seemed to be about done.

The case against the mayor fell apart when Stan died. Courtney Baker decided it was no longer in her best interests to testify against the mayor, so Michael Andelfinger walked away without being charged with a thing. For the mayor, though, the damage had been done; he lost the Democratic primary to Laura Adler.

Courtney slipped into the background after the case against the mayor fell apart, but rumor has it that she's been quietly advising Adler and could be her next chief of staff, should Adler win in the general election. Over in Galena, Melissa Potts is running unopposed for another term as mayor and is as popular as ever.

Right after the mayor was arrested in July, the Bakers quietly removed *Portrait of a Woman* from the Dubuque Art Museum, and soon afterward they replaced it with another Picasso they bought at auction from Sotheby's, apparently with no help from Richard and Lynn Johns.

The Johnses might have been busy consoling their daughter anyway, not because of anything related to the death of Jake Horgan—she never confessed to them—but because Frozen Expressions, her ice cream business, closed after just a couple of months. Seems that people preferred Stella's ice cream over Ashley's. Stella, in fact, has finally gotten a foothold in the Chicago market and is feeling bullish about her future.

A couple of weeks after I got home, I got a call from the editor of *Midwest Living.* She'd heard that I'd been researching the boutique food market in the Midwest and asked me to submit a query. I did submit it, and she liked the idea. I sent her a completed piece three weeks later that she promised to run after the first of the year.

With no plans to leave St. Louis for a while, I got into a routine. I start each day with a visit to the nursing home. Greg has never once recognized me; he barely even wakes up. After each visit, I've gotten into the habit of grabbing lunch at a barbecue joint down the street. They have killer brisket, which like all the meats they smoke, they buy from a local farmer. They even make their own condiments from scratch: sauces, pickles, ketchup, mustard. Some of those ingredients come from a small garden they keep on the side of their building. The food is damn good, with a freshness that you can find only in a place like that. All that is great, but what I like the best is the familiarity of it all. Every time I eat at that place, I feel like I'm home again.

Acknowledgments

I first visited Dubuque in 2007. It's not a place that you pass through accidentally; it's not exactly on the way to anywhere. My first impression was that the city had enormous potential but much of it was going to waste. It's amazing how quickly things can turn around.

The historic center of town may have never looked better than it does now. The multi-million-dollar makeover of the Hotel Julien turned a shady old lady into a prom queen. The Mississippi River Museum and Aquarium is a world-class facility that shows off the river's history and ecology. New housing downtown is bringing life back to the city center, and they have plenty of new restaurants and old bars where they can pass the time.

Across the river, Galena shines on as an example of what happens when you maintain the structural and social integrity of an old city. The streetscape along Main Street, where rows of brick buildings curve along the Galena River, is striking. Even more impressive is that the businesses that fill those storefronts are almost entirely locally owned. The money you spend in Galena, stays in Galena.

I've had many memorable experiences over the years exploring these two cities and the surrounding countryside. I've always found the local tourism folks to be knowledgeable and eager to help. I'm grateful for their assistance over the years and for tolerating what must have seemed like an endless supply of silly questions.

I'm also grateful that Allan Edmands agreed to be my editor. He was thorough with his review and with his explanations. Thanks to all the brave beta readers, too many to mention by name, who gave valuable feedback about earlier drafts. Thanks also to Peggy Nehmen for creating a captivating cover.

And thanks to my husband, John, and to the rest of my family for their continuing support and patience as I plod my way through the world of professional writing.

Dean Klinkenberg

St. Louis

Author's Notes

I'd love to tell you exactly what inspired this story, but I can't. Honestly. Let's just say that the central premise—a dispute between two women who ran their own boutique food businesses—was inspired by actual events. I just can't tell you what city it happened in (it wasn't Dubuque or Galena!) or even what type of food they each made.

Part of the reason their story caught my attention is that I love food, so naturally, Frank Dodge does, too. Dodge also shares some of the same skepticism I do about food trends and contemporary attitudes toward food. We've prioritized convenience at the expense of flavor and health. We've let fads invented by marketing professionals distract us from the simple, timeless practices, namely, that there's no substitute for cooking from scratch with fresh, seasonal ingredients. If more of us did that, our health (and the environment) would be better off.

I first visited Dubuque in 2007. It's not a place one passes through accidentally; it's not really on the way to anywhere. My first impression was that the city had enormous potential—scenic setting next to the river; stout, beautiful buildings—but much of it was going to waste. It's amazing how quickly things can turn around.

The historic center of town may have never looked better than it does now. A multi-million-dollar makeover of the Hotel Julien a few years ago turned a shady old lady into a prom queen. The Mississippi River Museum and Aquarium features a world-class facility that shows off the river's history and ecology. New housing downtown is bringing life back to the city center, and there are plenty of new restaurants and old bars where folks can pass the time.

Across the river, Galena shines on as an example of what happens when you maintain the structural and social integrity of an old city. The streetscape along Main Street, where rows of brick buildings curve along the Galena River, is striking. Even more impressive is that the businesses that fill those storefronts are almost entirely small, locally owned operations. The money you spend in Galena, stays in Galena. (Although that's probably not so true for your secrets.)

Both places have outsized histories. Galena gave us nine men who served as generals in the Union Army during the Civil War, for example. As always, I drop in a few Easter eggs here and there for my fellow history nerds. I'll share an obscure one. In this book, the mayor of Dubuque is a man called Mike Andelfinger. I didn't choose his name randomly. A man named Martin Andelfinger served as mayor of Dubuque in 1929 and 1932. I don't believe they are related.

We get to know Ruby much better in this book. Her character is based on a real person, my dear friend Lucille Keil. I met Lucille when she an energetic 84-year-old spitfire. She guided me around the small-town museum where she volunteered, dropping occasional insults to people she considered prudes or ignorant (or both). We hit it off right away, and I went back time and again to visit with her. Lucille led a good life, an admirable life, so she made an excellent model for Ruby. Their lives overlap but they are not identical. For one thing, Ruby never helped solve any crimes. Lucille passed away in 2019 at 96. I miss her terribly, but every time I write a new Frank Dodge book, I bring her back to life through Ruby. Lucille would enjoy knowing that. (I wrote a brief tribute to Lucille after she passed away; you can read it here: mississippivalleytraveler.com/one-of-the-toughest-smartest-people-i-ever-met.)

Dodge and I share an affection for the older mom-and-pop motels, which I'm sure will be a theme in each book. These older motels are usually cheaper than chain hotels, plus they often offer unexpected benefits, such as a good story or two. There was that time, for example, I stayed at one such motel in a medium-sized city where I didn't get much sleep because of the noise of men coming (literally) and going all night in the room next to me. The walls were thin, so I can confidently say they weren't all there for a friendly game of gin rummy with the woman (women?) in that room. In the morning, I was eager to clean up and get the hell out of there, but the heat and steam from the shower set off the smoke alarm in my room. The bed, at least, had a trampoline-like spring to it, so I could easily fan the steam away to silence the incessant beeping. I don't recall having an audience for that performance, though. Maybe I've blocked that part out. I finished my shower and dried off, only to realize I had forgotten to pack underwear. So I dressed commando-style, checked out, then made a beeline for the nearest Walmart. You don't get that kind of experience at a Holiday Inn.

If this book piqued your interest in traveling to the Dubuque/Galena region, check out the links below to my Mississippi Valley Traveler website, where you can start planning your trip!

- MississippiValleyTraveler.com/Dubuque

- MississippiValleyTraveler.com/Galena

Dean

January 2025

LETTING GO IN LA CROSSE PREVIEW

The headline is explosive. The clock is ticking. Can he uncover the lies before a community self-destructs?

Freelance writer Frank Dodge vowed to stay by his estranged lover's side until the bitter end. But when he's offered a plum assignment covering the economic impact of frac sand mining, he's torn between his career and reconciling with his dying ex. Believing he can do both, he's midway through the gig when a bomb goes off, taking innocent lives.

Discovering that corruption runs fatally deep in the clash between greedy corporates and luckless locals, Dodge chases the story into high-stakes territory. But the investigation takes him far from his former partner's deathbed when he realizes his major national scoop could take down powerful forces causing widespread environmental destruction.

Will Dodge's exposure of greed-driven crime cost him more than a guilt-ridden promise?

Letting Go in La Crosse is the third book in the gritty Frank Dodge mystery series. If you like snarky heroes, dark humor, and communities battling for survival, then you'll love Dean Klinkenberg's engaging page-turner.

Buy *Letting Go in La Crosse* to reveal the truth today!

**Scan this QR code to find out how to get *Letting Go in La Crosse*.

ALSO BY DEAN KLINKENBERG

Frank Dodge Mysteries

Rock Island Lines (Frank Dodge mystery #1)

Double-Dealing in Dubuque (Frank Dodge mystery #2)

Letting Go in La Crosse (Frank Dodge mystery #3)

Murder on the Mississippi (Frank Dodge mystery #4)

Non-Fiction Books

Road Tripping the Great River Road, Volume 1: 18 Trips Along the Upper
Mississippi River

The Wild Mississippi: A State-by-State Guide to the River's Natural Wonders

Mississippi River Mayhem: Disasters, Tragedy, and Murder on Ol' Man River

About the Author

Dean Klinkenberg, the Mississippi Valley Traveler, explores the back roads and backwaters of the Mississippi River Valley, a place with an abundance of stories to tell, big characters, epic struggles, do-gooders, and evil-doers. Some of those stories inspire the Frank Dodge mysteries; others you'll find in his non-fiction books, including the Mississippi Valley Traveler guidebooks. He lives in St. Louis with his husband John and a parrot called Ra. Find out more about him and his books at the links below.

DeanKlinkenberg.com (Fiction)

MississippiValleyTraveler.com (Non-Fiction)